The Rebel [illegible]

Laura Dowers

ISBN: 1507825838
ISBN-13: 978-1507825839

To the memory of my mother and for
Dad, as always.

'I was ever sorry that your lordship should fly with waxen wings, doubting Icarus's fortune.'

- Francis Bacon

PROLOGUE

Ash Wednesday, 1601

It was early at the Palace of Whitehall and the winter sun had only just begun to lighten the sky.

Servants had risen to perform their duties, but all courtiers were still in their beds. All except Robert Cecil. He had been awake for hours, listening to the steady breathing of his wife beside him. What sleep he had managed to get had been broken and inadequate. As his back began to ache from immobility, he grew worried that he would disturb his wife if he turned over to find a more comfortable position and so rose, thinking that as he was awake, he may as well go to work.

Cecil went to his office, savouring the slightly musty odour of parchment and herbs crushed beneath the rush matting and the smoky, woody smell of the fire his manservant was kindling in the grate. He opened the wooden window shutters himself, and when the fire had caught and was beginning to warm the room, dismissed his servant, refusing the man's suggestion that he bring food so that he could break his fast.

Cecil was not hungry, not this morning. He stood at

the table that held pile after pile of state papers: reports from his agents, petitions for lands, requests for positions at court, and some that even asked for justice. He pulled out a file and opened it. He read a few sentences but their meaning did not register and he had forgotten them before he moved on to the next. The file was shut and thrown aside. In exasperation, he looked for something else in his office he could occupy himself with. His black eyes fell upon a small stack of items that had been delivered late the previous night by a Tower messenger. Two miniature portraits, a pair of leather gloves, a roll of parchment and a book, a book whose leather binding looked a little familiar.

Intrigued, Cecil opened it. He scanned the lines and recognised the story of Sir Gawain and the Green Knight. It was, he realised with surprise, his father's old copy of *Le Morte d'Arthur*. He carried the volume to his desk and sat, easing his misshapen shoulder into the padded rear cushion of the chair. Laying the book across his lap, he turned over the front cover. A memory came, immediate, without warning, making his eyes sting from the tears that pricked at their rims. He had forgotten what he had once written on the flyleaf: '*To Robert Devereux, Earl of Essex, from his loving friend, Robert Cecil.*'

He had been thirteen years old when he had written those words twenty-five years earlier. Had there ever been a time when he and Robert Devereux had been friends?

He re-read the inscription and the scene was suddenly, vividly, in his mind. He and Robert had been in his father's study at Burghley House on the Strand, he taking advantage of the old man's absence to show Robert some of the house's treasures. Robert had gravitated towards the room's collection of books that were kept on shelves in a recess. Cecil had stood at his father's desk, on the same spot he stood to watch his father work at his state papers.

Robert Devereux had only been at Burghley House a week, coming as a ward of court. His father, Walter Devereux, had died in Ireland, leaving his nine-year-old son the holder of the Essex earldom. Robert had been like all the other boys who came to the house to stay. Boys who laughed at Cecil's limp and pointed at the hump in his back, boys who rode horses and practised archery while Cecil stayed indoors and worked hard at his lessons, telling himself he enjoyed them because he could not join in with the others in their sport. He had dismissed Robert as just such another creature until the handsome boy had spoken of poetry and shyly shown some of his own scribblings to the stunted son of the house. The poetry had been poor, he remembered, but the gesture had been rich, and Cecil had felt warmth towards a fellow boy for what may have been the first time in his short life.

That day in his father's study, Cecil had obeyed an unfamiliar impulse and taken down the book from where it sat on the lowest shelf, believing Robert would enjoy it more than any other. He had shuffled back to the desk, dipped a quill into the inkpot and, dripping ink over the dark-brown oak desk, written the inscription. Drying the writing with a shower of sand from the shaker, he had closed the book and held it out to Robert.

Robert, his light brown eyes twinkling in the sunlight, had taken the book, read the inscription and thanked Cecil, declaring it to be a fine present.

It was also a costly one, as Cecil found out later that evening when his father returned from court and noticed the Devereux boy deep in study with the book in his lap. His father had taken Cecil aside and reminded him that the books on the shelves were not Cecil's to give away. But Lord Burghley, not being a mean man, had not embarrassed his best-loved son by making him ask for the book's return. Instead, Cecil had to pay for the book, which meant eight months without his allowance. It had been a memorable punishment, but the boy Cecil never regretted the present.

Cecil turned some of the book's pages at random. There, in the margins, was Robert's handwriting. It had not been done recently for the letters were almost clumsy, lacking the style of the adult. He had written words such as *wonderful*, *heroic*, *foolish* and Cecil thought how aptly they could be used to describe the man Robert Devereux had become.

He heard a click, loud in the quiet room, and looked up to see the latch on his office door lift and the door open.

Elizabeth Tudor stood in the doorway, dressed in a linen nightshift, a green silk dressing gown, and with a nightcap covering her thin, grey hair. It was only the second time Cecil had seen her look so unadorned, devoid of finery, devoid even of the white lead paint that he could now see hid several liver spots on her forehead and cheeks. The shock of her appearance passed and he realised he was still seated. He moved to rise, but she waved him to be still and stepped into the room.

'You are here early, Pygmy,' she said, shuffling past him to the window and pressing her forehead to the glass, sighing softly as it cooled her skin.

'I have much work, madam,' he pretended.

'You are always working. Such a busy little elf.' She turned and pointed to the book. 'But that does not look like work.'

Cecil laid his fingers almost protectively over the leather cover. 'No. It's Malory. *Le Morte d'Arthur*. It belongs to the earl.'

'His favourite book. Many nights he read to me...' She

broke off and turned back to the window. 'What time is it?'

Cecil glanced at the clock on his desk, a gift from the Queen to his father, given some ten years earlier. 'It is not quite the hour. Madam, I must ask. Were you not minded to rescind the order?'

She looked at him over her shoulder, one plucked eyebrow arching. 'Would you have had me do that, Pygmy?'

He shrugged as if it were a matter of little importance. 'By law, he is rightfully condemned. I merely thought your fondness for the earl—'

'My fondness ended when he tried to depose me,' she snarled. 'Would you have me free such a traitor?'

'I would not have you free him, no,' he protested, getting to his feet, 'but why not imprisonment? Would that not be punishment enough?'

'Why, Pygmy, are you playing the advocate for your old adversary?'

He opened his mouth to answer, but church bells across London began to toll the eighth hour, the small clock echoing them with a more delicate chime. As the eighth bell died away, Elizabeth turned away from the window.

'You are too late, Pygmy. If you wanted Essex to live you should have appealed to me sooner. It would have been a pleasant surprise to discover you possessed a heart after all.'

She knocked a quick tattoo on the windowsill and left his office, closing the door behind her. Cecil sank slowly into his chair. He heard the rustle and drag of Elizabeth's dressing gown on the floorboards, the slap of her slippers as she made her way to the music room a few doors along the corridor. Moments later, he heard her playing a merry tune upon the virginals.

Cecil turned the book's pages back to his inscription, read the words once more, and held the book to his chest. He breathed in the smell of the paper and the leather, fancying he could detect the smell of Robert himself.

Elizabeth continued to play while Cecil wept.

I

1588

Elizabeth Tudor forced a wan smile onto her face as the young man sat opposite her at the table glanced up and shuffled the pack of cards.

It had been only a few days since she had unlocked her privy chamber door and allowed her ladies and counsellors in to tend her. She had not cared that her thin body was covered only by a soiled shift, her magnificent dress having been torn off, nor that her lustrous red wig had been discarded upon the floor. She had not cared, for Leicester was dead. Her dearest, truest friend was gone.

When she had first been given the news of the Earl of Leicester's death, she had locked herself in her rooms. She had cried, not quietly, not like a woman, but like an animal that had been mortally wounded, with savage sounds that forced their way up from the very core of her body. Her howls had scraped the sides of her throat, leaving it raw and capable only of mewling noises that came once her initial anguish had subsided.

For the first two days of her seclusion, she had not

eaten, only drunk the wine she had found in a cabinet, not bothering to dilute it with water as was her normal practice. For once, she wanted to be drunk, to feel that sense of numbness, that insensibility to pain that alcohol offered.

On the third day, her stomach had begun to ache for lack of sustenance and her fingers had grabbed at the few walnuts that had been left over from a four-day-old meal. But they could not satisfy her long.

On the fourth day, having experienced enough of solitude, she had let the world back in.

Her ladies, hurrying in, had viewed with shock the chaos of her bedchamber: the books scattered upon the floor, her jewels, earrings and necklaces tossed aside, the stench of her piss and shit as it festered in the close stool. Her older female companions who understood better what she was feeling had fluttered around her, fussing without asking any questions, while the younger ladies held back, willing to concern themselves only with the tidying of the room, not the emotional crisis of an old woman.

Silent and distant, Elizabeth had let her ladies bathe and dress her. Silently, she listened to Lord Burghley and Sir Francis Walsingham express their condolences at the Earl of Leicester's death, while she secretly scorned them for their poorly hid relief at her reappearance. They were there even now, at the periphery of her vision, huddled together, anxiously looking out for any further signs of weakness from her. They need not have worried. Elizabeth had her mask back on.

So, here she was, dressed in one of her most glittering gowns, her face and bosom covered with a thin layer of white lead paste, her cheeks and lips smeared with red cochineal, her wrists daubed with civet perfume and her thinning ginger hair covered with a tightly curled red wig, playing cards as if Leicester had not died. Playing with

Robert Devereux, his stepson, who she knew had been sent for to cheer her up. Robert was grieving too, for he had loved Leicester dearly. Elizabeth thought kindly of him for that.

Robert had dealt the cards and was looking at her expectantly. His brown eyes were kind, enquiring. He did not ask her if she were well. She would never be well again, and he, this boy of soft countenance and sweet charm, somehow realised that.

'I wish I could take the pain away,' he said, his hand reaching across the table to hers, not considering, or perhaps not caring, that it was not permitted for a subject to touch a sovereign uninvited.

'You ease it, my lord,' she replied, sliding her hand away to pick up her cards, 'which is all I can hope for.'

Robert spread his cards, fanlike, in his hand and began the game. 'My mother is broken-hearted.'

He mentions his mother ingenuously, she thought. *There is no inflection in his voice that points to a caution, the holding of a hidden meaning. He does not mention his mother, that she-wolf Lettice who stole Leicester from me, to wound, so I cannot be unkind to him.* 'Is she?' she murmured.

'I did wonder if I should be with her,' he continued, 'but then I realised she has my sisters for company, and of course, I could not leave you.'

To Elizabeth's ears, he actually sounded as if he meant what he said. *Does he? Can he? Is it possible?* 'You are very kind to think of me, my lord.'

'Please,' he said, leaning forward a little, 'will you not call me Robert? 'My lord' - it puts me at such a distance from you.'

She smiled, a true smile this time. 'Not Robert,' she said with a little shake of her head that set her pearl earrings jiggling, 'Robin.'

He frowned, his smooth, high forehead becoming marred by a single, deep crease. ‘Did you not call the Earl of Leicester so?’

‘I did,’ she nodded sadly. ‘He was my bonny sweet Robin. But it would please me to call *you* Robin. Do you object?’

‘If it please you, madam, then, of course, I do not.’

Elizabeth nodded and laid down a card. No man could ever replace Leicester, but if any man could lessen the loss of him, she felt that perhaps Robert Devereux was that man.

Cecil opened the door of his father’s private office and entered. Of all his father’s offices in every of the Queen’s palaces, it was this one at Whitehall with its small, diamond-leaded windows and panelled walls hidden behind piles of papers that he loved the most. He loved it for the feeling of comfort and security it gave him, folding around him like a fur cloak. He sat down in the special chair his father had brought in from home for him, custom-made so that his humped shoulder was cushioned as he sat.

‘What is she doing?’ Lord Burghley asked, not looking up from the papers he was working on.

‘Writing poetry with the Earl of Essex, Father.’

Burghley pondered this for a long moment, tapping his quill against his lips. ‘Good,’ he decided eventually.

‘Is it good?’ Cecil wondered quietly, glancing at his father from beneath lowered lids.

‘What harm can it do?’

‘Well, that’s the question, is it not?’

‘My boy,’ Burghley put down his quill and looked at his son, ‘the Queen has her favourites. It took me a long time to accept it but accept it I did. I had to. For thirty years, her favourite was the Earl of Leicester. In the beginning, I felt him to be a problem, distracting the Queen from her duties and giving her ill advice, but it became obvious to me that the Queen would not countenance parting with him. I found I had to either work with Leicester or forsake the Queen. And I must admit Leicester did have his uses.'

'But the Earl of Leicester was of a similar age to the Queen. Essex is so much younger than she.'

'The Queen is missing her favourite, so she has found another to keep her company, that is all. Essex is a plaything, an amusement for her leisure hours. She has always had a need for handsome young men about her.'

'Which I am not,' Cecil said bitterly.

He knew he was not handsome, disfigured as he was with a hunched back and a shortened left leg that made him limp and could not help but envy his handsome peers who were. It seemed to him that people were ready to believe, forgive or excuse a great deal if a person had been blessed with a beautiful exterior. And it certainly did nothing for Cecil's self-esteem to be called Pygmy by Elizabeth. When Elizabeth had first called him so, even Burghley had been shocked and upset at so unkind a nickname, but he had tried to persuade his son that with Elizabeth a nickname was a mark of favour. Cecil knew that his father spoke true, but the name still hurt.

'What you are is better, my son. These handsome young men like the Earl of Essex are only good for entertaining and flattering the Queen. They cannot govern her kingdom for her, but *you* can, Robert. It is what I have trained you for all these years. When I'm gone—'

'Please, Father,' Cecil said, holding out his hand and closing his eyes, 'please do not talk of it.'

Burghley sighed and picked up the quill again. 'It will

come, my boy, whether you allow me to speak of it or not. And when my time comes, you will be able to serve the Queen as I have done. She will have need of you then.'

'And what am I to do in the meantime? I cannot dance nor write poetry—'

'We will have to see. You will continue to help me with my work, I trust?'

'Of course, I will, Father.'

But, Cecil thought, *I would have liked it if I could have been made just a little bit handsome. Not to attract the Queen, but because... well, just because.*

As if he knew what his son was thinking, Burghley reached across the table and patted Cecil's small hand. 'Let the Queen have her young men, my boy. Your time will come.'

His wife was already in bed when Cecil returned to his rooms. Like many women of her generation, his wife was named Elizabeth after the Queen. In the short time they had been married, she had grown used to her husband's late hours and always left a candle burning by his bedside.

Cecil entered the bedchamber as quietly as he was able and began undressing, groaning softly as the action of taking off his shirt stretched the atrophied muscles in his shoulder.

A light sleeper, Elizabeth awoke. 'Husband?'

'Oh, did I wake you?'

'Yes,' Elizabeth yawned. 'Is your back hurting?'

'A little. It's been a long day.'

'Shall I rub it?'

Cecil shifted further up the bed and presented his bare

back to her, unconcerned as he would have been with others that she would find the deformed shape of it unpleasant. Their marriage, like all alliances of their class, had been arranged, but Cecil could not have hoped to be conjoined with, in his eyes at least, a more perfect woman.

'Did you talk to your father?' Elizabeth asked as her fingers probed and rubbed his shoulder.

'I did,' he said, closing his eyes and wincing as her ministrations caused him both pleasure and pain. 'He said I should not worry about Essex.'

'You sound like you think he is wrong and you should worry. There, that's enough. Get into bed.' Elizabeth patted his pillows to plump them up.

Cecil leant back against them, a weariness creeping up on him. 'He doesn't see things the way I do. Father thinks that all I have to do is work hard and the Queen will reward me.'

'He has known her for a long time, Robert.'

'But he has a biased view of her. I am sure he still thinks of her as she was when she first became queen. But she is different now. I have seen the change in her. I remember her when I was a boy and Father let me come to court and watch him work. The Earl of Leicester was alive and everyone knew how close they were. She was, I am not sure… kinder, somehow.'

'She loved Leicester and maybe she was happier then. And with Essex, well, perhaps she feels she still has something of Leicester. I believe Essex and Leicester were very close, even though there was no blood tie.'

'Yes, I think they were. It surprises me though, that the Queen should welcome Essex as she does.'

'Because he is Lettice Devereux's son?'

'Elizabeth hates the woman for marrying Leicester and I know she is eager to do that lady all the ill she can.

Why, as soon as Leicester died, she was calling in his debts so that the countess would have to pay them. Elizabeth may have been grief-stricken at Leicester's loss, but the Queen is never sentimental when it comes to money. So, you would naturally think that she would not wish to favour any of the Devereux children, would you not?'

'Perhaps she does so for Leicester's sake?'

'Perhaps,' Cecil said doubtfully. 'But I think she just likes the looks of Essex.'

'He is very handsome. So tall. He stands a full head above everyone else at court.'

'Does he indeed?' Cecil muttered. 'How very impressive.'

'Oh, husband,' Elizabeth scolded, slapping his arm lightly. 'What does he matter? I think your father is right to counsel you not to worry. You have no wish to be a favourite, do you? To be entirely dependent on the Queen? To have to write love letters to her? To be on hand at all hours of the day and night? To not be allowed to show interest in other women for fear the Queen will grow jealous?'

'Well, I already have my wife, and no other woman will look at me twice, so there is no fear of that.'

'Oh, shush. Why must you always think that I made such a bad bargain in our marriage? I love you, Robert, though you think you do not deserve it. I do not care that you are only a few inches taller than me or that your back is crooked. You have a fine mind and I know that you love me. It is enough. Had I made another marriage, who is to say that my husband would love me so well as you?'

'You would not have preferred the handsome Earl of Essex?' he asked playfully.

'No, I would not. I do not know him well, but I think he is not so pleasant as he appears.'

‘He can be cruel,’ Cecil said quietly, his mind travelling back to his youth. ‘But then he can also be kind. In fact, he can be whatever he has in his mind to be. That is his attraction.’

‘Do you know, I cannot work out whether you like him or not?’

‘I admire him, and the truth is, I envy him, Elizabeth. He is loved by many, he has favour, he has beauty, he has talents. I could like him better were he not so proud. When we were young, he was always boasting about his family, how the Devereuxs could trace their ancestry back to the Conquest. “Mine is a proud and lofty heritage,” he would say. “We Devereuxs are destined for great things. It is in my blood”.’

Elizabeth laughed. ‘He said that?’

‘I swear he did,’ Cecil laughed too. ‘So you see, how can I possibly compete with his glorious destiny?’

II

Chartley, 1589

Sir Christopher Blount uncrossed his legs, careful not to tread on the skirts of Lettice Devereux sitting by his side. He looked sideways at her, wondering if she was going to speak, but her profile appeared resolutely silent. Her chin, somewhat marred by a bulge of sagging flesh, was thrust forward, her lips pursed, and her eyes fixed on her son as he stood by the window.

Christopher followed her gaze, wishing he knew what Robert was thinking. Anger, of course, and resentment, that was to be expected upon hearing such news, but what else? Christopher had known Robert since he was a young boy and had lost his father, Walter, to the flux in Ireland. Christopher had been in service to Leicester as his Gentleman of the Horse and had often taken Robert riding. He knew all too well of Robert's changeable moods that were almost impossible to predict and thought it best he remain silent, at least until it was clear what Robert's attitude to him was going to be.

Robert, dressed in travelling clothes, had arrived at

Chartley, his country home in the county of Warwickshire, a quarter of an hour earlier, a little weary from the long journey from London, but otherwise looking fine and healthy. Lettice had greeted her son with a tight embrace and a smacking kiss that had left a patch of red cochineal on Robert's cheek. Christopher had followed at Lettice's heels into the entrance hall, and before Robert and he had had a chance to greet one another, Lettice had introduced him as her husband. Robert had stared at them both in astonishment, then stalked past them without a word into the room all three now occupied.

'Do you not think it unseemly, Mother?' Robert said at last, keeping his back to Christopher and Lettice. 'You have been but six months a widow.'

'Would you have me alone for the rest of my life?' Lettice retorted shrilly, grabbing Christopher's hand and holding it firmly in her lap.

Was it a gesture of defiance, Christopher wondered, *or was she worried I would bolt?*

Robert turned to face them. 'But you are not alone, Mother. You have Dorothy and Penelope and Walter. You have me.'

Lettice drew in a deep breath. 'Robert, my darling, as much as I love you, you cannot give me what a husband can.'

Christopher saw Robert's cheeks flush and felt the heat in his own, but he knew that if Lettice's cheeks flushed beneath her paint, it was through determination, not shame. He felt it was time he spoke. 'Do not criticise your mother, Rob, she is not the only one to blame. I know you think that I have betrayed our friendship and I am sorry for that.'

'And Leicester?' Robert demanded, coming towards him and almost knocking over a small octagonal table.

'Did you betray *him*?'

Before Christopher could reply, Lettice threw his hand away and rose. 'I loved your stepfather, Robert, but even you must have realised he was no husband to me by the end. I turned to Christopher for comfort.'

There, it was out, Christopher winced. *Did Lettice have to admit that we cuckolded Leicester?*

'Did Leicester know?' Robert asked, horrified.

Lettice's narrow shoulders shrugged. 'I think not. If he did, he never mentioned it. And remember, Robert, before you condemn me, that for all the time I knew him, I had to share Leicester with Elizabeth. I was never allowed to have him all to myself. Have you considered that?'

Robert raised his eyes to hers and Christopher saw that they had softened. 'You are right, Mother. I have no right to criticise you. Nor you, Chris. Forgive me.'

Lettice moved towards Robert and tugged his sleeve, an instruction for him to lower his head to her to receive another kiss. 'Good. I do so hate to quarrel. Now, I shall leave you two boys to talk while I have a lie down. I am feeling tired. Be sure to eat something, Robert, not just drink. Christopher, my dearest, see that he does.'

Christopher assured her he would and Lettice withdrew, closing the oak door behind her. Christopher waited a moment until he heard her footsteps on the wooden stairs and then turned to Robert. 'Shall we have that drink first?' he asked mutinously.

Robert nodded, smiling at the conspiracy. 'We must toast your marriage. No,' he held up a hand as Christopher opened his mouth to speak, 'let us say no more on the matter. It is done and cannot be undone.'

Christopher handed him a cup of wine, realising by the last statement that could the marriage be undone, Robert would be happy to see it. 'Thank you, Rob, very generous of you.' He returned to his seat. 'It is happening again, of course.'

Robert took a seat opposite and stretched out his long legs towards the fire. 'What is?'

'Your mother having to share with the Queen. We hear you are greatly in favour.'

Robert smiled shyly. 'In truth I am, Chris. Elizabeth must have me near her, no matter what time of day or night. We talk, we write, we ride, we play games.'

'That does not sound very arduous. How wonderful. Tell me, what do you think of the Queen?'

'She is not unlike Mother,' Robert said and they both laughed. 'It can be quite disconcerting. They even have the same laugh.'

'Well, they are cousins. But I hope it is not all take take take on the Queen's part?'

Robert looked away, swirling the wine in his cup. 'I have the Master of the Horse.'

'You got that post from Leicester. What is Elizabeth doing for you? You must get something from her, Rob, else your attendance at court is all for naught.'

'I know, Chris, and I am sure something will come.'

'Then you must needs be patient? Is that how it is? You have many virtues, Rob, but let me tell you, patience is not one of them.'

'I am trying. I ask for this and that from Elizabeth, but I am not the only one petitioning her. There is Ralegh.'

'Still? I would have thought he would have disappeared on one of his voyages or swaggered back to Devon by now.'

Robert sighed and gestured hopelessly. 'He appears immovable. The Queen graces him with favour, yet I cannot understand why. After all, what is Ralegh? A lowly knight from some backwater in the West Country. Why should he enjoy sovereign favour the same as I?'

'Well, as for that, I am but a lowly knight myself,

Rob,' Christopher reminded him, 'yet here I am, husband to a countess. I have risen.'

'Yes, my mother has certainly raised you,' Robert nodded, unaware of any offence he might cause, 'yet still you know your degree and pay me all due deference as your better. Ralegh is no respecter of rank. He seeks to rise, but what has he to recommend himself?'

Christopher shrugged. 'A handsome face, a ready wit, and a willingness to please. What else does he need?'

Robert grunted. 'Elizabeth has made him Captain of the Guard. He is always nearby. If I am in the chamber with her, then Ralegh is at the door. If the Queen and I walk in the gardens or ride in the Chase, Ralegh is there, not ten feet away. Remember when the Queen and I visited Warwick Castle? Dorothy was there too and when Elizabeth found out, she said she must stay in her room because she didn't want to have to look upon her, and just for marrying without her permission. My sister, Chris! I told Elizabeth that she was being cruel and she just laughed at me. I saw her look past me to Ralegh – he was standing by the door – and they both laughed. At me! I could not bear it.'

'You left, didn't you?'

'Of course, I left. I wasn't going to put up with such an insult, not just to my sister, but to me. And I certainly wasn't going to be made the butt of jests between Elizabeth and that bastard Ralegh.'

'You made your point though, Robert,' Christopher assured him. 'After all, Elizabeth sent someone after you to fetch you back, didn't she? She obviously knew she had upset you.'

'Aye, brought back like a wayward child. I shouldn't have allowed myself to be treated in that way. And there was no rebuke to Ralegh. Elizabeth did nothing, though I insisted she punish him.'

'If she is that keen on him, you may then have to put up with the fellow.'

'I cannot bear to. The man is odious. I did think perhaps I should try to discredit him in some way.'

Christopher grunted and rubbed his temple. 'Be careful, Rob. That may take more practised hands than yours and such manoeuvring needs a subtler, more cunning nature than you possess. I would not want you to undo yourself.'

'Perhaps you are right. I have not the courtier's nature,' Robert said proudly. 'I should not concern myself with the Raleghs of this world. I must rise by my own merits, not by doing down another, an unworthy fellow. Let us talk of other, happier things. Mother gave her order and we have failed to obey, Chris. Let us eat.'

III

Hampton Court Palace

Sir Walter Ralegh weaved his way around the box hedges of the palace gardens, nodding greetings to the men and women of his own station that he passed, bowing elegantly to those in rank above him. As he cleared the formal gardens with their beautiful roses and aromatic herb beds and painted figures of unicorns and other mythical creatures mounted on posts and entered into the wooded area, he looked about him to make sure that he was not observed.

'There you are, at last.' Bess Throckmorton pushed herself away from the tree she had been leaning against and waited for Ralegh to move nearer.

'My my, Bess, how very impatient you are,' he said, bending to kiss her lips.

Bess turned her head away, so that his lips brushed against her cheek. 'You know I will be missed if I am away too long.'

Less than an hour earlier, they had both been in the Queen's privy chambers, Bess in attendance on the Queen and Ralegh being given his instructions for the day as Captain of the Guard, receiving a list of who had an audience with the Queen so that they would be seen in the correct order. Ralegh had not looked in Bess's direction, had not greeted her or engaged in a pleasant exchange. It was not wise to pay attention to other ladies in the Queen's presence, though Bess would have been happy to receive even a fleeting glance from her lover. She had hastily scribbled a note while Ralegh talked to the Queen, then slid it into his hand under pretence of passing him a cup of beer. With consummate ease, he had placed the note inside his cuff, Elizabeth never realising that an assignation had been made.

'I can leave,' Ralegh said carelessly, 'if you think you ought to get back.'

Bess's throat constricted. How could he say such a thing unless he did not truly love her? She knew that there were plenty of women at court who would gladly submit to his caresses, but he had picked her out from all of them and she was not sure why. 'Do you not want to see me?'

'Of course, I do, my love, but not if you are going to nag me. There are far pleasanter things we could be talking about. Or doing.'

He leant in towards her and Bess felt herself melting as she breathed in the smell of his skin. She allowed herself to be kissed.

'There now, is that not better?' he said, nuzzling her neck.

She moaned, bending her body to his, only stopping when his hand began to lift her skirts. 'No, Walter, I must not.'

Ralegh let her skirts drop, disappointed but not displeased. She had said 'must not' when she could have said 'cannot' or 'will not'. There was hope yet. He sat down at the base of the tree, choosing a spot between its large, protruding roots. Bess settled alongside him and he lifted his arm to place around her shoulder.

'Walter, you will be careful, won't you?' she asked.

'Careful about what, you silly little thing?'

'The Earl of Essex. He means you ill.'

'I know he does, but I fear nothing from that quarter.'

'He has the Queen's favour.'

'As do I.'

Bess wanted to say that that was all very well, but as Essex had pointed out to anybody who would listen, he was an earl and Walter only a knight. Essex, by his very rank, was entitled to command the Queen's affection, and favour could be withdrawn as easily as it was bestowed. But she knew that such talk would only anger Walter and she did not want their tryst to be spoilt. 'It makes me furious to hear him talk of you,' she said instead, playing with a gold button on his doublet.

'What does the Queen say when he does so?'

'She rebukes him, but not strongly enough, if you ask me. I think you should criticise him when you are with the Queen.'

'And make me seem as petty as he?'

'Why not, my love?'

'I shall not do it, Bess, and do not entreat me to. Besides, I have better things to talk about when I am with Elizabeth. I am not going to waste my time talking of Essex when I could be furthering my own causes. I want her to fund expeditions to the New World, Bess. I need to convince her that they are worthwhile ventures. I cannot do that if all I do is complain about Essex.'

'Do you love her?' Bess asked.

Ralegh glanced down at her. 'Is this a trap? If I say I do love her, then you will ask whether I love you? If I say I do not love her, will you hurl abuse at me for being such a hypocritical wretch?'

'No,' Bess protested, 'I just wondered, that is all.'

'She is the Queen, Bess, so of course, I love her. She is an intelligent woman and I admire her for that. She is a survivor and I cannot help but think her great. When I consider what she has been through…' His voice trailed off as his mind considered the threats on Elizabeth's life, her questionable birthright, her dangerous adversaries and how she had outwitted them all in the end. 'She is a queen for a man to be proud of, that you cannot deny.'

'You would not say so if you were one of her ladies,' Bess replied sourly. 'What we have to endure! Boxings, tantrums, harsh words, and I know not what else.'

'She does not like women,' Ralegh laughed, patting her hand.

'You sound as if you understand her.'

'I do understand her for I have known other women like her. She does not like women because she sees them as rivals. Especially young women, like you.' He kissed her forehead. 'She is growing old, Bess, and the men who helped her in her youth are leaving her service to retire or else are dying. Look who she has to serve her these days, look who are all the old men's replacements.'

'You?' Bess teased.

'Yes, me, but I am the exception,' he said, only half in jest. 'Look at Essex. He aspires to a great office of state – I know he does, though he hasn't dared or thought to ask her yet – but would you honestly feel safe with the fate of the country in Essex's hands? And his friends, too. The Earl of Southampton, for instance. That young man only cares for himself. Cannot pass a mirror without examining his pretty face. And Cecil,' Ralegh drew a breath in through his teeth, 'that one. He has his eyes on the main chance. I doubt his own father knows what is going on in his mind, but it is not total subservience to the

Queen, despite what old Burghley believes. I wouldn't be surprised if Cecil were already communicating with King James up in Scotland. Getting ready for when Elizabeth is gone.'

'Maybe so, but not all of the young men at court would make such ill servants for the Queen. If only she would allow them the chance to prove themselves.'

Ralegh was surprised and impressed by Bess's perspicacity and told her so, suggesting that Elizabeth should make her one of her counsellors for Bess would prove able in the post. Bess laughed and agreed with him, saying if she were a counsellor, she would speak of nothing but Ralegh, if only she could be sure that Elizabeth would not think her words suspicious. Ralegh became serious and holding her at arm's length, cautioned her against saying anything in his favour, telling her that unfortunately, it would be better for them both if they acted as if they did not know one another.

'But will it always be so, Walter?' Bess pouted. 'Will we never be able to meet unless in secret?'

Ralegh sighed. 'It does not please me, Bess, you know that. But until I have what I want from Elizabeth, it is necessary. I must write my poems to her, and yet in truth, it is no chore, for I enjoy the writing of them. And I must dance attendance on her. But know that it is only because I must, not because I will it, despite my fondness for her. Do you want to know what is in my heart?' he asked, running his finger down her cheek.

'I do, Walter,' she replied earnestly.

'Well, I shall speak truth, my love, and tell you that I hope one day we can marry.'

'Oh, Walter. Then there are no other women?'

Ralegh frowned. 'Of course, there are no other women, you silly goose. Why do you ask that?'

Bess looked away, feeling foolish. 'Because I do not

know what you find to love in me. It cannot be my face for it is as plain as can be, I know that. So what?'

'For all of you,' Ralegh said. 'I am not so stupid a man as to love a woman purely for her face. Youth passes, Bess, and beauty fades. There has to be something more for a man and woman to be happy with one another. We have that, do we not?'

Bess nodded. 'But it is natural for a man to have mistresses and I would not blame you for it, though it would pain me greatly. Essex has mistresses, I know. Several of the Queen's ladies have been in his bed. Walter,' she sat up, an idea suddenly occurring to her, 'why do you not tell the Queen of his mistresses? That will put you in good favour with her.'

'And put several of your friends in danger of the Queen's wrath and cause harm to their reputations. Bess, do not be so unkind to your fellows and do not ask me to be a telltale. It is not gentlemanly.'

Bess sighed and stood, brushing dirt from her pale green skirts. 'I love you even more for that sentiment, Walter my dear, though I wager if Essex knew about us, he would not hesitate to do us harm. Now I must get back or else she will box my ears. Adieu.'

'Adieu, sweet Bess,' Ralegh said and blew her a kiss, watching her as she entered the gardens and disappeared from sight.

She was right. Essex would use everything he could against him. But Ralegh had seen Elizabeth's face when she had grown tired and could not maintain the pretence of being charmed and amused by Essex's words and changeable moods, and her manner had exhibited signs of irritability and frustration. It was entirely possible, he supposed, that Essex would do himself harm without any help from him.

Although small in comparison to some other houses – Burghley's Theobalds, Hatton's Holdenby, Bess Talbot's Hardwick Hall – Chartley was undeniably pretty. It sat amongst the green, almost endless fields of the Warwickshire countryside, a decorative moat encircling the house where willow trees dipped their branches in the water.

Penelope Rich, hearing of Robert's return to their family home, had begged leave of her husband to visit her brother. She and Robert now lay on their favourite spot on the whole estate, a shaded area close to the stone bridge that crossed the moat.

'Do you really not mind about our mother and Blount marrying?' Penelope asked, twining a strand of chestnut brown hair around her finger. 'I thought you would be furious.'

Robert waved a bumblebee away from his nose. 'I think Mother could have made a happier choice. Christopher is only a knight, after all, but no, I do not mind.'

Penelope giggled. 'He is half her age, though. Our mother,' she shook her head in admiration. 'I only hope I will still have men willing to marry me when I am as old as she.'

'Have you not enough admirers already, Pen? Sidney worshipped you, you know?'

Sir Philip Sidney had been Leicester's nephew and heir and one of Elizabeth's most accomplished courtiers: urbane, witty, highly literate, and loved by all, except those men who considered him a rival. Sidney had, despite their respective spouses, fallen in love with Penelope and she had been the inspiration behind some of his most beautiful poetry.

Robert knew that his sister's marriage was far from happy. Her husband, Lord Richard Rich, had a vicious, suspicious nature and kept Penelope on a very tight rein. She hated him but was powerless to change her situation. His other sister, Dorothy, Robert reflected, had been only slightly more fortunate in her marriage. She at least loved her husband, but her elopement had earned the disapproval of the Queen, and like their mother, was forbidden to go to court.

'I do not suppose you are allowed to have any admirers of your own, are you?' Penelope said, determined to change the subject. 'Not with Elizabeth's eagle eye on you.'

'She makes it difficult,' Robert admitted, 'but assignations can be managed as long as I am careful.'

'I think it's awful that you have to be careful. You are a young man and you should be allowed to love where you please. Just because she is a dried-up old maid, she refuses to let anyone else love. Elizabeth is a true tyrant.'

'Only if I allow her to be, Pen. I do not intend to let her rule me as she did Leicester. I loved him and it pains me to criticise him, but he should not have let a woman have such complete mastery over him.'

'Why did he allow it, then? He was no milksop. He argued with Mother often enough and often refused to let her have her own way. If a man can refuse Mother, he can refuse any woman.'

'I suppose Leicester felt he had to be careful. The Dudleys were not a distinguished family. Everything Leicester had he got from Elizabeth, so he had to do all he could to please her.'

'There must have been more to their relationship than that, Robert. I always felt Leicester cared deeply for Elizabeth.'

'He may have done.'

‘But not you?’ Penelope probed.

‘No, not me,’ Robert cried indignantly, propping himself up on his elbows. ‘She is the Queen, Pen, not my paramour. Elizabeth cannot be treated the same as other women, I grant you, and I respect her as my queen, but I will not lose my head over her.’

She reached for him, her expression grave. ‘Promise me, Rob.’

Robert laughed at her seriousness. ‘I promise.’

IV

Greenwich Palace

The sun shone bright, warming the steel of Robert's armour. Sweat clamped his shirt to his body, the helmet flattened his auburn curls against his skull and his eyes, peering through the slits, were gritty from the sandy dust of the tiltyard floor. Robert's horse pawed the ground as they stood at the end of the tilt, perhaps feeling as he did, hot and impatient.

Robert held out his arm and his oak lance was placed in his hand. He gripped the pole, pressing his gauntlet up against the coned guard and anchoring the butt beneath his armpit. His muscles ached as they strained to hold the heavy weapon and he squeezed his arm tighter, afraid he would drop it and look like a fool.

The master of the tilt raised his warder to signal that the jousting knights should make ready, and Robert soothed his mount, guiding the mare up to the mark. The warder was dropped and Robert squeezed his heels against the mare's flanks, and then all he could hear was the reverberation of the animal's hooves, loud inside the steel helmet, bruising his skull. His opponent was coming up fast, the tip of his lance juddering with the rise and fall of the horse.

And then Robert felt a numbing thud against his left shoulder, which threw him backwards and made him tumble from the saddle. He hit the sandy floor with a crunch of metal that did nothing to cushion the fall. All was noise for a few, long seconds, and then he felt hands helping him to sit up. His helmet was pulled off, the riveted metal scraping the skin of his cheeks. Robert's vision blurred from the sudden harsh sunlight, then cleared, and he could see the spectator stands with their coloured awnings flapping in the breeze, their occupants staring down at him with concern. His eyes sought out Elizabeth and they found her, risen from her seat and leaning forward on the wooden barrier rail.

'Is he hurt?' she called and someone at his side asked him the same question.

Unsure how he felt, Robert tried to rise, but the weight of his armour was too great and he fell back on the ground. Strong hands grabbed him beneath his armpits and hauled him to his feet. Robert found he could stand unaided and heard his unknown helper call out, 'The earl is unhurt, Your Majesty.'

Assured of his condition, Robert saw Elizabeth straighten. 'Well done, sir,' she called, and Robert thought it odd for him, an earl, to be called sir when he realised she was not speaking to him but to his opponent, Sir Charles Blount.

Blount, a distant cousin of Robert's new stepfather, was a young man with dark hair, a thin moustache and a handsome face. Blount stepped up to the wooden rail and bowed, his armour clanking as his body bent. Robert watched Elizabeth throw something, something that glinted and caught the sunlight. Whatever it was she threw, Blount caught it deftly, closing his gauntlet possessively around his prize.

Robert drew near the rail, wanting to know what it was Elizabeth had thrown. Blount, seeing him approach, held the favour in his open palm for him to witness and Robert saw a chess piece, a golden queen. He looked up at Elizabeth, who returned his gaze with equanimity. He held out his hand, ready to catch the favour she would bestow on him, but nothing came falling through the air, and Robert withdrew his hand in embarrassment.

'I applaud you, Sir Charles,' Elizabeth said and Blount made a clumsy bow, dropping the gold chess piece and scrabbling in the dirt to retrieve it while the spectators giggled.

'Now I see that every fool must have a favour,' Robert said loudly and the rising chatter hushed.

The favour safely back in his gauntlet, Blount turned on him. 'I do not deserve such an insult, my lord.'

'Do you not, sir?' Robert said, squaring up to him. 'Yet I have said you are a fool and none here gainsays me.'

Blount raked his eyes over the stands. Robert and he had an audience, an audience who was waiting eagerly to hear his next words. 'I cannot let this pass. Honour demands—'

'Are you challenging me to a duel, sir?'

Blount paused only a moment. 'I am, my lord.'

'What's that?' the shrill voice of Elizabeth cut in. 'Did I hear talk of a duel?'

'Honour demands it, Your Majesty,' Blount called to her.

'To the devil with your honour, sir,' she sneered. 'I have forbidden my courtiers to indulge in duels and I make no exceptions. Ladies, away.'

The spectators rose as one, her ladies and her counsellors following Elizabeth from the tiltyard stands and onto the gravel path that led back to the palace. Fuming at his impotence against the insult, Blount moved away, savagely pulling his gauntlets from his sweating hands.

Robert cast a glance towards the palace and the party that was disappearing through its gates, well out of earshot. He hurried after Blount. 'Name the place.'

Blount halted and stared at him. 'The Queen has forbidden a duel.'

'The Queen need not know.'

'I… I…,' Blount stammered, wanting to say to Robert that he was as ready as he to prove his manhood, but that he was wary of the Queen's wrath, too.

'Come, man, what does a woman know of honour? Are you a man or are you not?'

'I am a man, my lord,' Blount returned the taunt with vigour. 'I'll meet you, whenever and wherever you please.'

Robert drew himself up, satisfied. 'Tomorrow morning at seven in Marylebone Park.'

Lord Burghley, standing in front of Elizabeth as she sat at her desk in her private chamber, winced as his gouty foot throbbed and he waited for the pain to ebb away before speaking.

'Madam, I have been informed that the Earl of Essex and Sir Charles Blount engaged in a duel this morning in Marylebone Park.'

Elizabeth looked up from her book, her amber eyes darkening. 'They did what?'

'They fought a duel—'

'I expressly commanded that they were not to do so. How dare they?'

'I have no doubt that it was at the earl's instigation rather than Blount's. Indeed, I have been told that Blount protested it was contrary to your orders, but the earl challenged him on his manhood.'

'By God's Death,' Elizabeth tutted and reached for her cup of watered wine. 'Oh, sit down, Burghley, I know you are suffering. The earl needs taking down and taught better manners, or he will never be ruled.'

'He is young, madam,' Burghley suggested, sinking into a chair one of Elizabeth's ladies promptly provided. 'I remember him when he was my ward of court. He was always willful. Perhaps this incident should be put down as a youthful indiscretion.'

Elizabeth tapped her long fingers rhythmically against the cover of her book and grunted, sliding a sideways glance at him. 'A wild stallion indeed. Am I to be plagued with reckless youths at my time of life, Burghley?'

Burghley nodded, raising his bushy white eyebrows. 'The court is a very different place from when Your Majesty first came to the throne.'

Elizabeth's lips crooked in a rueful smile. 'Were we ever that young, my lord?'

'Some of us still are, madam,' he replied, bowing his head towards her.

'Oh, you flatterer,' she reproved, enjoying the compliment.

'And perhaps the earl's injury will cool any further impetuosity.'

'His injury?' Elizabeth said sharply, her eyes opening wide in alarm. 'Robin was hurt?'

Burghley consulted a paper. 'Blount pierced him in the thigh, it seems. A great deal of blood ensued from the wound and required medical attention, but it poses no danger to his health. He will recover.'

Elizabeth slammed her book down on the desk. 'But the fool could have been seriously hurt, Burghley. What would I have done then? Does he never think of me? I shall send my doctor to him. I would have Robin well.'

'And is there to be any punishment, madam? For either the earl or Sir Charles?'

Elizabeth sighed and shook her head. 'No, no punishment for either of them. Blount is not to blame. Robin provoked and publicly humiliated him with that foolish remark. And yes, I know what you are thinking, that I should punish Essex, but he is headstrong, Burghley, and does not always think before acting. He is a young man and young men should act a little wild now and then, I think.'

She was right. Burghley did think that there should be punishment for the two men, even if it was only a token punishment to show that the Queen would not allow her subjects to disobey her without incurring retribution. He feared that such forbearance on her part would only encourage similar acts of disobedience and these young men around the court were already too sure of themselves for his liking. But he knew it would be pointless to argue with Elizabeth. He had seen that Robert was necessary to her, how she brightened and seemed to forget her cares when he was with her. To pursue a course of punishment would only anger her and make him seem vindictive.

So, Burghley squashed his feelings and merely sighed before saying, 'As you wish, madam.'

V

1589

A deep, lusty laugh boomed above the sound of chatter in the Presence Chamber of Whitehall Palace and everyone turned to look at the source, the stocky Devonian, Sir Francis Drake.

The room was crowded and Drake was short, so Robert had not noticed the hero of 1588, the man who had saved England, almost single-handedly so the ballad-makers claimed, from the Spanish Armada. Robert excused himself from the men and women who surrounded him, drawn by his fresh looks and charm, not to mention his closeness to the Queen, and cut through the crowd to Drake.

'Sir Francis, may I speak with you?'

Drake looked up at the tall stooping figure. His dark, suntanned brow creased as he tried to place his interlocutor. He was not often at court and was not familiar with all the young gallants. But the Queen's new favourite had been the subject of many a conversation and Robert was so unlike other men, being unusually tall, strikingly auburn-haired and who walked with an unusual forward stooping motion, that Drake was able to recognise him. 'My lord Essex, of course.' Drake's companions made way for Robert and Robert moved closer.

'I have heard a rumour you are forming a fleet to attack Lisbon.'

Drake's dark brown eyes twinkled. 'Have you, my lord?'

'Is it true?'

Drake cleared his throat, folded his arms across his chest and widened his stance. 'It is true. We thought we should give those Spanish dogs an English beating. We'll never have a better chance. Their armada no longer exists and we should attack before they have time to build another. We even have an excuse for attacking if we need one. The Portuguese want the Spanish invaders out of their country and Don Antonio, the poor usurped king, wants his throne back.'

'I wholeheartedly agree, Sir Francis. Can you find a place for me?'

'For you?'

'Yes, for me. I want to be included.' Robert noticed Drake's hesitation and was a little hurt. 'I am an able soldier, Sir Francis, I assure you. I have been in battle in the Netherlands with the late Earl of Leicester and Sir Philip Sidney. You must not think I would be a liability.'

'And I assure you, my lord, I was thinking no such thing.' Drake had in fact been thinking that Elizabeth would want her favourite close by her side, as she had with Leicester, rather than dashing off to war. 'No, indeed, you would be very welcome.'

'You will take me then?'

'With the Queen's permission, of course.'

'Why with the Queen's permission?' Robert asked

irritably. 'Can you not just tell the Council I am required?'

'I can tell the Council that, my lord, but the Queen must approve you all the same, as she must approve every officer in the fleet.'

'Oh, I see,' Robert said, his chin sinking upon his chest.

Drake leant forward and tilted his head up to Robert. 'Don't despair, my lord. The Queen has not gainsaid any of my officers yet.'

Robert nodded glumly. 'If you'll forgive me, Sir Francis, there is none other so placed as I.'

'Ah,' Drake's shoulders jerked with a laugh. 'And I have always thought it an honour to be so favoured by Her Majesty.'

'It is an honour,' Robert agreed, 'but it has its drawbacks too, Sir Francis. If you could make it clear how valuable I would be as part of the fleet when you petition the council, it might help.'

'I shall do my best, my lord,' Drake assured him, thinking that he wasn't going to put himself out too greatly and risk a telling-off from the Queen just to have this eager young pup in his fleet.

Drake did petition the Council as he promised, but Elizabeth said Robert could not go and Drake let the matter drop.

Robert felt unable to let it drop quite so easily. He begged, he pleaded, he even argued and shouted, but Elizabeth was adamant. Robert was not to join the English fleet. He was not to risk his life in such a venture. He was not to try to gain a fortune by wresting it forcibly from the Spanish.

Robert did not listen. Elizabeth was not going to tell him what he could and could not do. He needed money and there was gold just waiting for him in Lisbon.

So, he made his plans secretly and drew friends into his plan, Sir Philip Butler and Sir Edward Wingfield, men who were, unlike him, not the favourites of the Queen and were, therefore, free to do as they pleased. They made arrangements on his behalf with Sir Roger Williams, captain of the *Swiftsure*, who was also a friend to Robert and had been since their days in the Netherlands campaign, and who was keen to help him escape from Elizabeth's clutches. Sir Roger would anchor the *Swiftsure* at Falmouth, a few miles away from the main English fleet at Plymouth, and wait for Robert to arrive in the early hours of the fifth of April. Robert would have slipped away from the court without any fanfare, without anyone even noticing he had gone.

This plan arranged, Robert sat down in his apartments to write dozens of letters, letters that would be delivered once he was safely away from the court.

One of his letters was to Elizabeth, explaining why he had disobeyed her, that he was sure she would forgive him, and assuring her of his undying love. He had gone to Lisbon to make her England safe and he promised he would bring back Spanish booty that would swell the coffers of Elizabeth's treasury for years.

The news of his departure soon spread, not just through the court, but through the city. Robert's departure was being talked about and being cheered in the alehouses of London. The young and handsome Earl of Essex had thumbed his nose at the Queen, so the talk went, and dashed off to sea to teach the hated Spanish a lesson they would never forget. And the people loved him for it, loved his youth and his daring, were proud of his courage in defying the Queen and were proud to call him one of their own.

Elizabeth did not share their admiration. She had told Robert he was not to go to sea and he had defied her. She screamed at her Council, at their stupidity for letting Robert leave the court. She ordered Robert's grandfather, the elderly Sir Francis Knollys, into her presence and demanded that the poor old man ride after his wayward grandson and bring him back to court. And, she told him with an emphatic jab into his shoulder, if that disobedient Welsh cur, Sir Roger Williams, had not already hanged himself in shame for aiding Robert's escape, he was to be brought back in chains and thrown into the Tower where some suitably dank dungeon awaited him.

Poor Sir Francis spared his aged body nothing in riding after his grandson but when he arrived at Falmouth, the weather had turned and the small ship he set sail in to pursue Robert was tossed about by storms and forced back to port. Unhappily, he had to report to the Council that his prey had eluded him and he could do no more.

Robert, for his part, had begun to regret his action, for he and Williams on the *Swiftsure* had problems in finding the rest of the English fleet and sailed around hopelessly for more than a month before they had a sight of their sister ships. Robert climbed aboard Drake's ship expecting to be greeted with warmth and admiration. Instead, he had to endure a severe rebuke from Drake for putting him in such an awkward position. Drake showed him a letter from the Queen, which stated that when Lord Essex was found, he was to be told to sail straight back to England.

Robert opened his mouth to protest, but Drake halted him, telling him there was no need. As much as Drake wanted to obey his queen, the wind was against them and sailing back to England was not possible. The only way was forward, to attack the Spanish-held towns and ports in Portugal. Robert could hardly believe his luck. He had got away with it.

Another week passed and the coast of Portugal came into view. The English force clambered into their small boats and rowed towards the beach. One boat was lost, overturning in the tumultuous sea, but Robert kept his face forward, determined to be the first to land on foreign soil.

The Spanish saw them coming and the Spanish garrison at the castle of Peniche, just beyond the sand dunes on the beach, left their stronghold to see off the English invaders, leaving the town undefended. Robert, with the aid of Sir Roger Williams, outflanked the small party and forced the Spanish to flee. Robert and his men reached the town, took control and raised the flag of St George in victory.

But the main target of the whole expedition had been and still was Lisbon, sixty miles to the north. Sir John Norris took command of the land army and Robert insisted on going with him. They marched through the Portuguese countryside for seven days, the soldiers happily plundering every Catholic church of its gold as they went. But the early promise of the campaign soon dissipated as the army's supplies ran low and foraging parties often returned empty-handed.

And when the English army reached the gates of Lisbon, they found the Spanish occupiers disinclined to come out and fight. With nothing to do and no one to fight, a strategic withdrawal was suggested by the English captains, but Robert protested. He had not risked the displeasure of the Queen simply to turn tail and run away when things became awkward. If the Spanish would not fight voluntarily, then they must be made to.

He rode alone to the city, his pike lowered like a

jousting lance, and thrust it into the wooden gates. He shouted up into the air, challenging any Spaniard inside the gates who would dare to question Elizabeth's honour to come out and fight him, man to man. Robert waited, but no one shouted back. He called again. Still silence. He rode back to the English camp, complaining to Norris that all Spaniards were cowards.

Meanwhile, Drake had sailed the fleet to Cascais and been delighted to encounter sixty Baltic trading ships full of valuable cargoes. These were quickly appropriated by Drake and his comrades. Drake had laid his hands on the fortune that Elizabeth would so delight in.

But Elizabeth had other things on her mind and still wanted Robert back. The army rejoined the fleet and another letter arrived demanding the return of the Earl of Essex and Robert felt he could not ignore the command. He boarded the *Swiftsure* one last time and landed back in England before the month of June was out.

As he rode back to London, Robert found his countrymen waving to him from the side of the roads and from out of their windows, cheering him and praising his name. He even heard ballads sung about his exploits in Portugal and read broadsheets that proclaimed him as the Shepherd of Albion's Arcadia. The people of England loved him. It didn't seem to matter that the adventure had failed to achieve its objectives. Many of the Spanish ports in Portugal were still in the enemy's keeping and Don Antonio, the usurped king, was still without his throne.

And it seemed that Elizabeth did not mind either, for when Robert came before her, there were a few sharp words from her, but there was also warmth in her looks. Elizabeth had her Robin back by her side, and she was content. All she needed to do was find a way to stop Robert seeking his fortune elsewhere.

Cecil re-read the paper his secretary had just handed him, sighed inwardly and dismissed the man.

'This is it,' he said, handing the paper to his father.

Burghley ran his eyes over the wording. 'The Queen is entitled to bestow monopolies on whomever she wishes, my boy.'

'I know, I know,' Cecil said, picking at a splinter in the wood of his father's desk.

'Then what is your objection?'

Cecil raised his eyes to the ceiling and shook his head. 'Why does it have to be to him? He has done nothing to deserve it.'

'If the Queen were to reward only those of her subjects who deserved a reward, she and we would be a great deal richer.' Burghley laughed at his own joke.

'This is a ten-year grant, Father,' Cecil persisted. 'Ten years of revenue from the import and export of sweet wines. It is a small fortune and the Queen has just given it to the Earl of Essex. For what? For playing cards with her, and dancing, and writing poetry.'

'Someone had to have the monopoly,' Burghley pointed out, 'and the earl needs money. A very great deal of it if he is to live as befits an earl. You know this, Robert. Why am I having to explain it to you?'

'Am I sounding petulant, Father?'

'A little, my boy. This is a lesson you should learn. Poor men with rich tastes should be given money to stop them from trying to acquire wealth through other means. An ambitious young man with a great deal of promise and no money with which to achieve it is a dangerous combination.'

Cecil pulled up a chair alongside his father and looked him in the eye. 'Did you suggest the Queen give Essex the sweet wine monopoly, Father?'

'Now you understand, Robert,' Burghley nodded, patting his son's hand. 'What has it cost us? Nothing. What do we gain by it? A great deal. Elizabeth is happy to give her favourite a means of income. She is grateful to us for allowing her to make the gift. And Essex is given the money he needs to wear fine clothes and travel around town in a coach, so that he is not finding other ways to make money, such as demanding gifts that are in the Queen's prerogative and that may soon come your way instead of his. Think of the future, Robert, always be thinking of the future.'

Burghley looked into his son's face, saw the doubtful look in his sharp eyes, and realised he had failed to convince him. 'I know you do not like the earl and I know why. Ah, you look at me like that, but I was not blind when Essex was my ward. I know you wanted him to be your friend and I know how hurt you were when he dropped you in favour of others. No, do not blush, not in front of me, there is no need. You are my son and I know what you are thinking and what you are feeling. What hurts you hurts me. But you are not a child anymore, Robert, and I do not want your thoughts and actions to be governed by the resentments of the child you were. Do you understand?'

Yes, Father, I understand,' Cecil said reluctantly. 'And I know you are right.' He took a deep breath. 'So, the Earl of Essex is to be granted the monopoly on sweet wines for a ten-year period. I will take this to the Queen straight away and have her sign it.'

Burghley watched his son rise awkwardly from his chair, the paper in his hand, and limp out of the office. He felt the twinge of pain he always felt when contemplating his son's misfortune, but he also realised with another part of his brain that he still had much to teach him.

VI

Hampton Court Palace

Robert had enjoyed his morning. He had met his childhood friend, Henry Wriothesley, Earl of Southampton, in the palace's tennis courts and they had spent an enjoyable couple of hours hitting balls at one another, with the competitive spirit of the first hour relaxing into boyish humour in the second. Now, washed and wearing a fresh suit of clothes, he came out of his chamber and skipped down the adjacent stairs that led to the Queen's Privy Chamber. Two Yeoman Warders stood either side of the double doors, one of which stood partly open. As Robert drew nearer, he heard laughter. He recognised the Queen's voice and, with a stab of resentment, Sir Walter Ralegh's.

He looked through the gap in the door. Elizabeth and Ralegh were sitting upon cushions on the floor. Elizabeth sat upright, her stiff corset refusing to allow her to slouch and her orange skirts billowing around her, while Ralegh rested on one elbow like an ancient Roman, his long legs, encased in silver-threaded hose, stretched out and crossed at the ankles.

'Why, Robin,' Elizabeth said, noticing Robert standing in the doorway. 'What are you doing there?'

'I... I...,' Robert stammered, feeling like a child who had been caught spying on his parents. He pushed the door farther open. 'I heard... I wondered who you were with.'

'I am with my dear Walter,' Elizabeth said, smiling at Ralegh as she drew out the 'a' sound, a pun on his Devonshire country accent. 'He's been amusing me.'

'If you wanted amusement, madam, you need only have sent for me,' Robert said primly.

'I was on hand, my lord,' Ralegh said, pushing himself up to lean back on his hands. 'There was no need to bother you.'

Robert scratched his head and frowned. 'I am at a loss to conceive how a mere Captain of the Guard has anything to say to a queen that can be so very amusing.'

Ralegh's handsome face lost its geniality. 'Wit is not a quality only the nobility possess, my lord. In fact, I have known it to be wholly absent in some members of that rank.'

Robert felt the insult warm his cheeks. 'You mean me, sir?' he demanded, stepping into the room and moving towards the pair, only stopping when his boot nudged one of the embroidered cushions. He paid no attention to Elizabeth, who watched her two favourites with a thrill of satisfaction at their manly enmity. This was a scenario she had always enjoyed, two men fighting over her, and she encouraged such rivalry whenever possible, but always putting a stop to it before matters progressed too far.

'Why would you imagine I mean you, my lord?' Ralegh said, a smile curving his pink lips. 'Have you not wit?'

'More than a Devonshire peasant, I assure you, sir,' Robert countered, his hand curling around the hilt of his sword.

Elizabeth saw the movement and decided the encounter had played its course. 'Enough,' she said. She lifted her arms and both Ralegh and Robert bent to take her hands and help her to her feet, no easy task for her dress was heavy and cumbersome. 'Have you not had your fill of fighting, Robin? Your wound from your encounter with Sir Charles can have barely healed.'

Robert did not want to be reminded of losing a duel, especially not in front of Ralegh. He glared at Ralegh, who was still holding Elizabeth's hand.

'I insist you remove your hand from the Queen's person,' he said, pointing at the offending appendage.

Elizabeth's lips twitched in amusement. Robert could truly find an offence in the smallest of incidences. Ralegh made no move to comply, so she pulled her hand gently from his. 'There, Robin. Does that satisfy you?'

'It does not satisfy *me*, madam,' Ralegh protested in mock outrage.

Standing there in his habitually casual, self-assured manner made Elizabeth think of the differences between the two men and the opposite ways in which they responded to her. Robert sulked while Ralegh teased, and she knew it was the difference between a boy and man. But a man's character was already formed, and Ralegh, she had come to suspect, was not a man she could ever tame, though it irked her to admit it. But Robert, still so young in many ways, was made of wax, ready to be shaped into whatever she chose to make of him. She had power over him and the power pleased her.

'It was not to you that the question was addressed, sir,' Elizabeth rebuked Ralegh sharply, having made a decision to favour Robert.

Ralegh saw that Elizabeth was in a playful mood no longer and decided there was no profit or amusement in prolonging the encounter. He could make better use of his time elsewhere. 'Then I must ask your forgiveness, and if you wish it, take my leave.'

'Yes, you may go,' she said, her head already turning away from him.

Ralegh bowed, deeply to Elizabeth, less so to Robert, and left the room, signalling to the Yeoman Warder to close the door.

'You see how I do your bidding, Robin,' Elizabeth said, moving to a table by the window and selecting a sugared almond from a gold platter.

'I wish you would dismiss him altogether,' Robert said, pleased at his victory. 'He has no virtues that I can see.'

'Of course, he has virtues. I would not waste my time on him else. You do not believe me, I see. Shall I list them for you? Well then, he is a clever man, Robin, adventurous, courageous, charming—'

'Enough,' Robert protested, putting his hands over his ears. 'He may, indeed, be all these things, I know not, but you have nobles who have these virtues, too. Why give your company to one of such low degree?'

Elizabeth laughed. 'Because I am my father's daughter, Robin. He never put breeding before brains when it came to his servants and nor do I. I recognise virtue in all stations of Man.'

'Recognise it, use them, by all means, but do not keep them so close about you. Such a man sullies you by his presence.'

'Would you alone have access to your queen, Robin?'

'Of course. Why would I not want to keep the most beautiful queen in the world all to myself?'

It was a banal statement, lacking invention, but

Elizabeth welcomed it all the same. 'You should have seen me in my youth,' she said, her eyes glistening in remembrance. 'I made a pretty maid then.'

Youth has its own beauty, so the statement may have been true, Robert could not say. All he knew was what his mother had told him of Elizabeth's early days as queen. That Elizabeth had managed to convince many a man she was beautiful by virtue of her sovereign station and the magnificence of her clothes and jewels. 'It was incredible how beautiful even a plain maid could look when she wore diamonds and emeralds,' Lettice had remarked in one of her more catty moments, Robert remembered, probably when Leicester had praised Elizabeth for some trifling reason.

Elizabeth, ignorant of his thoughts, picked up the plate of sugared almonds and invited Robert to stay and sit upon the cushions. The cushions that were, he noted irritably as he obeyed, still warm from Ralegh's arse.

'Gelly,' Robert shouted, striding into his apartments and throwing off his sword and baldric to land in a corner of the room.

Gelly Meyricke hurried through from the adjacent antechamber where he had been enjoying a quiet cup of beer with his feet up on a stool. Meyricke, a man whose Welsh heritage was everywhere exhibited in his person, in his short stature, his black hair and eyes, had been with Robert for many years, having served in the Devereux household for more than two decades. So long a service meant the Devereuxs were more like family to him than his own and Robert like a young brother. Meyricke cared deeply for his master and was concerned by the Robert he now encountered. 'Something the matter, my lord?'

Robert groaned and fell face down on his bed. 'What am I doing, Gelly?'

'At this very moment?'

'Here at court,' Robert punched the mattress and flipped himself over, disarranging the silk coverlet, one leg hanging over the side of the bed. 'What am I doing *here*?'

'Where else would you be?' Meyricke said, picking up the sword and baldric, wondering if this was the onset of one of Robert's notorious moods.

Throughout his life, Robert had been troubled with sudden changes in his temperament. For seemingly no reason, he would become melancholic, locking himself in his room and refusing all company. When his family asked what was wrong, he would truthfully be unable to answer, unable to identify the reason or the harsh word that had caused his sadness. And there were also the other times when Robert would laugh and be merry, almost to the point of hysteria. At such times, everything seemed possible to him, nothing was beyond his reach. The Devereux family had grown used to these changes of moods but were keen for no one else to find out about them. Indeed, part of Meyricke's job as Robert's manservant, as ordered by Robert's mother, was to keep an eye on him and even, if necessary, protect Robert from himself.

'What is it I do all day?' Robert asked, staring up at the canopy of the bed, his arms above his head. 'I play games. I win and lose money at cards. I see to the horses in the stables. I dance when music plays. I make the Queen smile.'

Meyricke moved to the side of the bed and leant over him. 'These are not insignificant things, my lord.'

'But are they work for a man, Gelly?' Robert demanded. 'Waiting on women?'

Meyricke held up a cautionary finger. 'I am not sure the Queen can be considered the same as other women, my lord.'

'Oh, do not be fooled about Elizabeth, Gelly. She *is* a woman. You have only to look beneath her skirts.' Robert sat up and hung both legs over the side of the bed. 'A man should perform deeds of honour. There are battles being fought in the world, you know, Gelly.'

'Not by England, there aren't.'

'No, indeed, not by England. The Spanish are overrunning Europe, enforcing their Papist creed and terrorising entire countries, but we,' Robert gestured at himself with both hands, 'stay in England and do nothing.'

'You want to go to war?'

'What else is a man fit for? If we men do not fight, we are no better than women. We may as well all wear petticoats and spin wool.'

'We have been to war before, my lord, if you remember, and not all that long ago, neither,' Meyricke remarked, reminding Robert that they had both served with Leicester in the Netherlands campaign against the Spanish. The campaign had been far less than successful, especially for Leicester who had been humiliated and disappointed while there, the former by Elizabeth when she had made him renounce a prestigious title the Netherlanders had bestowed upon him, and the latter by the later ingratitude of the Netherlanders themselves when the English army failed to achieve its objectives. The country was still trying to rid itself of its Spanish invaders.

'I remember, Gelly.'

'You will remember then a great deal of hardship. Men falling sick, men dying. Your friend, Sir Philip Sidney, among them.'

'I know. As if I could forget the death of Sidney. But I remember too, the riding into battle, the meeting of an enemy face to face. That feeling, Gelly, tell me you felt it too.'

'The thrill of battle?' Meyricke smiled and nodded. 'Oh yes, I felt it. Being a hair's breadth away from death, your heart beating so fast you fear it will burst out of your chest. A rapturous moment when you have nothing else in your mind but running your enemy through with your sword.'

'That's it,' Robert said excitedly, 'you do know what I mean.'

'I know,' Meyricke admitted, moving to the buffet and placing Robert's sword on its cradle. 'But I do not long for such a feeling again.'

'You are growing old, Gelly,' Robert scoffed. 'And I am sure I will be old before such an opportunity arises again.'

Meyricke, seeing that the conversation was going round in a circle and Robert growing more despondent, sought to change the subject. 'Come, my lord, your time here is well spent. You already have the license on sweet wines that brings you in a pretty penny. Your closeness to the Queen will provide more material rewards soon.'

'You speak only of coin,' Robert said sourly.

'Indeed, I do not. I see I must remind you of your stepfather.'

'Which one? I have a new stepfather now, Gelly.'

'The Earl of Leicester,' Meyricke continued doggedly, ignoring Robert's sarcasm. 'He was Master of the Horse, as you are now. He rose to become a Privy Counsellor and died the Lieutenant and Captain-General of the Queen's Armies and Companies, the highest title there is.'

Robert's eyes brightened. He rose and gripped

Meyricke's shoulders with both hands. 'That's right, Gelly, he did. And what were the Dudleys? Mere parvenus. Why, Leicester's grandfather was nothing more than King Henry VII's tax collector. But you know I am a Devereux. I have more royal blood in my veins than the Queen herself. How high might *I* not rise?'

Meyricke glanced towards the door, relieved to see it was shut. He wished Robert would not say such things, or at least if he must say them, say them less loudly. If Robert had only given his words more serious thought, Meyricke reflected, he would have realised that the only title higher than the Lieutenant-General was King, and how could he aspire to such a position? Did he think he could marry the celebrated virgin queen? He put his hands over Robert's and removed them from his shoulders.

'Perhaps it would be best, my lord, if you were to keep those kinds of ideas to yourself.'

VII

Robert had heard Lady Frances Sidney was in London, visiting her father, Sir Francis Walsingham. Meyricke's mention of her husband, Philip, had reminded Robert of a promise he had made to the dying young man. As Sidney lay on the army cot bed in the cold surgeon's tent in the Netherlands, the smell of his gangrenous leg turning Robert's stomach as he sat at his side, he had reached for Robert's hand with his own clammy extremity and held it tight to his chest. Sidney's cracked lips had opened and asked Robert to look after his wife when he was dead. Robert had readily agreed, most willing to do all he could for a man he so admired. But the promise made, it was soon forgot, and Frances Sidney had seen her husband's deputy only once since he had returned from war. The realisation of his neglect made Robert ashamed and he determined to pay Sidney's widow a visit as a means of making amends. So, he had made the short journey from the court to Walsingham's house in Seething Lane and had been shown into a small chamber with a meagre fire and little comfortable furniture, so unlike his own abodes. He looked out of the diamond-leaded window while he waited.

Robert heard behind him the soft pad of footsteps on the rush matting, the rustle of silk, and turned. Lady Frances Sidney was dressed in a handsome mustard yellow damask dress that complimented her olive complexion, an inheritance from her sallow-skinned father, and a Venetian headdress that covered most of her dark brown hair. She was slimmer than when he had last seen her and he suddenly remembered she had been carrying Sidney's child when he died. *How could I have forgotten that?* he scolded himself.

'Lady Sidney.' He took her hand and pressed it to his lips. 'You must forgive me for not attending on you sooner.'

'I understand you are very busy, my lord,' Frances said, indicating a chair. 'There is no need to apologise.'

There was a moment's awkward silence between them. Now he was here, Robert had little idea of what he should say to this woman. He had only become a close friend to Sidney during the Netherlands campaign and had met Frances on only a few occasions before that when Sidney had brought her with him when he had visited his uncle Leicester.

'Your child?' was the subject Robert settled on. 'He… she?'

'She,' Francis confirmed with a smile, sensing his awkwardness. 'She is well, I thank you. I can see her father in her.'

They endured another silence while they both paid mental homage to Philip's memory.

'Will you be coming to court while you are in London, my lady?'

'On Friday. I must pay my respects to the Queen and I understand there is to be an entertainment.'

'Yes, a play by my late stepfather's company, Lord

Leicester's Players. That is, they used to be called that. They're now under the patronage of Lord Strange, but they are still very good.'

'Indeed? I shall look forward to it then. I rarely see quality entertainment in the country.'

'Perhaps you would care to sup with me after the play?' Robert asked on impulse. Frances's colour deepened and Robert expected, almost hoped for, a refusal.

Instead, she raised her head and looked him in the eye. 'Thank you, I would like that. It is kind of you to think of me.'

'Not at all. It pleases me to be able to keep my word to your noble husband. I promised him I would look after you.'

Robert did not understand why the pleasure seemed to leave Frances's countenance. He could not know that she wished he had asked her to supper because he wanted to spend time with her, not out of duty to the husband who to all the world had seemed the perfect knight, but who in truth, had cared little for her.

Frances accepted another cup of wine from Gelly Meyricke and drank half of it down in one gulp. She had enjoyed the play, despite her disappointment at having to take a seat in the second row behind Robert and the Queen. She had been worried that Robert would be called upon to keep company with the Queen, but the German ambassador was in London and protocol demanded Elizabeth sup with him.

Frances had chosen her newest dress for the occasion, a green silk with gold thread embroidery and cut in the latest French fashion. She told herself that it was for no one's benefit but her own, that she had wanted to make a good impression at court, but as supper had begun she had had to acknowledge that it was not true.

To her dismay, Robert had not noticed her new dress. He had greeted her in the Presence Chamber before the play's commencement and they had talked of nothing, in particular, just pleasantries and a little court gossip. She, and perhaps Robert too, was very conscious of not only the Queen's penetrative stare but her father Walsingham's all-noticing eye. They had had only a few minutes together before Elizabeth had summoned Robert to her side and she had not relinquished him until the players had danced their final jig. During the short walk to his private apartments, Robert had seemed distracted and Frances had wondered if he was regretting his invitation, keeping him, as it did, from the Queen's presence. Through supper, she watched him eat without seeming to notice what he put into his mouth and noted with apprehension the quantity of wine he drank.

Her concern faded, though, as Robert relaxed, no doubt aided by the alcohol. He ceased to look at the door as if hoping or expecting a summons and Frances allowed herself to believe that he enjoyed her company after all. She even began to flirt with the handsome earl, a practice she had not been able to exercise since before her marriage. It made her feel desirable. Robert made her feel desirable. And she was grateful.

The expensive silk dress had been discarded, tossed in a crumpled puddle on the floor. Her skin was tight with dried sweat, her lips bruised and her throat dry. Frances turned over onto her side in the bed and ran a finger down Robert's spine, its tip bumping over each cartilage, coming to a stop only when it reached the base of his spine. A body so different from her husband's, the only other man she had known.

Frances knew that she would have to leave and resented it. She had not felt so content, so happy, for such a long time, but moments of pure pleasure could not last forever and she slipped from beneath the blankets to search for her shift. She crouched low and twisted her limbs as she searched because even though Robert had explored every inch of her body with an almost inconsiderate self-indulgence, she felt embarrassed now their passion was spent and did not want him to see her naked.

She struggled into her shift and dress, knowing that she would be unable to lace herself and wishing she had kept it on. *Just like a whore from the Southwark stews,* Frances mused. She winced at the thought, the full realisation of her actions filtering through to her just as the dawn leached in through the shutters and daubed the bedroom a sepia hue. She pulled on her stockings and slipped her small feet into her shoes. Her bodice flapped open, hanging upon her, and she had a moment of panic that someone in the palace corridors would see her in such a state of undress and know what she had been doing.

Frances moved towards the door and hesitated. She did not want to leave like a whore, creeping out in shame, nor did she want to think of the past few hours spent in Robert's bed as a sinful act. Wise it may not have been, but her heart refused to believe that it was wrong.

She tiptoed to the other side of the bed and bent over Robert, listening to his breathing. She kissed his cheek and his eyelids fluttered sleepily open.

He mumbled her name, but his head did not rise up from the pillow. Frances told him she was leaving and he nodded. Disappointed that he did no more, she left his room, pausing at the door to check the corridor before making her way quickly to her own chamber, situated next to her father's. Her maid, sleeping on a pallet pulled out from beneath the four-poster bed, awoke at her entrance, but thankfully said nothing as she helped her mistress undress once more and climb into her own bed, even though Frances could have sworn she saw the girl smile.

VIII

Thomas Pope pulled the painted curtains of the Theatre's tiring house an inch apart and put his eye to the gap. The theatre was filling up; it was going to be a full house. Perhaps it was the draw of the new play, or maybe the talent of their leading man, Richard Burbage. Pope raised his eyes to the wooden galleries to see how many of the seats were taken. Plenty of ruffs and silk gowns, he noted happily. The company could truly claim to play to the quality. He looked back to the stage, where stools were being set down for the young noblemen who paid to sit on the raised platform to have a good view of the play, but more importantly, to be seen. William Sly called from the rear of the tiring house where he was climbing into his costume to ask how the house was and Thomas replied that it was busy and let the curtain fall. He started towards Sly to help him tie his ruff, but a ripple of applause drew him back to the gap in the curtain.

A group of three young men were making their way through the groundling pit, the crowd parting to create a narrow, uneven corridor to the stage. They were dressed magnificently, the rich colours and quality of their doublets and hose a striking contrast to the workaday garb of the commoners of London.

They reached the edge of the stage and unhesitatingly mounted the steps to the platform. The applause became augmented with cheers. Two of the young men acknowledged the acclaim with a raising of their hands before settling themselves onto the stools. The third turned to face the crowd, just as if he were one of the actors about to perform before them. His gaze travelled around, up and down the horseshoe of the theatre, his hand raised and his face shining with pleasure. He bathed in the people's adoration for a few glorious seconds longer, then joined his companions.

'What's happening out there?' Sly said, almost falling over as he pulled on a knee-length leather boot.

Pope turned to Sly, grinning. 'Guess who's arrived.'

'Who?'

'The Earl of Essex.'

It had been a long day for Elizabeth. She had risen at her usual hour of six, attended chapel, heard a sermon and then breakfasted. She had ridden out in the Chase, taking with her some of her younger ladies who did not object to being in the saddle, as well as a few of her courtiers. An exceptional horsewoman, she had never lost her love of riding, but she had had to reluctantly accept that her body could not endure its vigorous exercise as it once did. She was still in good shape, it could not be denied, but Elizabeth had entered her fifth decade and now her bones ached in cold and damp weather and an hour on horseback was all she could bear. Her dinner had been a simple, even meagre affair, and feeling weary, though not wishing to admit it, had declined to take part in the afternoon's dancing.

Cecil had appeared as the afternoon turned into evening, the usual stack of papers beneath his arm. In the early years of her reign, Elizabeth had attended assiduously to the business of governing, revelling in the power and yes, the problems that came with it, but as the years passed, she knew she could trust her counsellors and would let them get on with their work, so that now she only insisted on a daily report from her secretary.

Elizabeth had felt half-inclined to tell Cecil to go away, that business could wait until the following day, but decades of being a queen made even this small act of indolence unthinkable. She nodded to Cecil and led the way through to her private apartments so that they could attend to business.

Elizabeth signed the document and handed it back to Cecil who tucked it into his leather folder.

'And the last item, Your Majesty. A report from the Master of the Revels,' he said. 'Several new plays are being performed this week. *A Knack to Know a Knave, The Seven Deadly Sins,* and *Henry the Sixth.* The Master has passed them all fit for performance, nothing seditious in any of them, and suggests that *The Seven Deadly Sins* will please Your Majesty and recommends it for a court entertainment.' He paused to look at Elizabeth and, gauging her mood, decided it was safe to continue. 'He also writes that the playhouses are attracting some of your courtiers. The Earl of Southampton and the Earl of Essex, along with Lord Mounteagle, attended a performance of Master Kyd's *The Spanish Tragedy* at the Theatre on Wednesday, and the Master writes that the Earl of Essex was greeted with much acclaim by the playgoers.'

Elizabeth, whose body had begun to droop, jerked alert. Her bones ached, her eyes were heavy and she had been thinking only of her bed, but now she was wide awake. *Acclaim for Essex? Since when have any of my courtiers, my subjects, deserved acclaim for merely showing up at a play? That is my prerogative. I am Gloriana. My subjects cheer me.* 'So the people love Essex, do they? Why do they so?'

Cecil shrugged, a little surprised that her response had not been harsher. 'He is young, handsome, courageous. He is everything the people always love.'

'They see a hero, I suppose. He glitters, he shines,' Elizabeth laughed savagely. 'What is it Walter Ralegh wrote? "Say to the court it glows and shines like rotten wood".'

'A rather unfair simile, in my opinion,' Cecil murmured.

'No? I think it rather apt. These days, anyway. It was not always so. Time was my subjects knew their place.'

This is more like it, Cecil thought with glee, *here is the jealous queen*. 'Should I suggest to the earl that he refrain from visiting the theatre?'

'Upon what grounds, Pygmy?' she demanded sharply. 'I cannot forbid him from seeking out entertainment. He would simply do it all the more, like a petulant child. Leave him be. Do nothing, but instruct the Master of the Revels that I want to hear of it should any similar incident occur.'

IX

Frances Sidney was in her bedchamber at her home in the country when she should have been supervising the making of butter in the dairy. She had consulted her almanack, not just once but three times, just to be sure. The moon had come and gone again, but not so her menses. It had been two months since she had shared a bed with Robert Devereux and Frances knew her body. She had been pregnant twice before and she recognised the signs of being with child.

She was such a fool. She had not been some green girl, a coy virgin, unaware of what she was doing when she climbed into bed with Robert. She was a mature woman, a mother of two children and a respected widow. She was not a stupid woman either; she had known what would be the likely outcome of their encounter.

Frances sat on her bed and told herself to breathe deeply, else she was sure she would weep. She was so lost in her thoughts that she cried out when her bedchamber door opened, squealing on its hinges.

'Frances, what do you think of this clo—'

Her mother, Ursula, ceased abruptly and looked into

her daughter's face, her maternal sense knowing something was wrong. 'What is the matter?'

Frances had feared, yet at the same time, wanted her mother to ask the question, and now she burst out with, 'Oh, Mother,' and held out her arms.

Ursula immediately took a seat beside her daughter on the bed and put her arms around her. Frances cried against her mother's neck and Ursula patted her back, cooing soothingly, 'There now.'

When her sobs were spent, Frances unbent her body and relaxed her hold on her mother, sniffing to stop her nose running.

Ursula provided a linen handkerchief and told her daughter to wipe her eyes. 'Now, tell me what the matter is.'

'You will think me wicked,' Frances promised.

'No doubt, but I will hear it all the same.'

It took several moments but, at last, Frances confessed. 'I think I am with child, Mother.'

'Oh, Frances,' Ursula breathed, shutting her eyes, 'you foolish girl. Who was it?'

'I cannot tell you.'

'You will tell me, Frances,' Ursula declared, in no mood to brook any nonsense, 'or I will throw you out of doors.'

Frances knew it was a hollow threat, that her mother would not commit such an unnatural and brutal act, but it salved her conscience to be forced to tell the truth rather than volunteer it. 'The Earl of Essex, Mother. When I went to London.'

'Oh, Frances,' Ursula said again, 'of all the men at court, you had to choose the one closest to the Queen. And he! What was he thinking?' A thought suddenly occurred to her. 'He did not force you, did he?'

Frances shook her head. 'I cannot blame him.'

'Have you told him? Does he know?'

'No. How can I tell him?'

'How can you not, you silly girl?'

'Well, what good would it do?' Frances asked, wiping her nose. 'Surely, it would be best if I stayed here until the child is born and then I give it to one of the women on the estate to look after.'

Ursula was shocked. 'I will not have any grandchild of mine unacknowledged by this family, Frances. Give it to a woman on the estate, indeed. I am ashamed of you for thinking such a thing. No, we will write to the earl at once and say that he must wed you.'

Frances caught her breath, half-hopeful, half-fearful. 'But Mother, he is an earl. He will not want to marry me. And there's the Queen. She may not allow it.'

'You are the daughter of one of the Queen's most trusted counsellors, Frances, not a nobody. And quite frankly, as far as his and your status is concerned, if my daughter is good enough to be bedded, she is good enough to be wedded, by anyone. I do not care that he is an earl, he could be the tsar of Russia for all I care. And as for the Queen,' Ursula bit her lip, 'well, yes, that will be a problem, but we will have to think about that later.'

'And Father?'

'We shall go to London to tell him. I do not want to write to him of such a matter.'

'Would it not be best to wait and find out what Robert… what the earl says before telling Father?' Frances suggested, knowing that the news would greatly disappoint her father.

'He has a right to know, Frances. This is not the kind of secret we can, or should, keep.' Ursula disentangled herself from her daughter and rose. 'We were going to London next week in any case. We shall just bring our arrangements forward. We should be able to leave for

London on Friday. Now, you write that letter to the earl and do not seal it. I want to read it first.'

Ursula strode out of the room in a determined manner. Frances, feeling much better now that her mother knew of her shameful condition, moved to her table by the window and began to write to her one-time lover.

ೋ ೋ ೋ

Gelly Meyricke ducked his way through the crowd in the Great Hall at Hampton Court Palace, the press of so many bodies making him feel hot. He made his way to the raised platform at the end of the chamber where the Queen and the highest peers in the realm sat.

Robert, seated at Elizabeth's left hand, saw Gelly approaching and wondered what had brought him to the chamber. Whatever it was, it was important and from the look on Gelly's face unwelcome. Robert didn't want the Queen hearing anything he would rather keep quiet, so he excused himself to Elizabeth and stepped down from the table. Gelly saw his master rise and halted to wait where he was.

'What is it, Gelly?' Robert asked.

'I am sorry to disturb you here, my lord, but this letter has just been delivered. The messenger said it was urgent. He came from Lady Frances Sidney.'

Robert took the letter from Gelly without a word, apprehensive of its contents. He felt he had acted dishonourably with Frances, seducing the widow of a man he had so admired, and he had written to her apologising for his conduct and asking for her forgiveness. Frances had replied, assuring him he had nothing to apologise for and trusting to his discretion. He had heard nothing more and had hoped to forget the incident altogether. He opened the letter and read the contents.

Gelly saw his master's expression darken and knew that the letter contained ill news. 'Something amiss, my lord?' he asked quietly, so as not to draw the attention of those nearby.

'Yes, Gelly, something amiss.' Robert refolded the letter and tucked it inside his doublet. He glanced back at Elizabeth. She was talking to Burghley, but her eyes were on Robert. He smiled bravely at her before turning back to Gelly. 'You cannot help me.'

'Are you certain?' Gelly probed, curious.

'It is not fitting that I speak of this matter to you,' Robert snapped, angered by the letter's contents and careless of who he took his anger out upon.

But Gelly was used to being reminded of his inferior status and his master's temper and was not upset by Robert's words. He said, 'The Earl of Southampton is approaching. Perhaps he can help.'

Robert looked around just as Henry Wriothesley slid his arm through Robert's. Robert dismissed Gelly with a sour nod.

'I sense something is wrong,' Henry, who had been watching Robert and was curious to know what was going on, said playfully. 'Will you tell me or must I guess?'

Robert drew Henry towards the side of the chamber, brushing against the magnificent tapestries that Henry the Eighth had commissioned from the tapestry weavers of Belgium fifty years earlier. Woven with gold and silver thread, they demonstrated the weavers' great skill and still had few rivals in England, but the central fire of the hall had caused the tapestries to blacken in parts and they shone less brightly than they once had.

'Lady Frances Sidney has written to me,' Robert said. 'She is with child, Henry.'

Henry, who had been told of Robert's tryst with the widow, said simply, 'Yours?'

'She says so.'

'Have you reason to doubt her?'

'No,' Robert was vehement. 'Heavens, no, Henry. She is not every man's mistress.'

'I am only asking,' Henry said, putting out his hands in mollification.

'She is Sidney's widow. Do you think he would have married an unchaste woman?'

'No, of course not.' Henry thought it best not to add that for all of his married life, Sir Philip Sidney had hardly been a paragon of fidelity and had been less than loyal to his wife. 'Well, what will you do?'

'What can I do, Henry?' Robert asked hopelessly. 'She's bound to tell her father and then he will tell the Queen. Elizabeth will be furious. But I cannot, in all honour, abandon Frances. That would make me a blackguard.'

Henry drew delicate fingers across his smooth forehead and shrugged. 'But you will mar your fortunes if you displease the Queen, Rob. You know how she feels about her favourites marrying, especially without her consent, if that is what you are thinking.'

Robert sighed. 'Must I be in thrall to a woman? Why must I watch what I say and who I dally with? Damn, Henry, I am a Devereux, yet I am kept chained as any prisoner in Newgate.'

'The curse of our times, Robert. It is how we gallant young men must make our money,' Henry said with an exaggerated sigh, a trick he had picked up from the theatres he so liked to visit. 'If we had a war to fight, we would be able to make our fortune on the battlefield rather than at the court.'

'There's the Spanish, Henry. They are a bloodthirsty

lot. They may threaten England again.'

'And hope too that the Queen will act? That is a fantasy, Robert. The Queen loathes war. And besides, she would never let you go. Look how she kept Leicester by her side for all those years.'

'I'll hide behind no woman's petticoats, Henry, queen or no.'

'I hear you, Robert, calm yourself.' Henry laid a hand on his friend's arm, wary of provoking his temper. 'Forget the prospect of battle. That is far off and we drift off course. The matter in hand is Lady Sidney.'

Robert said, 'I must marry her.' His tone was full of despair. He did not want to marry Frances Sidney; he had no love for her and no urgent desire for an heir. But he could not forget Philip. His conscience pricked and he knew he had no choice but to wed his dear friend's widow.

'But think, Rob. She is only the daughter and widow of knights. Hardly a fit wife for a Devereux.'

'Yet, she is a respectable woman, Henry.'

Henry pondered the virtue of pointing out that if Frances were a respectable woman, she would not be pregnant by a man who was not her husband, but he refrained. 'Marry her then, if you must.'

'I must because I have wronged her, do you not see that?'

Yes, I see and I agree,' Henry said, growing bored with the subject. 'Marry her, if it please you, but do not blame me for the Queen's wrath when she finds out.'

Sir Francis Walsingham returned home earlier than usual. The customary pain he felt in his stomach had been great during the day, making him cry out and double over in agony. His secretary, Thomas Phelippes, had pleaded with him to leave his work and retire to his bed, assuring him that England's security could wait until the morning. For once, Walsingham had allowed himself to be persuaded and he was looking forward to climbing into his bed, resting his aching head against the cool pillows and holding a cloth-covered hot stone to his tormenting side. He was to be disappointed.

Walsingham was surprised when his wife came into the hall while his servant was divesting him of his cloak and gloves, not having expected her until the following week. She said that she had brought Frances with her as if that was explanation enough for her premature visit, and asked him to follow her to her closet. Ursula led the way, her heels clicking on the bare floorboards with a rat-tat-tat in her haste. They reached her closet and Ursula held the door open for him to enter.

Frances was standing by the small fireplace, staring down into the dancing flames. She looked up as her father entered, greeted him and made a curtsey. Walsingham noted that his daughter avoided his eyes, looking instead behind him at her mother, who also entered and closed the door. He felt his body stiffen in apprehension, knowing there was bad news coming, and the pain in his side intensified in a way he had not thought possible.

'Will one of you tell me what is wrong?' Walsingham said impatiently. 'Why have you come to London?'

'I have some news to tell you, Father,' Frances said after a terrible pause and at her mother's prompting. She took a deep breath. 'I am with child.'

Thank God, the news is not that she is ill, Walsingham thought, but his relief passed almost instantly. His daughter, his widowed daughter, was carrying a child! He had heard correctly, had he not? 'Your husband is dead, Frances.'

'Husband,' Ursula said quietly, placing a restraining hand on his arm.

He pulled it gently but firmly away. 'Tell me, am I wrong in that belief?'

'No, Father, you are not,' Frances admitted. 'The Earl of Essex is the father.'

'The Earl—', Walsingham's voice cracked and he put his hand to his mouth to clear his throat. 'The earl is the father of your child?'

'We wrote to him before we left for London, telling him of Frances's condition,' Ursula interjected. 'He would have received our letter by now.'

'And what do you expect him to do once he knows of our daughter's condition?' Walsingham wondered.

'Well, of course, we hope he will suggest marriage,' Ursula said, her tone unconvincing.

'And if he does not?'

'He is an honourable man, Father,' Frances said desperately.

'Is he, indeed?' Walsingham said, taking a seat. He leant forward, his elbows on his knees, an attempt to squash the pain that was making his upper lip perspire. 'I do not have the confidence in the earl that you seem to have. If he were honourable, he would not have seduced you, Frances.'

Frances could not admit to her father that she had been ripe for seduction and her cheeks flushed at the memory. 'Do you not think he will marry me, Father?' she asked quietly.

'How can I say, Frances?' Walsingham looked up at his daughter. 'This news has quite upset me.'

'I have disappointed you,' she said unhappily.

Walsingham looked away.

Ursula spoke. 'Go to your room, Frances. I must speak with your father.' When their daughter had gone, she said, 'You *are* disappointed in her, aren't you?'

'Of all the men she could choose, Ursula, why him?'

'I know. I said the same.'

'How could our daughter go from being the wife of a great man like Philip Sidney to being the mistress of Robert Devereux?'

'I know you do not think much of him—'

'With good cause, Ursula.'

'But he has the Queen's favour.'

'Which is another reason why I wish Frances had not… had not forgot herself.'

'But the earl is a favourite, like Leicester. The Queen forgave Leicester his marriage to Devereux's mother.'

'Essex is not Leicester, Ursula.'

'Frances must marry him, husband. She, and we will be shamed else. You must insist Essex marries her. In secret, if necessary.'

'Yes, I know. Of course, she must marry him. But I could have wished for a better son-in-law.'

'She…,' Ursula swallowed, 'the Queen will not punish Frances for marrying Essex, will she?'

Walsingham stared into the fire. 'I do not know, my dear,' he murmured.

X

Elizabeth was grinding her teeth and it hurt. She had lost four on the left side of her mouth and those she still had were decaying. *But*, she thought, *if I do not clench my jaw or grind my teeth, I am going to scream, I am going to roar because it has happened again. A man has once again betrayed me!*

'They did not obtain my consent to marry,' she hissed.

'No, Your Majesty,' Walsingham admitted, keeping his eyes on the ground and wondering whether he dared to shift his weight onto his other foot. Movement had the potential to draw Elizabeth's wrath that was, mercifully, directed against Essex and not him at this moment. To his relief, Robert had agreed to marry Frances and the ceremony had been hastily arranged. Whether to tell Elizabeth of the marriage had cast a shadow over the celebrations, with Frances, Robert and Ursula wanting it to be kept a secret. But Walsingham knew that it could not remain so and decided that the best course would be to face the danger head on. He had hoped that Robert would accompany him to tell the Queen, but Robert had declined, finding that he had other matters to attend to elsewhere.

'Your daughter, Walsingham,' Elizabeth said accusingly.

'Circumstances, Your Majesty. This course of action would never have happened but for circumstances.'

'And what circumstances were they?'

Walsingham's dark face coloured. 'My daughter is with child by the earl.'

Elizabeth's throat constricted. Swiving. Always country matters. What was the matter with men that they were so ruled by their loins?

'I see,' she snarled, rising from her chair. Her ladies cowered, keeping their eyes low and pressing their backs against the walls. 'And where is the wretch?'

'Madam?'

'Essex,' she screamed, losing her control at last. 'Where is he?'

'He is at court, Your Majesty.' Walsingham looked around as if expecting, almost hoping, Robert would appear.

'Then you tell him to get himself from my court. I do not want that vile seducer anywhere within my walls. And as for his wife, you can look after her,' she spat at Walsingham. 'I won't have them living in the same house as one another. I'll teach them to go behind my back. They should think themselves fortunate I do not send them both to the Tower.'

It was the best offer Elizabeth was going to make, Walsingham knew. Better his daughter live with her family than languish in the Tower. He bowed, backing out of the room, and went in search of his new son-in-law.

'What a fool you are,' Lettice said, pinning her needle to her embroidery and moving to sit beside her son in front of the fire.

Robert had retired to Drayton Bassett, his mother's home in Staffordshire. When he had first arrived, he had been indignant, proud, haughty that Elizabeth should punish him for such an act as daring to marry, but as the days passed and no news came from the court, he lost his bluster and his old melancholy settled upon him. He had never liked to be mocked, not even in play, and he was fretting over how he was being talked about by his peers at court. *No doubt*, he thought ruefully, *they are calling me a fool as Mother has just done, and they are right. I am a fool. And what galls me most is the thought that that rogue Ralegh will be making the most out of my absence with Elizabeth.*

'Mother,' he said wearily, resting his aching head on his hand and closing his eyes against the brightness of the day, 'it is done now. I am married. Help me make it better.'

'Why ask me?'

'Because you know Elizabeth. What must I do to win her favour again?'

Lettice sighed and pushed the embroidery stand aside. 'You forget how long it is since I saw her, my boy. God's Death, but I have not been at court for,' she raised her eyes to the ceiling as she searched her memory, 'twelve years or more. But I suppose she has not changed a great deal.' Her voice grew low as she reflected, 'Just grown older, as we all have.' She looked to her son. 'She is a vain old hag, Robert. Do what Leicester always did. Flatter her. Write her long letters of love.'

'I have just married another woman. She will not believe them.'

'Of course, she will,' Lettice could not keep the

contempt out of her voice. 'She sincerely believes, and expects, every man at court to be in love with her.'

'I cannot tell such lies, Mother.'

Lettice slapped his hand, growing angry with him. 'Now, you listen to me, Robert. You do what you have to do.'

'I would rather stay here or go to Chartley.' The lie came defiantly. 'The court is no place for me.'

'How do you expect to make your fortune in the country, my darling? And what of your wife? You must write to the Council and be humble if you want Elizabeth to relent and allow you to have your wife at your side.'

'Oh, do not plague me with such questions,' Robert shook his hands at her in frustration. 'I cannot be thinking about Frances now. She can stay where she is, with her family.'

'Why, Robert! Do you not love her?' Lettice teased, a smile playing upon her lips. 'What is she like, this new wife of yours? She always seemed a very dull creature when she was married to Leicester's nephew.'

'She is pleasant enough, Mother.'

'You could have married better, my darling.'

'Perhaps,' Robert nodded in agreement, 'but there are advantages to this marriage that I had not considered before. I have elevated Frances from a lady to a countess and made Walsingham kin to me. He must therefore needs do what he can for me for his own family's good.'

'Silly boy. What can he do for you when you are banished from court?'

How Robert hated it when his mother was in the right. 'Oh, very well,' he said, moving to a desk and snatching up a quill, 'I will write to the Council, to Walsingham, and to Elizabeth, to anyone you want and abase myself. Will that satisfy you, Mother?'

Lettice raised her eyebrows, unappreciative of her

son's resentful conformity to her suggestions. 'Do not concern yourself with satisfying *me*, Robert, when it is for your own good.'

Lettice returned to her embroidery stand and Robert wrote his letters to Elizabeth. He wrote words he did not mean, feelings he did not own. The words came to him far easier than he had imagined they would. Once begun, his declarations of love and loyalty, his pleas for forgiveness, flowed easily. He was almost able to convince himself that he meant every word.

Elizabeth's eyes opened stickily. She blinked, trying to focus. She pulled her arm from beneath the coverlet and pressed her fingers to the delicate skin beneath her myopic orbs. She felt wetness there and realised that had been crying in her sleep. She lay perfectly still on her side, listening to the sound of even breathing coming from the woman asleep on the pallet at the side of her bed, sleeping there for her safety and security.

The dream was already fading, even as she stared into the semi-darkness of her bedchamber, but she remembered how it had made her feel, why she had awoken with tears running down her face. Lonely. Unloved. Frightened. She had been experiencing dreams of this sad nature for some little while, but it was the first time one had carried over into reality.

Elizabeth was growing afraid of falling asleep, wary of the dark night and what it would torment her with. Her bed only held horrors and she wanted to avoid it as much as possible. She needed someone to sit up with her into the small hours, someone who would not complain that they were weary or become taciturn because they could not think of anything to say that would amuse her. She had had someone like that once.

Oh Leicester, she moaned into her pillow, *how I miss you, how I need you still.*

Thoughts of Leicester led inevitably to Robert, his replacement. He had betrayed her by marrying, it was true, but at least he had never claimed to love the woman. Robert had married Sidney's widow as an act of honour, as the unhappy consequence of fumbling beneath her skirts, and Elizabeth could not blame him for that. She knew how important honour was to him, had seen his eyes glisten when he read passages from books on chivalry and recalled the deeds of his ancestors. And, in truth, what real harm had been done? she asked herself. She had had letters from him professing regret that he had hurt her and assuring her of his unwavering love and devotion. She had no reason to doubt he was sincere. No, she decided, if Robert asked again to be allowed to return to her, she would let him. He would have to be punished, of course. He could not betray her and expect not to suffer a little, but there was no need to make the punishment too harsh.

Elizabeth slid her arm back beneath the coverlet as her skin grew cold, pulling the covers up to her chin, drawing her legs up to her stomach. She closed her eyes, prepared to risk sleep now that she had made a decision.

Walsingham came to her later the next morning with a letter from Robert that once more begged Elizabeth's forgiveness. Elizabeth read the letter, re-read it, held it to her breast and thanked God for it. She did not hesitate.

She looked up at Walsingham and, to his surprise, he found no malice in her eyes. He was even more surprised, but nevertheless pleased, to hear her say, 'Tell Essex he may return.'

XI

Robert hurried back to the palace at Whitehall as soon as he received word he would be welcome. He had been granted a private audience and felt Elizabeth's steely eyes upon him as her attendants filed out. He had to be humble, he reminded himself and so he had not just bowed, but knelt to Elizabeth, and she had kept him on his knees for at least three minutes by his reckoning.

'You may rise,' Elizabeth said at last, just as his knees were beginning to hurt.

He got to his feet. 'Thank you, Your Majesty. May I say—'

'How is married life?' she cut in. The words were solicitous but the tone in which they were delivered was decidedly not. Unsure how to answer, he hesitated. 'Do you find it amenable, sir?' Elizabeth persisted.

'I hardly find it anything at all, madam,' he returned, 'as I live as if I were not married. The lady, as I understand you know, remains with her mother in the country.'

'Do you miss her company?'

'I find I do very well without it, madam.' He gave

Elizabeth his most charming smile and it worked its magic now. Her amber eyes widened and the thin-lipped mouth twitched. In pleasure? In amusement? Robert could not tell.

'And it pleases me to have you back at court, my lord. I have had so little company to offer me distraction.'

'Oh, you mean Sir Walter has not amused you? I find that odd. He always makes me laugh.'

'Now, Robin,' she said, deciding she would grace him with the old familiarity, 'do not say so. I will not have our reunion spoilt by jealousy.'

'As Your Majesty commands. Of what then shall we talk?'

'Of what you will, Robin.'

'Why then,' he said, emboldened by her warmth and wanting to press his advantage, 'may I speak of France?'

The coquettish smile fell from Elizabeth's face. She had expected love talk from Robert, not politics. 'France?'

'King Henri,' Robert explained. 'Has he not sought your assistance in his military endeavours against the Catholic League?'

The Catholic League was a society formed by Henry I, the Duke of Guise, in 1576, which sought to remove all trace of Protestantism from France. Many French nobles were Huguenots, defenders of the Protestant faith, and the Catholics in the country were concerned over the power they had. Henri, although the legitimate king of France, had been unable to enter its capital, Paris, because it was held by Catholics, and was forced to retreat into the southern part of the country. He had been appealing to all of Europe's Protestant leaders, but especially to Elizabeth, to help him take control of his realm.

'What if he has?' Elizabeth's voice had acquired a sharp edge. 'And how the devil do *you* know of it, anyway?'

'If he has,' Robert ignored her questions, judging it was not wise to admit that the French king, knowing him to be a champion of Protestantism, had written to Robert personally asking for him to plead with the Queen on his behalf, 'then I would dearly love to represent you in the field, Your Majesty.'

'What?' she scoffed. 'You go to war? Do not be absurd.'

'I am not being absurd.' Robert fell to his knees once more and looked up at her. 'See how earnest I am.'

'I do not care for your earnestness, Robin. Get up.'

'I will not, Bess,' Robert declared. 'I will stay on my knees until you give me leave to go to France.'

'Then you will be on your knees a long time, my lord.'

'At least allow me to speak to you on the matter, I beg you.'

It would not hurt to listen to what he has to say, Elizabeth thought, *and he does make a very attractive supplicant, kneeling there at my feet.*

But she had forgotten how persuasive he could be and, though she tried to resist him, Elizabeth found herself eventually agreeing to Robert going to France after he had petitioned her for two hours on his knees. Any qualms she felt at the prospect of his leaving were assuaged by the ardour with which he thanked her.

And, in fact, Robert had done her a service. He had reminded her that she need not be lonely without him, for he was not the only interesting young man at court, though he had been her most attentive and malleable. No, there was also Ralegh. With Robert to keep her company, Elizabeth had not thought of calling on Ralegh to stay up with her into the early hours. His attendance at court could be erratic. Though he held the position of Captain of the Guard, he often delegated his duty to others, convincing Elizabeth he needed to travel to some distant country on explorations, and she like a fool would let him go, inspired by his talk of strange encounters and riches. Well, that would change now. Ralegh would stay at court while Robert was away and keep her company.

And now Elizabeth thought harder, she found Ralegh sometimes easier to be with than Robert. Elizabeth understood Ralegh and Ralegh understood her. Perhaps it was because Ralegh was a decade or so older than Robert. Robert was such a boy and she enjoyed his enthusiasm and his youth, for it made her feel young again, but Ralegh was a pragmatist at heart, just like her. Elizabeth understood that Ralegh paid her the compliments she loved to receive because he wanted things from her. This, of course, was how the relationship between sovereign and subject worked. A subject swore allegiance to a sovereign, and in effect, allowed them to remain on their throne in exchange for material rewards.

And because they understood one another, Elizabeth knew she could bestow her attentions on others and not upset Ralegh too greatly. When she was bored with her other men, she could pick up with Ralegh where they left off, without there being rancour or bitterness on either side. Ralegh was also interesting, able to talk about life outside the court, about other people, about lives that she could not possibly know of or experience for herself. The conversations Elizabeth had with Ralegh were quite unlike those she had with any other. Robert, for all his charm, had an irritating tendency to talk only of himself. Ralegh had a thrilling intellect and sense of adventure that she could only admire and envy. He wrote poems as easily as he breathed, while other courtiers, Robert included, would struggle and agonise over every word. He talked of distant places and strange people, of getting on board a ship and sailing to lands that did not exist on any map but that he knew must exist. He talked of travelling to the New World and creating a new England, so that she, Elizabeth, would not just be a queen of one little island, but of a country whose undoubted wealth had not yet been tapped. Oh yes, Ralegh was a fine companion for her. And he, like all the others, did profess to love her, to adore her. For all she knew, he was speaking the truth.

I may not say that Walter is all mine, but he understands the game, she thought. *I will send for him and he can do his duty by me and keep me company while Robert goes to his wars. I never have to wake up crying again.*

‘You would do far better to stay in England,’ Henry Wriothesley said when Robert told him that he was going to France to help the French king regain his territory. ‘Why go to France? You could become a statesman like your wife’s father.’

‘Oh, Henry, pens and paper are not for me,’ Robert said dismissively. ‘What glory is there in that?’

Henry shrugged, unlike Robert, not being particularly concerned with acquiring martial glory. He moved to Robert’s desk and picked up the royal commission, rubbing his finger over the elaborate signature of the Queen. ‘When do you leave?’ he asked, watching Robert as he moved about the room, checking the flypages of books, choosing ones to take with him on his journey, discarding those he did not.

‘Saturday, leaving from Dover. I will catch the noonday tide.’

‘I think I shall come and see you off.’

‘You could come with me, you know. Do you not

fancy a spell of soldiering?'

Henry laughed and held out his hands. 'Thank you, Robert, but I am well enough here. My inclination at the moment is for the playhouse and the delightful whores I find in the taverns. If ever that changes, I will let you know.'

Robert laughed and playfully threw a shirt at him. 'You will get the pox and then where will you be?'

'Not dead on the end of a pike or with an arrow through my throat, which is where you may be heading.'

'Not I, Henry. I am not destined to die on the battlefield.'

Henry's expression changed to one of derision and told Robert that it was impossible to know what lay ahead for any of them.

'I do know,' Robert assured him, opening the cover of a book and taking out a folded parchment. He handed it to Henry and told him to take a look. 'Mother had my fortune foretold. You can see from that, glory awaits me, Henry, and you do not achieve glory by sitting at home and scrawling figures in account books.'

'Or playing the lover to an old woman,' Henry smirked, glancing over the esoteric diagrams and charts on the paper.

Robert glared at him, all mirth gone. 'Why do you say that?'

'Well,' Henry half-laughed, a little taken aback by Robert's angry expression, 'that is what you do, is it not? Flatter the old bird, tell her you love her?'

'I do only what others do,' Robert protested. 'The Queen likes to be spoken to of love. Tell me, who does not like to be admired and flattered? Elizabeth need not believe it. Maybe she does not.'

'I understand, Robert, really I do. It is a game, we all know that, and you play it well.'

'Then do not mock me for it, Henry.'

'You mistake me, I do not mock you. Forgive me, I am merely full of envy. The Queen will never look on me with such favour as she shows you. You are loved by the gods, Robert.'

Placated, Robert's grin returned. 'Of course, I am, Henry. I am a Devereux and I have a glorious destiny.'

XII

July 1591

Sir Henry Unton laid his gloved hands on the window embrasure and looked down into the courtyard of Burghley House, where one thousand men under the command of the Earl of Essex had gathered to be inspected by the Queen.

Unton had to admit that Robert had done well. He had heard that upon receiving his commission from the Queen, Robert had written to his stewards, instructing them to recruit every willing and able-bodied man on his estates for his campaign in France. And they had come, nay, they had flocked to the earl's banner as, Unton reflected, was often the way with young men desperate for a taste of battle. He could understand it. Elizabeth had, for the most part, brought peace to England, but while her people rejoiced at the benefits, particularly in trade, that peace brought, her nobles grew restless and frustrated by the lack of action. Were he still young, Unton would have felt the same way, too.

A few minutes later, Sir Thomas Leighton joined him

at the window, Sir Henry Killigrew a step behind. Unton nodded a greeting and all three looked down on the courtyard as the Queen stepped out of her carriage, her gloved hand in Robert's.

'You have had your instructions?' Killigrew asked, giving Unton a sideways glance.

'Regarding the Earl of Essex?' Unton, his eyes still on the couple below, raised his eyebrows understandingly. 'Indeed, I have.'

Leighton chuckled. 'Essex may be her favourite, but Elizabeth does not exactly place much trust in him, does she, Unton?'

'I think it a very wise precaution to send us as advisers to the earl. Essex has little military experience and we,' Unton looked at his companions, 'have plenty between the three of us.'

'Ah, but will he listen to us?' Leighton wondered.

'The Queen commands that he does,' Unton said, taking a folded paper from the purse that hung from his belt and handing it to Leighton.

Leighton read: *'The Queen commands Sir Henry Unton, Ambassador to the Court of King Henri IV, take especial care of the Earl of Essex and his actions in the French campaign. He is to disregard the difference in their respective stations and deal in the plainest manner with him.'*

He handed the paper back to Unton. 'I am very glad that it has been so set down. Will you show that to the earl?'

'I think not, Leighton,' Unton said, tucking it back in his purse. 'I doubt the earl would care to know that he is only in titular command of this campaign.'

A cheer drew the trio's attention back to the courtyard. The Queen had made her inspection and was now entering the house to take dinner with Burghley. They saw Robert eagerly relinquish her hand to stay behind with his troops and throw an arm around a young man who trailed at his heels.

'Is that the earl's brother?' Killigrew asked.

'Walter Devereux. Yes, that's him.'

'He looks very young.'

'Not all that young, but he does not come to court often. I heard he prefers the country. But Essex insisted he come on the campaign,' Unton said. 'I can only imagine the earl wants the Devereux name to be amply represented.'

They watched as Robert gave orders to his captains and the troops began to disperse.

'Well, gentlemen,' Killigrew said with a sigh, 'the earl will no doubt be impatient to sail and I still have matters to attend to. I will see you soon at Dover.'

A summer storm had blown up in Dieppe and the rain was battering down on the canvas of his tent as it stood with all the others in the French field. Robert could have enjoyed its steady, soothingly soft rhythm were his mind not sorely troubled.

He had been so eager to leave England and fight in the French Protestant cause that he had not considered what his absence might mean. Elizabeth's favour was such a precarious thing as he had already found out. He had done what others had struggled to do before him, marry and retain the favour of the Queen, so he knew she regarded him highly. But he also knew Elizabeth was entertaining Ralegh with renewed vigour, and he suspected Sir Walter would attempt to put him out of favour, and the suspicion troubled him.

But his relationship with Elizabeth was not the only

matter on Robert's mind. He needed action to ward off the depression he could feel lurking. It hovered at the edge of his thoughts; when he awoke, it was there to greet him, and when he climbed into his bed, it was the last creature to bid him good night.

And yet, action seemed determined to elude him. King Henri was on the move, marching onto Noyen, and despite Robert's repeated pleas to Elizabeth to be allowed to follow him, her permission had still not been granted. Robert's army had been forced to stay where it was, and Robert was beginning to wonder why Elizabeth had agreed for him to come to France if she were not prepared to let him do anything else. Robert had also written to King Henri, hoping that a request from a fellow sovereign might force Elizabeth's hand, but he had heard nothing from him either. Was it a foible of monarchs to withhold communication from their subjects and allies, he wondered?

Robert was irked too that he was under the thumb of an old man. Unton was a decent fellow, but damn it all, a mere knight. He had been ready to march onto Noyen, with or without the Queen's permission, but Unton had told him the uncomfortable truth of his commission that Robert must follow his advice. Robert had stared at Unton, almost unable to believe his words. Unton had authority over him? It hurt, it actually caused him physical pain to discover that Elizabeth had so little faith in him. She had humiliated him before Unton, and what galled him more was that he didn't know who else knew his queen did not trust him and that he held no real power in the campaign. Elizabeth was treating him like a boy, sending guardians out with him to war to make sure he didn't get into any trouble.

Robert poured himself another cup of wine from the jug and downed it in one gulp. He knew he was drinking too much, but it was the only thing that helped, the only thing that stopped him thinking and feeling things he should not and did not welcome.

Unton poked his head through the tent flap and asked if he could come in. Robert waved him to enter, swaying a little.

Unton frowned, wondering, then saw the wine cup and understood. 'I have something that will please you, my lord. Finally, a letter from King Henri.'

Robert snatched the letter Unton held out and broke the seal. His vision was a little blurry and he had to narrow his eyes to bring the words into focus. 'King Henri's captured Noyen. The town is his.'

'That is indeed wonderful news, my lord,' Unton said.

'He is inviting me to join him there.'

'Ah,' Unton stroked his beard thoughtfully, 'I am not sure that would be wise. The journey to Noyen would take you through enemy territory.'

'God's Death, Sir Henry, I cannot ignore an invitation from the King of France,' Robert said, appalled at the suggestion.

'No,' Unton agreed reluctantly, 'I do not suppose you can.'

Robert was determined. 'Make the arrangements. We leave in the morning.'

Despite Unton's concerns, Robert and his entourage made the journey to Noyen without encountering any opposition. With each mile covered, Robert's mood improved, glad to be finally doing what he had been sent to do. His pride was bolstered even further when a messenger rode up to his horse carrying the French standard and informed him that the King intended to leave his prize of Noyen in order to meet with Robert at a castle in the nearby town of Compiegne. *The king riding out to meet me*, Robert thought and shouted excitedly to Unton of the honour King Henri was doing him.

Unton, pleased for Robert, nevertheless advised his charge to wait. They had been riding for several hours and, in truth, Unton could do with a rest, but Robert would not hear of it. King Henri was waiting and Robert would not brook any delay.

So, on they rode and Unton found himself cursing Robert as his bones begged for release from the saddle. A few more hours hard riding and they arrived in Compiègne. Not even stopping to wash or change his clothes, Robert presented himself in the castle's Great Chamber and was immediately conducted to the King, who was walking in the castle's pretty gardens.

Robert, as protocol demanded, knelt and bent his head before the French king, but Henri held out both his arms and welcomed the man who could, so everyone said, persuade the Queen of England to do anything. Robert, whose only experience of sovereignty had been Elizabeth, had been ready to flatter and praise King Henri as he had been used to doing with her, but was delighted to find that no such nonsense was necessary.

There was even familiarity and the sense of an almost brotherly bond between them as King Henri put his arm through Robert's and the pair walked in the gardens, talking in French of military matters. Robert enjoyed their conversation immensely. It was such a relief to not to have to speak of love and be able to talk instead of military strategies and battles won and lost.

This is how it should be between sovereign and subject, Robert thought as King Henri led him back to the castle where a feast had been prepared. *Not an endless round of tease and taunt, of insincerity and false emotions, but mutual respect between men. What a shame England has a queen and not a king. How much simpler things would be then.*

XIII

The Council chamber was darkening and candles were being lit by pages as the counsellors settled down to business.

Burghley hemmed, his face crumpling in distaste as a gobbet of phlegm slid down his throat. 'Have we any news from the Earl of Essex?'

Cecil sighed, an involuntary reaction to any dealing with Robert, and showed his letter to the Council. 'The earl has written to the Council. King Henri has been successful in capturing the town of Noyen and is pressing on towards Rouen, his army enlarged by the forces of the Duke of Nevers and the Mareschal d'Aumat. If all goes well, writes the earl, once Rouen is taken, the whole of Normandy will surrender to the French king. And the earl assures us if and when this event takes place, the King will not forget what he owes to the Queen of England.'

'The Queen will not allow the French king to forget,' Walsingham said without a trace of humour. 'She wants English ports on the French coast again.'

'The earl does not mention any such intended remuneration in his letter.' Cecil continued, glancing up at Walsingham. 'The English force is now at Pont de l'Arch, but will move to Ravilly within the next few days.'

'But the French king does know what the Queen expects in exchange for our alliance, does he not?' Walsingham persisted.

'The Earl of Essex was instructed to make it clear to him, Sir Francis, but whether he has or not, I cannot say.'

'The question is,' Burghley cut in, 'should the army return to England if the French cause is so close to victory? The Queen is concerned by the cost of the army's maintenance.'

'The Queen is always concerned about money,' Walsingham said impatiently. 'I think it far more important that we remain in France to ensure the Catholic threat is completely eradicated.'

'We all know your hatred for the Catholics, Sir Francis,' Burghley said wryly, 'but our remit was to provide assistance to the French king and, I believe, that has been done. It is also the Queen's desire that the Earl of Essex be recalled to court.'

The counsellors seated around the table looked at one another, all privately thinking that the Queen missing her favourite was a poor reason for recalling Essex.

'But will Essex come, Father?' Cecil wondered. 'You know what he is like. He has defied the Queen's orders before.'

'That, fortunately, is not our concern,' Burghley said, taking the earl's letter from his son and filing it away in his folder. 'The Queen has written a letter instructing the earl to return and it is our duty to send it on. See to it.'

Unton entered the tent gingerly, ensuring the flap closed

completely, not wanting to let any chill night air in. He moved to the far side of the tent and looked over Meyricke's shoulder, down to the cot bed where Robert lay. Robert's forehead was slick with sweat and his hair lay flat against his skull. His eyes were closed, his mouth open and his head moved fretfully from side to side.

'How is he?' Unton asked.

'He is still delirious, Sir Henry,' Meyricke answered quietly. 'The campaign must be preying heavily on his mind. He talks even though he is not awake and runs through the lists of the men and our armaments, of reaching towns and besieging them. But his mind seems fixated on the Queen and those he believes wish him ill.'

'The poor young man,' Unton said. 'God forbid this should spread to the army.'

'No, no, sir, do not fear that.' Meyricke led Unton away from the bed. 'This is not a camp fever. I trust you will not speak of this, but my master has suffered from such torments of the mind since his youth.'

'Indeed? What is the cause?'

'I cannot say. The doctors who have attended him supposed it to be a nervous affliction. Worrying, you see, sir, can make him ill.'

'I did not realise he was so sensitive to trouble.' Concerned though Unton was for Robert, he was also worried for the army that it should have so weak a leader. *Should I write to the Council of this nervous affliction?* he wondered, giving Meyricke's pleas for discretion no thought.

'Do you know if my master's brother has returned yet, sir?' Meyricke asked as he sorted through Robert's soiled clothing.

There had been constant skirmishes between the French and English allied forces and those of the enemy, the French Catholic League, and before he had fallen ill,

Robert had sent his brother, Walter, out on a patrol into their territory of Ravilly. 'Only Master Walter can calm him better than I.'

'No, his party has not yet returned.'

'Do you think they have run into trouble?'

'How can I know?' Unton replied irritably. 'Of course, it is possible. We have been lucky so far that our losses have been so slight.'

Robert began to mumble, drawing Meyricke and Unton to his side.

'I hope for his sake his brother returns soon. Do what you can for him, Meyricke,' Unton said and left before Meyricke could point out that he had hardly left Robert's side for the past four days and needed no prompting from Sir Henry Unton to continue.

❧ ❧ ❧

Robert's eyes opened and quickly shut again, for the light hurt and caused an intensely sharp pain at the back of his eyeballs. He waited for the pain to fade and then once more dared to open his eyelids, slowly this time. The pain was not so great and he kept his eyes open, waiting for his surroundings to come into focus. He experienced a moment's confusion at the walls that billowed and the shouts and strange noises from beyond them. Then he remembered where he was. His tent. Ravilly. France.

A head entered his field of vision. The mouth opened and said, 'My lord?'

Robert licked his lips, his tongue finding them rough and dry. 'Gelly?' he croaked.

The head smiled. 'Yes, my lord. Here, sit up and drink some water. You need it.'

Meyricke helped Robert to a sitting position, cradling his head and tipping a horn cup of water towards his lips.

Robert sipped the water at first, then greedily. The cup was soon empty and Meyricke helped him to lie back down.

'Have I been ill?' Robert asked as Meyricke tidied the blankets.

'You have had a fever.'

'How long?'

'Five days.'

Robert groaned. 'The army?'

'Being taken care of, never fear.'

Robert allowed his eyes to close. A moment later, they snapped open again. 'Walter. I remember. I sent him on patrol. How long ago was that? Five days, you said. He must be back by now. Where is he, Gelly? Why is he not here?'

Meyricke's breath caught in his throat. 'I… I… I will get Sir Henry.'

Robert caught hold of his arm and held him fast. 'Where is Walter?'

Meyricke placed his hand over Robert's and squeezed. 'His party was ambushed. Your brother was shot. He is dead, my lord. The survivors brought his body back.'

Such terrible news. Robert had sent his only brother to his death while he had been lying useless on his bed, ill from a mere weakness of spirit. So much for a glorious destiny, he could not even protect his own brother. Robert's face crumpled, tears falling from the corners of his eyes to create damp spots on the pillow. Meyricke, afraid the fever would return, attempted to soothe his master, but Robert felt he did not deserve kindness and pushed him away. He turned on his side and cried into his pillow.

Terrible though his grief was, it provided a release, and when all Robert's tears were spent, Meyricke could see that weeping had done his master good. He ordered meat and wine for Robert and made him eat, watching until more than half of the beef broth had gone and Robert said he could eat no more. The effort of eating and the effects of a full stomach that had shrunk over the past five days soon made Robert sleepy, and Meyricke laid another blanket atop the other and shaded the lantern so that the light would not disturb him. He felt that he too could afford to rest now that Robert was through the worst. He spread out on his cot bed, now bereft of blankets, and folded his arms across his chest to keep warm. As he did so, Meyricke heard the crinkle of paper and remembered the letter from the Queen that he had placed in his jerkin earlier.

'Damn,' he scolded himself, wishing he had remembered its existence before. Robert, he knew, would have been pleased to hear from the Queen.

Never mind, Meyricke told himself. He would give it to Robert in the morning. He strained to listen and satisfied that Robert was sleeping soundly, turned on his side and quickly fell asleep.

Meyricke gripped the back of the chair, his knuckles turning white in his anger. Damn the Queen. She was going to make Robert ill again.

Meyricke had given Robert Elizabeth's letter and he now watched in dismay as Robert's face changed. The brown eyes, a little sunken and purplish from his recent illness, hardened and his jaw tightened, a vein twitching in his cheek. Robert seemed to have become dizzy and Meyricke saw him stretch out a hand and grab the central pole of the tent to steady himself. Meyricke stepped towards him to help, but Robert insisted he was well and stopped his friend's and Unton's advance with an outstretched arm. He waited for his head to stop swimming, then held out the letter to Meyricke.

Meyricke read. No words of praise, none of concern, not even of friendship did Elizabeth write. She wrote instead words of criticism, of reproof, of disappointment.

'I wish I had never given you this letter,' Meyricke hissed and looked at Unton. 'The Queen does nothing but criticise my master, Sir Henry.'

Unton said nothing, trying to remember what he had written in his own letters to the Council. Had he been overly critical of the earl? Was the Queen's disfavour with Essex his fault?

'How can the Queen write such things, Sir Henry?' Robert wondered. 'Does she not know what I have suffered?'

'I assure you I wrote to the Council informing them of your illness and the situation here, my lord,' Unton replied indignantly.

'Then why, why does she berate me in such a manner? She calls me rash, negligent. And undutiful, Sir Henry, undutiful. Me! I, who have done nothing but in duty to her. She complains that I have not kept her informed. For heaven's sake, I am in command of an army. I have been ill. Does she not know all of what has happened? That I have lost my brother? Has no one told her all?' Robert demanded, suddenly doubtful. He searched his companions' faces for an answer. 'She cannot know, I am certain. *I* will write and tell her.'

He pulled out the chair from beneath the rickety table, and drawing a fresh sheet of paper towards him, dipped his pen in the inkpot and began to write.

'My lord,' Unton said, eager to return to army business and prevent any more accusatory questions, 'how are we to proceed? King Henri's man, Marshall Biron, wants us to help him capture Gournay, but the

Privy Council—'

'We shall assist Marshall Biron, Sir Henry, never mind the Privy Council. It is what we came for. And we must do it at once, for the Queen commands that I return to England by the end of the month. And the Queen must not be gainsaid, must she?'

Unton winced at his sarcasm. 'No, indeed she must not, my lord.'

Capturing Gournay proved difficult. The town maintained their defences for an entire week, but their walls were unable to withstand a constant battery of cannon and two breaches were made by the French and English forces. At the sight of armed troops marching towards them, the townspeople realised the futility of continuing the fight and surrendered.

The action cheered Robert tremendously. Meyricke was pleased to see his master throw off his grief and his anger in the thrill of battle, and even more pleased to see Robert defy the Queen and refuse to return to England after all. In the explanatory letter he had written to Elizabeth, Robert claimed that it would be a dishonourable act to leave the French king after such a victory, but in truth, it was an act of defiance, a young man making a stand against a cantankerous and ungrateful old woman.

XIV

Robert Carey, recently returned from the battlefields of France, stood at Burghley's left side at the end of the Council table. He was waiting, like the rest of the Privy Council. Each member seated at the table looked towards its head where Elizabeth sat, one hand holding a letter, while the other drummed its fingers on the wooden surface.

Burghley's milky eyes stared hard at her face, trying to make the blurred area of her eyes and mouth sharpen so he could tell what was about to happen. It was at times like this that he missed the Earl of Leicester. Leicester, who knew how to handle Elizabeth, who had been able to predict her mercurial moods, pacify her and make her see reason when she had had her tantrums and been blinded by rage.

'How dare he!' Elizabeth's voice was hard, controlled. 'How dare he send this letter!'

'Madam,' Burghley began but was silenced when Elizabeth grabbed her nearest neighbour's wine cup and threw it against the wall.

'You, Lord Burghley,' she jabbed a heavily ringed

finger at him, 'you write to the Earl of Essex and you tell him that he is to return to England immediately or I will use him as an example of what can happen when a subject of mine loses my favour.' Elizabeth got up from her chair, causing all those present to rise as well. Her skirts whipped around their chair legs as she stalked the room. 'I should have expected this behaviour. He gets it from his mother, of course. She always was a disobedient bitch.'

'Your Majesty,' Carey blurted, visibly shaking as Elizabeth turned to him, 'I will, of course, deliver any letter you or this Council sends, but I know the earl will think he returns to England in disgrace and he will not be able to bear it. He will retire to the country, unable to show his face and he will diminish. His heart is already broken from the loss of his brother. The loss of your favour will surely kill him. But perhaps you require that satisfaction, Your Majesty. Indeed, I do not know.'

'CAREY!' Burghley cried, as loudly as his cracked octogenarian voice would allow.

'Calm yourself, Burghley,' Elizabeth said, her eyes locked upon Carey. Her gaze made his blood run cold. 'Well, Master Carey, you have courage, I allow you that. The earl certainly manages to inspire loyalty in his associates. Would I could say the same.'

'Madam, you have the most loyal of—,' Burghley began, but Elizabeth cut him off.

'In truth, I had forgot young Walter Devereux's death. Perhaps the earl is not himself and this is why he disobeys my command. I shall write to the earl in my own hand so he can understand how concerned I am over his conduct and how vital it is for his wellbeing that he obeys my command. I trust, Master Carey, that you will convey my feelings to your friend.'

Carey nodded, letting out the breath he had been

holding.

'And know, too, Master Carey,' Elizabeth added before resuming her seat, 'that I will not tolerate such a disrespectful outburst from you twice.'

Elizabeth tapped her right foot against the ground impatiently as she waited, seated in her velvet-upholstered chair and shaded by her canopy of estate. She felt the anticipation in the Presence Chamber, knew her courtiers were all wondering and eager to see how the returning Earl of Essex would be received by the Queen who had so recently made known her displeasure with him.

A cheer and applause were heard in the chamber and the courtiers looked around to see who had committed such a daring act. Seeing no one responsible and realising that the sound was coming from outside, the courtiers, almost as one, raised their eyes to the windows. The people of London were cheering and clapping, the way they did when they saw the Queen. Except the Queen was here in the Presence Chamber. So, who were the people cheering?

A notion struck the courtiers as to who it might be and they returned their attention to Elizabeth, whose foot had stopped its tapping. The cheering died away and the courtiers, and Elizabeth, waited for the Earl of Essex, the only man in the country who enjoyed such public acclamation, to appear. When he did, positioned perfectly between the double doors of the Presence Chamber and flanked by liveried men on either side, Elizabeth had to admit that Robert looked every inch a hero.

He had some sense, she noted, not to solicit admiring looks from her courtiers as he processed towards her.

Instead, he kept his face forward, his stride unfaltering, measured and unhurried. She knew that walk. She had walked it for more than thirty years.

Robert was before her now, his handsome face showing only the faintest signs of the past troubled months. It irritated her, the fact that he was young and handsome and popular with her people, even in her very presence.

'Your Majesty,' he bowed, elegantly, of course.

Elizabeth made a decision. She would show them all. 'My lord Essex. You are returned.'

'As you commanded, Your Majesty.'

'As I commanded several months ago, sir.'

'I could not leave your army without its commander, madam.'

'A convenient excuse, my lord, and not a credible one. Had you not three good knights upon whom you could rely? Were they not commissioned in this enterprise for that very purpose?' It pleased her to see his clear, unwrinkled brow crease. 'Did you think I would send out an untried cub alone to a battlefield? Did you flatter yourself I would place all my trust in such a rash youth as you have proved time and again to be?'

Robert's cheeks turned a gratifyingly deep red, and Elizabeth heard a whisper hiss around the chamber.

Robert shifted his feet, wanting to kick at Elizabeth's legs and truly hurt her, cause her as much pain as she was causing him. He drew his shoulders back. 'I see Your Majesty is determined to ruin me. If that is your will, I can do naught but yield to it, but I contend, madam, that I do not deserve such a welcome. And if you were to ask the people,' he pointed to the windows, 'the people out there, they would agree with me.'

'Unfortunately for you, sir, those people, *my subjects*, can do nothing for *you*. Your future, if you have one, lies in *my* favour.' She saw him swallow and his shoulders droop a little.

'I am your humble servant, Your Majesty,' he forced himself to utter.

Elizabeth rose and stepped down from the dais until her face was no more than a foot from his. 'Yes, my lord. I know you are.'

XV

Hampton Court Palace, 1591

Elizabeth had wanted to listen to music and practice her dance steps, so the dancing master had been called for. She enjoyed dancing, enjoyed the closeness it brought with a man, feeling his breath upon her cheeks and neck, his hands around her waist. She reflected that it was the only intimacy she was allowed to enjoy. She found her mind drifting towards memories of Leicester: his hand in hers, her head upon his shoulder. She would never feel such warmth again. She pushed the thoughts of him away for they were too painful. She hurried towards her chair and fell into it, waving her hands at her ladies that they should continue with the lesson.

First, Elizabeth Vernon moved into the centre of the room, her pretty face turning coy as the dancing master placed his hands around her slender waist. His fingers spread and pushed against the heavy fabric, and Elizabeth knew he was feeling the bumroll beneath her lady's skirts, knew too that Mistress Vernon enjoyed his chaste exploration. *What a little trollop*, Elizabeth thought, biting into a hazelnut. *Painting, already, I see. I did not paint when I was her age. I did not need to.*

'You! Enough!' she pointed at Mistress Vernon, waving her aside peremptorily to stand in the corner of the room. 'Bess, your turn.'

Another hazelnut was rolled around her mouth while Bess Throckmorton, almost shyly, stepped up to the dancing master. *She is a good creature*, Elizabeth thought. *Not at all pretty, so no man is going to try and take her away from me.*

'Faster, dancing master, faster,' she instructed with a laugh.

The dancing master drew Bess in closer, putting the whole length of his arm around her waist and half-lifting her from the ground, whirling her around. He set Bess back on her feet and Bess held out her hands, her eyes on the floor. He took hold of them and spun her around again, according to Elizabeth's orders. At last, he stopped, but Bess continued to turn. She could not stop. Her vision was blurry, her head was spinning, and she felt vomit rise up her throat. And then the ground came up to meet her, and she felt her knees crack against the hard wooden floor.

'What is the matter?' Elizabeth called, rising from her chair and signalling Mistress Vernon to see to the fallen woman. She watched as Bess placed a hand against her forehead, then moved it to cover her mouth. 'Oh, for heaven's sake, unlace her. She is going to faint.'

Bess's stays were cut by Mistress Southwell, while for decency's sake, the dancing master was shown out. Mistress Vernon tugged the dress from Bess's body, who whimpered and tried to hold onto the masses of fabric. But Mistress Vernon was enjoying herself, taking delight in the little adventure, and Bess's dress was tossed aside.

'Get her up,' Elizabeth called, still from her chair.

'She needs to walk about. Open the window.'

Supported on either side, Bess was walked slowly around the room. She wanted to stick her head out of the window to breathe in the fresh air, but she was steered away from it. It was a relief to stand only in her shift, her body no longer tightly bound. She straightened to ease a crick in her back, and when that did not work, disengaged her arms and placed her hands on the small of her back, bending her body backwards, forgetting why her tight lacing had been so necessary.

Elizabeth's eyes widened and she started from her chair. A long, thin finger pointed at Bess's belly, which was round and pronounced beneath her shift. 'You little slut,' Elizabeth screeched, and Bess shrunk away, trying to hide her stomach.

'Your Majesty, please,' she begged, already crying.

'Your belly swells,' Elizabeth continued mercilessly, advancing on the cowering young woman. 'Fornication! Fornication! Who is he? Who is your seducer?'

'Madam, no.'

'Tell me. I command you.'

'He is my husband.'

Elizabeth stopped, her frown creasing. 'I have not given you permission to marry.'

'We married in secret, Your Majesty. We love one another. Forgive us.'

'Who?' Elizabeth demanded, fearing the answer. 'Who is he?'

Bess was snivelling and could not speak. Elizabeth moved towards her and raising her hand, brought it down upon Bess's head, slapping her again and again. The ladies in the room looked on, horrified. None spoke or moved to intervene. They knew better than to get involved when Elizabeth was in a rage.

'You will tell me who he is,' Elizabeth shouted,

emphasising each word with a blow. When Bess crawled out of the way of her hands, Elizabeth lifted her skirts to aim a kick at her rump.

Bess cried out in pain. 'Sir Walter. Sir Walter is my husband. Please, please stop.'

Elizabeth did stop. She stopped in bewilderment. No, it was not possible. Walter Ralegh, this ugly girl's husband? But he was Elizabeth's lover, wasn't he? He wrote love poems to her, said he loved her, talked to her in private, made her laugh, made her dream. She looked down at Bess, at the girl's rumpled red face, tears and snot making it even uglier. How was it possible that Sir Walter, handsome Sir Walter, funny Sir Walter, intelligent Sir Walter, could love such a creature?

'Sir Walter Ralegh is your husband?' Elizabeth whispered, bending low.

'Yes, Your Majesty,' Bess sniffed. 'And the father of my child.'

'Call the guards,' Elizabeth instructed coldly, straightening, and Mistress Southwell hastened to obey. The Yeomen Warders promptly entered the Privy Chamber and Elizabeth addressed them directly. 'You will arrest Sir Walter Ralegh and Mistress Throckmorton immediately. They are to be taken to the Tower and kept there.'

One of the guards bent and placed his hand beneath Bess's arm, lifting her gently but firmly upright. Mistress Southwell put Bess's dress in her arms and stepped back. The guards led Bess out of the room and Mistress Vernon closed the door behind them. She and Mistress Southwell looked at one another, neither daring to speak.

Elizabeth, standing in the middle of the room, suddenly let out a loud sob, her body bending as she covered her head with her hands. No one moved. No one dared. Blindly, Elizabeth stumbled back towards her chair, grabbing the cushion and holding it to her chest, crushing it beneath her hands. Betrayed again. Was it all lies? Could no man swear he loved her and mean it? Her handsome Sir Walter had been lying to her all this time. He had loved another and given his beautiful body to be kissed and caressed by an ugly woman. But his body belonged to Elizabeth. She had admired its leanness, its strength. She had dreamt of touching it, feeling his skin beneath her fingers, pressing her cold lips to it and feeling his heat. But now she couldn't think of such things anymore, for they were now exposed as fantasies. Bess Throckmorton had undoubtedly enjoyed the reality of such desires, while she, Elizabeth, was only allowed to dream them. Another dream tarnished, ruined.

Well, they would pay. They would be put in the Tower and kept apart. Bess Throckmorton would have her brat in prison and Walter would never get to see either of them again.

Oh yes, I can be cruel, Elizabeth reminded herself. *Let all who betray me know just how damn cruel I can be.*

∞ ∞ ∞

The news soon spread around the court. Sir Walter Ralegh, Elizabeth's darling, had got Mistress Throckmorton with child and they were both now imprisoned in the Tower. It was incredible, astonishing. It was worrying for all those young lovers who made assignations with one another and held each other close.

Robert was worried. Though he revelled in Ralegh's fall from favour and laughed about his imprisonment, he could not blame the man for acting as a man. He did wonder what on earth he saw in Bess Throckmorton. Robert had looked upon her and thought her very plain, not worth his attention. He had not guessed that she was

Ralegh's paramour, not guessed that she was any man's paramour. Mistress Howard was another matter. There was a handsome woman and one that was ready to defy the Queen's commands regarding chastity. Robert had had Mistress Howard on several occasions. In his apartments, while Elizabeth entertained foreign visitors next door, in the gardens when night began to fall and all was shadow. Hell, he had even had her on the Queen's bed when he had paid a visit to the Privy Chamber and found Elizabeth away. And there was Mistress Southwell, another young woman who had caught his eye and who was currently sharing his bed at every opportunity. Robert pulled Henry Wriothesley aside after a game of cards with the Queen and spoke of his anxiety.

Henry, surprised that Robert should worry about mistresses when he had married without consent and still escaped Elizabeth's wrath, laughed and asked what Robert was proposing. To become a monk? To forswear all lusts of the flesh? What a dull life he would have, Henry told him.

Robert agreed, shaking his head. He had got away with a relationship with another woman once. He was not sure Elizabeth would forgive him a second time. What to do then?

Henry told him to just be discreet. Swear the ladies to secrecy and not to take any unnecessary risks. And besides, Henry pointed out, with Ralegh gone, who else did Elizabeth have to keep her entertained? Robert would be more necessary to Elizabeth than ever before, so even if he was found out, she couldn't afford to imprison him. And, Henry reminded him with a jab of his finger, Robert was an earl, not a lowly knight like Walter. She could hardly imprison one of her nobles without trial, no one would stand for it.

Robert nodded his head, choosing to see the sense in

Henry's arguments. Yes, carry on as before, just be a little more careful. That is what he would do.

Cecil had heard the news of Ralegh's downfall with a similar pleasure. Ralegh had never been that much of a problem to him, for Elizabeth kept the man strictly on the periphery of government, but he had been an unnecessary nuisance when he inspired the Queen with talk of voyages to the New World and kept up a constant plea for funding, and it was better for Cecil that he was now out of the way.

Cecil laughed to himself. Perhaps there was some virtue in being unattractive to the Queen, after all. Ralegh, another handsome man who had been the instrument of his own downfall. His mind turned to Robert.

One down, he told himself, *one to go*.

XVI

Lincoln's Inn

Anthony Bacon tugged the fur collar of his black cloak around his neck to keep himself warm, the biting wind blowing harshly through the narrow passages of the Inns of Court. Dodging other lawyers who were scurrying like black rats to their chambers, he half turned as he heard his name called, but it was too cold to stop walking.

'Anthony, stop, damn you.' His brother, Francis, ran up to him and grabbed hold of his shoulder. Thinner than his brother, he was similar in almost every other respect, down to the pointed black beard. 'I was calling.'

'Oh, was that you?' Anthony said, moving on again. 'Walk then. It is too cold to stand around.'

'I want to talk to you.'

'So I imagined. About what?'

'Our future, brother. I think it is time we accept that our uncle will not be of any help to us.'

'Francis, I have told you before we must continue to hope. Lord Burghley—'

'Lord Burghley may be our aunt's husband but he will forever put his own son before us.'

'But surely he will do something for us. If not a Privy Counsellor, then—'

'Then nothing, Anthony. Lord Burghley will not foster rivals for his son. He will keep us down if he can, I promise you.'

They reached Anthony's chambers and hurried inside. Keeping their cloaks on, they huddled around the brazier, holding their hands over the hot coals. 'What do you propose we do?'

'It's simple. We must ally ourselves with another.'

Anthony stroked his beard. 'You mean the Earl of Essex.'

'Who else would serve us better?'

'There is merit in the notion,' Anthony agreed. 'And I suppose it makes little sense to tie ourselves to an old man not long for this world.'

'Who will no doubt be replaced by his son when he dies,' Francis finished his thought. 'Lord Burghley is already grooming Cecil to take over, whether the Queen realises it or not. And our cousin Cecil will never be a friend to us.'

Warmer now, Anthony snatched up a jug of wine from the table and poured out two cups. He handed one to Francis. 'Essex *is* the coming man, he is the talk of all of London. And in truth, Francis, I have often thought our ideas and thinking are more suited to the earl's circle. The Cecils are cautious creatures, always wanting to preserve things the way they are. They will never countenance change.'

'I am glad you are of my mind,' Francis said, sipping his wine, 'and agree we should approach Essex. I hear you are to journey to Germany at the end of the week?'

'Yes. There are details of a trade treaty that require clarification. I will be away at least three weeks, maybe longer.'

'I don't think we can afford to wait. I think it best if I try for an appointment with the earl as soon as possible.'

'You can manage it alone?'

'Of course, I can manage it alone,' Francis snapped. 'You are my brother, Anthony, not my tutor.'

'Why, Francis, do not be such a shrew,' Anthony laughed and stroked his brother's cheek. 'I trust you not to make a mess of it. Here, have another cup of wine.' He raised his own in the air. 'Here's to better times and better fortune, brother.'

Francis's backside was growing numb. He had been sitting on the bench in the Great Hall at Essex House for more than an hour. Some of his companions on the bench had changed over the course of the hour, while others remained as static as he. He had expected to have to wait to see the earl, and he knew of some people who had waited weeks, even months, but unlike him, most of them had nothing to offer.

The person to his left attempted to strike up a conversation but Francis offered only monosyllabic answers and the man wandered off to find a more voluble person to pass the time with.

Francis looked around and saw the steward with whom he had first announced his request for an audience with the earl. He jumped up from the bench and hurried to him. 'It is most urgent that I see the earl,' he pleaded.

The steward, who was used to being harassed in this manner, halted, his annoyance evident. 'Master Bacon, you *are* on the list.'

'I have been on the list for the past eight days.'

'It is a very long list, sir. You are not the only one. As you can see,' he waved his arm in a wide arc that took in the room, 'many people want to see the earl.'

'Wait,' Francis said, laying his hand on the steward's arm as he made to walk away, 'I am not like all these others. I do not want him to do something for *me*. I want to do something for *him*.'

The steward met his eye for the first time. 'Make it worth my while and I will see what I can do.'

Francis delved his hand into the purse that hung from his belt and drew out four groats. He slid the coins into the steward's hand. 'I must see the earl today.'

The steward dropped the coins into his own purse, told Francis to wait and exited through a door in the corner of the room.

Francis resumed his seat on the bench and rested his sweating hands on his knees. He tried not to measure the passing time, but he found himself counting. Four minutes, five. *How long does it take*, he wondered, *to move me to the top of the bloody list?* His head jerked around as the corner door opened and the steward came out, scanning the room for Francis. Francis got to his feet and strode over to him.

'Come with me,' the steward said and headed back the way he had come, throwing one quick glance over his shoulder to make sure Francis was following. Along a short corridor and into a much smaller chamber, richly furnished with colourful tapestries and gold plate, a central desk and chair, and a chest heaped with a great pile of papers. At the desk sat Robert. The steward announced Francis, waited a moment to be dismissed and left.

'How much did you give him?' Robert asked.

'My lord?'

'My steward. I can always tell when he has been bribed.'

Francis did not know whether Robert was annoyed or simply curious and took two seconds to decide whether he should tell the truth or lie. He told the truth.

Robert raised his eyebrows, impressed. 'Then I appreciate how much you wanted to see me. He would have accepted less. And I would have got around to you, you know. I make sure I see everyone who wants to see me.'

'I am sure you do all your admirers that honour, my lord, but I did not want to delay being of service to you.'

'You are Sir Francis Bacon, yes?' Robert asked, consulting a paper. 'Your brother is Sir Anthony Bacon, currently abroad on Her Majesty's service, and you are cousins to the Cecils.'

'That is correct, my lord.'

'A notable connection, kinship with Lord Burghley.'

'Notable perhaps, but the connection does neither my brother nor myself any good.'

'Yet, you are clever,' Robert said, rising from behind his desk and sitting on its edge. 'No, make no denial. I can see it in your face. Does not Lord Burghley covet clever men?'

'Not if they could be considered rivals to his son's interests.'

'Ah, I see. So, you come to me?'

'Not as a second choice,' Francis said hastily.

'No? I am glad to hear it. The thought had occurred.'

Francis shuffled his feet. 'While my brother and I could seek to ally ourselves with the Cecils, the reason for doing so would be purely one of blood and natural affinity. But offering service to you, my lord, makes plain common sense and accords with our true inclinations.'

'Why so?' Robert frowned and folded his arms, his badge of Master of the Horse nestling amongst his lace cuffs.

'If you will forgive my familiarity, my lord, you are a peer of the realm, a scion of an ancient and distinguished family. You have the favour of the Queen. You are youthful, brave, handsome and the people love you. Lord Burghley can claim to have only one of these assets – the favour of the Queen. His son has none. And there is no virtue in allying oneself with an old man when the future belongs to the younger generation.'

'Indeed, Sir Francis,' Robert said, both impressed and flattered. He was used to being complimented, but not in so bold a manner. It pleased him to hear another speak of his attributes, even as it embarrassed him. 'What is it you believe you can do for me?'

'Innumerable services, my lord. Secretary, lawyer, confidante, intelligencer.'

'Intelligencer?' Robert sprang up, suddenly serious. 'You mean in the manner of Walsingham's agents?'

'I do, my lord. The late Master Walsingham cultivated a strong intelligence web that both I and my brother played some part in. On occasion, you understand, not with any great regularity. But our involvement meant we were able to cultivate our own contacts and sources of information. If you want to know secrets, my lord, my brother and I can find them out for you.'

'I will not deny, Sir Francis, I am in sore need of such service. I cannot be the man I wish to be without having access to such intelligence, here and abroad.'

'Then if may speak boldly, you need my brother and I. I have my sources here in England. My brother, Anthony, has considerable contacts abroad. If I may ask, my lord, do you already have a secretary?'

'A man who writes my letters, no more. The position is yours if you can make good on your boasts.'

'I can, my lord,' Francis assured him, thinking that Anthony would be proud of how he had handled the interview, 'and I thank you. It will be an honour to serve you.'

XVII
Greenwich Palace

Cecil took the seat Elizabeth offered him in her Privy Chamber. He looked around the room, pleased that there were only two ladies present and they away in the far corner. The conversation he wanted to have with Elizabeth he wished to remain private and not be gossiped around the court. 'I have good news, Your Majesty.'

Elizabeth smiled back at him. 'I am very glad to hear it, Pygmy. From the Commons?'

Cecil nodded. 'Following the announcement of the renewed threat from Spain, this current threat being that they are considering the launch of another armada against England and are bribing disaffected Scottish nobles to join them in an attack against us, the Commons have agreed to double the subsidy granted to the Crown for the defence of the realm.'

Elizabeth laughed and clapped her hands. 'Excellent. I am glad they are so conformable to our wishes.'

'Indeed, madam. In fact,' he hesitated and tugged at his earlobe, 'I believe that we may be able to get a little more money out of Parliament.'

Elizabeth's eyes widened. 'More money?' she asked with interest.

Elizabeth always needed money, for the cost of maintaining her court and palaces was enormous and was the main reason why her ministers were not punished for accepting bribes, for while they were receiving money from other people, they were not demanding a salary from her.

'I believe so,' Cecil continued. 'If the House of Lords were to state to the Treasury that, despite the doubling of the subsidy, it is still not enough to defend the country against foreign threats, the Commons would be compelled, in their own interests, to increase the sum. I have the backing of the entire Privy Council in this matter, madam,' he added.

'Then pursue it, Pygmy,' Elizabeth said eagerly, waving him towards the door. 'There is always a need for more money for the Treasury. The defence of this country is my chief concern and I cannot defend it unless I am granted money. Make that clear to the Lords.'

'I will,' Cecil was happy to assure her and left to make his directions.

Unfortunately for Cecil, and for Elizabeth too, Robert sat in the House of Lords. He was present when the bill was read out in the chamber, and discussing it later with Francis Bacon, realised that Cecil was behind it. In truth, Robert did not care whether Elizabeth was given more money or not, for it would not be coming out of his household, but he was keen to thwart Cecil in any way he could. Francis suggested that as he was a member of the House of Commons he stand up and oppose the motion when Cecil rose to propose it, and Robert eagerly agreed.

Block him, he told Francis, say whatever you must, but block the little Pygmy.

Elizabeth had never liked this part of being a queen, having to sit and listen while the members of Parliament made their speeches. She remembered the early years of her reign when she had been harangued by her Members of Parliament to marry. Already convinced that she would never marry yet unwilling to lose her advantage of being an eligible bride for all the bachelors in Europe, she had exercised her lifetime's experience of avoiding awkward questions and kept her subjects, and her fellow royalty, guessing. She had continued to provide her answerless answers to Parliament, provoking its members sorely and often delighting in the knowledge that she did so. Although Elizabeth was not like her father – she had not his surety of the demi-divinity of the sovereign, nor his lack of hesitation in removing heads – she often wished that she did not have to deal with Parliament, that she could just make laws and demand money from her subjects without having to get their agreement first.

Lord Keeper Pickering was making his address, telling his audience that even more money was needed by the Treasury to keep England safe from Spain and Scotland. The Commons had already shown their loyalty to the Crown with the approval of the double subsidy but the Treasury needed more.

Elizabeth knew that Cecil's plan of trying for more money was asking much of her people, perhaps too much, but she desperately wanted his scheme to succeed. Money, money, money. She always needed it and always seemed to lack it, no matter how many economies she made in her household. She scanned the assembly, squinting to try and make out the various expressions on the men present, but she could only make out those nearest to her. What were they all thinking?

'The Member for Middlesex,' Lord Keeper Pickering declared, relinquishing the floor.

Elizabeth leant towards her secretary to her left and murmured, 'Name?'

'Sir Francis Bacon, Your Majesty,' he promptly replied.

'Bacon?' *Oh yes,* she thought, *Essex's friend.* She straightened, her ears pricked to catch every word.

'Honoured gentlemen,' Bacon said, 'this proposal goes against all custom. It is not the place for the House of Lords to put forward a proposal for yet more subsidies, but the privilege and prerogative of this House. The privilege and prerogative of we members to make the offer of an enlarged subsidy for the benefit of Her Majesty and to take care of this nation, not for the Lords to demand one from us. Have we not given enough? Have not the people of England, gentle people who have had to sell their plate, farmers who have had to sell their pots to raise the money for the subsidy already agreed, have they not given enough? Spain has always threatened England and we have always survived, against tremendous odds. What true need then of yet more money? Is this not just a stratagem of the Privy Council to gather more money to themselves?'

Bacon's fellow members chorused their agreement, glad that one of them had had the courage to speak up, even in the very presence of the Queen. A few cast surreptitious glances at Elizabeth, wary of drawing her attention. What would she think of such flagrant disrespect and suspicion of her Council?

'This proposal for yet more money,' Bacon continued, 'should be rejected to preserve the integrity and inviolability of this House.' He sat down, tugging his cloak straight, pulling the fabric out from beneath his buttocks before he finally dared to look at the Queen.

As he knew she would be, her eyes, mere slits in the pale oval of her face, were fixed on him. He could almost feel her hate.

~ ~ ~

'You failed.' Elizabeth stood before him in the Council chamber. She was majestic, magnificent and frightening. She did not sit, nor did she invite Cecil to take his ease. She was in no mood to be kind.

Cecil took a deep breath, keeping his eyes firmly on the buckles of his shoes. 'Unfortunately so, Your Majesty.'

'So, my Treasury does not benefit from the extra money you promised me—'

'I made no promises, Your Majesty.'

'— and now the Commons believe my Council to be avaricious and grasping, and will begin to suspect any motion put forward by them in the future. This has not been a good day's work, Pygmy.'

'No, indeed.'

'And I have had to suffer the indignity of being refused by my Commons to my face. I was there, Pygmy, in the chamber, and those wretches insulted me.'

'Most regrettable, Your Majesty.'

'Regrettable, you call it,' Elizabeth sneered. 'I agree, it is regrettable. How could you allow it to happen?'

Cecil looked up at last. 'I fear, madam, that certain elements within the House of Lords acted against the Privy Council's intentions and incited the rebellion in the Commons.' He fell silent, waiting for Elizabeth to make the inevitable connection.

'Certain elements,' she echoed, moving to stand before him, her sour breath coating his skin. 'And I suppose you know who these certain elements are?'

Cecil said he did indeed have an idea and Elizabeth commanded her Pygmy to speak, that she would not have him keeping his idea to himself. He raised one eyebrow, trying to give the suggestion that he was loathe to speak. 'The Earl of—'

'Essex, was it?' Elizabeth cut in, her mouth forming a pout. 'Eh, Pygmy, was it him?'

Cecil nodded.

'Yes, well, it would be, wouldn't it? That Francis Bacon fellow is in his service, I believe. I thought he was a cousin of yours, Pygmy?'

Cecil confirmed that he was related to the Bacon brothers.

'So, why is he not on your side, eh?' she asked. 'Why is Bacon not speaking up for *you*?'

Cecil shrugged. 'I and my father have not thought Bacon and his brother suitable servants.'

'You don't like them. Why not? Is it because they are sodomites? I have heard that about them.'

'I really could not say, madam,' Cecil, his nose wrinkling at such a distasteful subject.

'Are you certain Essex has had a hand in this?' Elizabeth said, her expression turning doubtful and eyeing Cecil suspiciously. 'Essex knows how important the subsidy is to me. I do not think he would do anything that would be an act against me.'

Cecil wanted to say to Elizabeth that she was wrong, that Robert Devereux would do and say anything that furthered his own ends, but he suspected his words would be misconstrued and he would lose what little faith Elizabeth had in him. So, he kept silent.

Elizabeth looked at him for a long moment, then

sighed. 'Well, never mind. We do still have the double subsidy. It will have to do. I trust in my Council to make the most of it. Can you do that, Pygmy?'

Cecil bridled at the insinuation. 'I will do my best, Your Majesty,' he said and backed out of the room at her dismissal.

And if nothing else, he thought as he walked back to his office, *this incident has taught me that the Earl of Essex has designs on playing politics against me. I shall not underestimate him again.*

Robert clinked his glass against Francis's and drank down the fine Burgundian wine. 'A victory, Francis,' he declared.

'For you and for the Commons, my lord,' Francis agreed, sipping his wine and taking a seat, pleased to have been invited to dine with the Devereux family at Essex House. Dinner was over and it had been a fine dinner, far better than he was accustomed to eating in his lawyer's room in Lincoln's Inn. He and Robert were now alone, sitting by the fire in Robert's private closet.

'Aye, we showed the little Pygmy, did we not, Francis?' Robert grinned, running his hand through his auburn curls. 'That was one in the eye for him.'

'The Cecils made a grave miscalculation,' Francis said, a touch smugly. 'They thought they could command the Commons. I am glad to say that they cannot.'

'What is more important, Francis,' Robert said, pointing his glass at him, 'is that they cannot command *me*. I know what they think of me. They think I am a boy, someone who knows nothing about politics and the running of a country.'

'They know different now, my lord,' Francis assured

him. 'And if I may be so bold, I think you should continuc to disillusion them.'

Robert licked his lips and frowned. 'What mean you, Francis?'

'Become a statesman,' Francis suggested with a small shrug. 'Indeed, what could be more natural?'

Robert tugged his earlobe. 'I already have a voice in Parliament, Francis.'

'But there you are one among many. If you were to become a Privy Counsellor, you would be one among a few.'

'A Privy Counsellor?' Robert sat up, a little of his wine splashing on his hose in his haste. 'I?'

'Why not? Are you not one of the foremost peers in the realm? Do you not have power and influence, both at court and in the country, as well as abroad? I can think of no better candidate for a Privy Counsellor. And it would certainly ensure that there is opposition to the policies of Lord Burghley and Robert Cecil. They would not have everything their own way. And since Walsingham's death, you have no one well disposed to you in the Council.'

Robert rose and began pacing the room. Francis watched him, wondering if he had said too much, gone too far. His words might seem to Robert an impertinence, a lowly gentleman telling a noble how he should act, what he should do. But someone had to tell him, Francis reasoned, and he had learnt that Robert always wanted to be more than a mere courtier, that he needed to be more to satisfy the expectations he placed upon himself as a scion of the Devereux dynasty.

'You are right, Francis,' Robert said at last, wagging a finger at him. 'I should be on the Council. In fact, it is a disgrace that I am not already. Why have I not thought of this before? I mean, good Lord, what is Elizabeth thinking, keeping me from it? Am I not right, Francis?'

'You are, my lord,' Francis returned, inwardly a little amused by Robert's indignation, so strong yet so recently acquired.

'Then I must tell her to appoint me,' Robert decided, nodding his head emphatically.

Francis rose, a little diffidently. 'If I may be so forward, my lord, ask rather than tell. As you have said so often yourself, the Queen is a woman and women, in my experience, never take kindly to being told what to do. They are contrary and inclined to do the opposite out of spite.'

Robert smiled a crooked smile. 'In your experience, Francis? I thought your experience did not extend towards women.'

'Still, my lord,' Francis said, the smile stiffening on his face, 'the principle is the same. Ask, rather than tell.'

Francis found that a little of his resentment for the tactless slur on his manhood faded as Robert patted him on the shoulder and said he would take his advice.

They were in the gardens of Hampton Court Palace, for the day was warm and Elizabeth had wanted to feel the sun on her face. She had commanded the archery butts to be set up and ordered Robert to join her.

'You have something on your mind,' Elizabeth said as she aimed her arrow at the target some twenty yards away. She loosed the bowstring and, a moment later, the arrow thudded into the outer ring of the butt. 'Damn,' she hissed, stepping aside for Robert to take his shot. 'Well, have you not?'

'I have,' Robert said, stepping up to the mark and taking aim. His arrow hit one of the inner rings. 'May I speak of it?'

Elizabeth, with a show of impatience, said he may and gestured for him to take another shot.

'I was wondering, hoping rather, that you would consider me for some greater service than Master of the Horse.'

'What is wrong with Master of the Horse?' Elizabeth said sharply. 'Leicester held that position for over twenty years. It was only with the greatest reluctance that he gave it up to you.'

'And I do not mean to give it up, Bess,' Robert said. 'But Leicester was not just the Master of the Horse, was he?'

Elizabeth's breast heaved with a great sigh. 'You mean you want a seat on my Council?' She was surprised that it had taken Robert so long to get around to the subject.

'It's not too much to ask, is it?'

'My turn to shoot.' Elizabeth's skirts brushed him aside. She took aim again, too quickly, and her arrow thudded into the grass a yard short of the target. She was a poor loser and angrily thrust her bow at an attendant. 'I have had enough of shooting for today. Let us go in.' She began walking back towards the palace, striding ahead of Robert. 'Oh, do stop sulking, Robin. I have not said No, have I?'

'You have not said Yes, either.'

She took a few more steps and then halted. 'Being a Privy Counsellor carries a great deal of responsibility, dedication—'

'I know that, Bess.'

'Do you, Robin?' she queried, looking him square in the face. 'Do you?'

'Damn it, Bess, you have made Robert Cecil a Privy Counsellor. If you can make that hunchback a counsellor, why not me?'

'Is that all it means to you?' Elizabeth asked, playing with her pearl necklace. 'A chance to be even?'

'No, but—'

'Sir Robert Cecil has been made a Privy Counsellor because he has proved himself worthy. And I did it in deference to his father.'

'Oh well, that is it, is it not?' Robert flung his bow on the grass and started pacing up and down before her. 'I have not got a father to plead for me. I have to carve my own way—.' He stopped, his mind suddenly full of memories.

He had hardly known his father, it was true, for Walter Devereux had been away more on the Queen's business than he had been at home, but Robert had found a second father in the Earl of Leicester and had welcomed the warmth and security he had provided. When Leicester had died, Robert had truly mourned him, not just as a presence in his life but as a support, someone who had looked out for him and tried to advance his interests. Robert now lacked that kind of man in his life and unlike Cecil, who had a father, had to sail the stormy waters of court life alone.

'Have you finished?' Elizabeth asked with a loud sigh. 'I do not want to hear of your pitiful excuses. If we are reduced to haranguing one another with our personal losses, then I can beat your number ten times over. You hear me, young man?'

'Yes, madam,' Robert mumbled, his eyes travelling aimlessly over the palace windows.

Elizabeth softened, affected by the image he cast before her. And he was right, in his way. He was due a reward. Her hunched shoulders dropped, her jaw unclenched and her eyes lost their intensity. 'I do not mean to be harsh, Robin. You must think of me as a mother who chides her child only to improve him.' She reached her leather-gloved hand up to his cheek and gave the blushing skin a gentle caress. 'There now. Look at me, Robin. Look at me.' She felt a thrill of pleasure that was almost maternal as his dark eyes looked into hers. 'You can have a seat on my Privy Council. You are one of my nobles and it is only fitting.'

Robert's face brightened. He grabbed both of Elizabeth's hands and kissed them each several times. 'You are my most gracious queen,' he swore, making Elizabeth laugh and feel inclined to return to the butts.

Burghley held the parchment close to his face and read aloud. 'You do swear by Almighty God to be a true and faithful servant unto the Queen as a member of her Privy Council. You will not have knowledge or understand any manner of thing to be attempted, done or spoken against Her Majesty's person, honour, crown or dignity, but you will stop and withstand the same to the uttermost of your power, and reveal it to Her Majesty or to her Privy Council. You will in all things faithfully and truly declare your mind and opinion, according to your heart and conscience; and will keep secret all matters committed and revealed unto you, or that shall be treated of secretly in Council. And if any matter touch upon any fellow counsellor, you will keep it secret until Her Majesty or the Privy Council make publication of it. You will to your uttermost bear faith and allegiance to the Queen's Majesty. And generally in all things, you will do as a faithful and true servant to Her Majesty, so help you God.'

Robert, kneeling, raised his chin a little higher. 'I do swear it.'

There was a polite round of applause from the spectators in the Presence Chamber who had gathered to witness Robert's appointment. Elizabeth took the quill her secretary proffered and signed her name at the bottom of the parchment.

'The Earl of Essex may take his place at the Privy Council table,' she announced and gestured at the corridor visible through the door at the side of the room and the Privy Council chamber that lay beyond.

Robert forced down a smile as he knew it would be inappropriate, not to say childish, to display such pleasure at his appointment. He bowed to Elizabeth and followed Burghley out of the Presence Chamber, shortening his stride so as not overtake the old man or step on his long cloak. When they entered the Privy Council chamber, Robert felt strangely bereft, his pride no longer bolstered by an audience and disappointed that this was to be a private moment and not a public one, with just him and the other counsellors present.

'Just one more formality, my lord,' Burghley murmured, struggling to hide his unhappiness at Robert's admission to the Council. 'Your signature is required.'

Robert sat down at the table and a secretary placed a parchment beneath his hands. His eyes swept over the names of the Queen's Privy Counsellors and he felt a thrill of pride as a quill pen was handed to him and he signed his name on the official paper – *Robert, Essex*. Sand was shaken over the wet ink by a clerk and blown away.

It was done. Robert was officially a Privy Counsellor. He was a man of substance, of government. He was now one of a select few, men who made important decisions about the governance of the country and advised the Queen on foreign matters.

Burghley bowed his head and smiled down at the

young man. ‘Welcome to the Privy Council, Lord Robert.’

XVIII

Whitehall, 1593

Elizabeth winced as pain shot up her cheek and struck her temple. *Damn that tooth*, she thought. *I suppose I shall have to have it pulled as Burghley says I should.*

She glanced at Robert sitting further down the table and allowed herself a small smile at his serious and eager face. The boy wanting to prove himself a man. Elizabeth supposed that being a husband and father he had already proved himself a man, physically at least, but to her, those two states were proof of nothing more than lust. To Elizabeth, a man was a man when he demonstrated intelligence and knew when to exercise caution, but a man's chief attribute should be loyalty. She looked around the table, at the old men sitting there. Old men, yes, she knew that was what they were, but she also knew that she could rely on them. These new men at her court, the young men, they frightened her with their ideas and their energy, and their constant desire for change.

Even now, Robert was talking about the Spanish threat

again. How he hated being at peace. She remembered Leicester when he was of a similar age as Robert. He had been just as keen to bloody his sword and the trouble she had had curbing his enthusiasm. Elizabeth felt too old to go through all that again, but she had the unpleasant feeling that with Robert she might have to.

Her gaze was drawn to Burghley, who was reaching for the Bible that habitually lay in the centre of the table, dragging it towards himself with his crabbed fingers. He turned the pages quickly, knowing exactly what he was looking for. He twisted the book around to face Robert and jabbed a finger at a passage. He knew the passage by heart and declared, '*Bloody and deceitful men shall not live out half their days*.'

Elizabeth looked at Robert, who sighed and rolled his eyes. 'You are too cautious, old man.'

'My lord,' Cecil got to his feet, his chair scraping on the floorboards. 'I will not have you talk to my father in such a disrespectful way.'

Burghley patted his son's hand, a temporising gesture, but Cecil was too angry and continued to glare at Robert.

Robert held up his hands in a gesture of contrition. 'Forgive me, Lord Burghley, that was rude of me. But please, gentlemen, you know that the Spanish are making plans to attack us again. They are the very reason for the grant of the double subsidy to the Crown.'

'For defence,' Cecil said grumpily, resuming his seat, 'not attack.'

Robert ignored him. 'The Spanish failed the last time because God knew we were in the right, but the truth is we are woefully unprepared for another attack. The Spanish are making their plans and construing their plots—'

'You cannot possibly know that,' Cecil scoffed.

'I can know that,' Robert insisted. 'You and your

father are not the only ones who have an intelligence network, Cecil.'

Ah, that has shut Cecil up, Elizabeth noted with interest. *So, Robert has his own spies, does he?* She watched Cecil look to his father, who shook his old white head and closed the Bible. Robert, who knew he had scored a point, was looking pleased with himself.

'I think that is enough for today, gentlemen,' Elizabeth said, noting that Burghley was looking tired. 'Essex, you will stay.' The counsellors filed out, leaving her and Robert alone. She chuckled. 'Why Robin, once again you look like a sulky schoolboy.'

'I am no schoolboy, Bess. I wish you would recognise that small fact. And am I now to be punished for speaking my mind?' Robert asked pertly. 'I thought I was allowed to do that. It is a perquisite of the Privy Council, is it not? Or perhaps you just want men who will say "Yes, Your Majesty" and "No, Your Majesty"? I hope so because that is who you have in your Privy Council. Pygmies, all of them.'

'Do not be insolent,' Elizabeth said, not as sternly as she knew she should. 'Cecil is right. You should have respect for your elders.'

'I cannot respect such a cautious policy in regard to the Spanish.'

'The Spanish have been our enemy since my accession,' Elizabeth said dismissively.

'Because they think we are weak, Bess. If we were to be the aggressors for a change, they would have to reconsider how dangerous we can be.'

'Enough, Robin. All you speak of is Spain this and Spain that. I have heard enough of Spain. I tire of Spain.'

Robert sighed and leant back in his chair. 'Must our conversations always be on your terms?'

'Should I allow *you* to dictate them, then?' Elizabeth

asked, raising a thin eyebrow.

Robert leant forward and reached across the table for her hands. 'If you will not countenance war, then I would like to speak of another matter, if you would allow it.'

The warmth of his hands pleased Elizabeth and she bid him speak, if only to hear the sound of his voice, pleading with her.

'The post of attorney-general is vacant. I would like to propose Sir Francis Bacon.'

She had not expected this. This was no trivial matter, the appointment of a secretary or a new groom. This was a matter of the governance of the country. Did Robert really think she was so foolish as to make such appointments on a whim, simply because he asked? Elizabeth pulled her hands from beneath Robert's and put them in her lap. 'I am already considering Sir Edward Coke for the attorney-generalship.'

Robert waved that aside. 'Oh no, consider Bacon, Bess. He is a clever fellow. Quick-witted, knowledgeable—'

'He is a friend of yours.'

'He serves me well.'

'And would continue to do so as attorney-general.'

Robert was affronted. He was proposing a man who would serve her better than any other. He was thinking only of her and here she was, insinuating otherwise. 'Why do you say such things?'

'Sir Francis Bacon has spoken against me in Parliament. When I asked for more money to defend this country against the Spanish, that subsidy you spoke of just now, he blocked it with a cry that it was against parliamentary custom.'

'Ah yes,' Robert said, jabbing his finger against the table top, 'but when Cecil proposed that subsidy, Bess, he was asking for much more than normal, and Parliament knew it was unlikely that all of the money would go to England's defence. Bacon was simply protecting the interests of Parliament. All he did was speak his mind.'

'Speaking one's mind seems to be a common trait amongst young men nowadays.'

'Would you censure us for that, Bess? I know what is best for you and this country. If you love me, as you profess you do, then you will grant me this small favour.'

'Do not talk to me of love when you talk of matters of state. Burghley has a high opinion of Sir Edward Coke, and I trust *his* opinion in this matter.'

'Burghley does not propose Coke because he believes Coke has the talent for the position. He makes no recognition of Coke's talent. He proposes him because he has Coke in his power and he is a man who will do as he is told. And you cannot throw age at me as a reason because even if Coke were fifty years older than Bacon, he would still lack Bacon's wit and intelligence.'

'I see I must remind you that I am queen here, Robin.' Elizabeth rose and headed for the door.

'Will you at least consider Bacon for the attorney-generalship, Bess?' Robert called after her. 'For me?'

'No, Robin, I will not,' Elizabeth said and left, leaving him alone.

Robert slumped in his chair, angry with Elizabeth for denying him. He had promised Francis the attorney-general post would be his and now he would have to tell him he had failed. Yet again, Elizabeth had made him look like a fool and exposed his inadequacies.

Francis Bacon was waiting in Robert's apartments and bowed as Robert entered.

'Have you been waiting, Francis?' Robert said,

untying his cloak, trying not to look him in the eye. He was embarrassed, ashamed of his failure. *What will Francis think of me?* he wondered unhappily.

'A short while, my lord. I was just wondering if there was any news on the post of the attorney-general?'

Robert poured himself a cup of wine before answering. 'I cannot get it for you, Francis. I am sorry.'

Francis frowned. 'But you said—'

'I know what I said,' Robert snapped testily. 'But the Queen is immovable. She has decided that the attorney-generalship will go to Sir Edward Coke.'

'I see,' Francis said, as calmly as he could, but the news was a blow. Robert had promised him that the attorney-generalship was as good as his and Francis had believed him. And why should he not? Robert was favoured by the Queen and had boasted that she would do anything he asked. Francis had trusted in his power and had even written to his brother to tell him of his imminent promotion. 'Then I shall not bother you any longer, my lord.'

'Wait, Francis. I will not let you go empty- handed.' Robert opened a small wooden box that stood on the buffet and took out a parchment. 'These are the deeds to Twickenham Park. The house and gardens are yours. It is a fair estate, worth two thousand pounds. Now, do not deny me this. I promised you a position and I have not been true to my word. You shall wound me if you refuse.'

Francis had no intention of refusing the gift, but took the parchment with a show of reluctance, thanked Robert and bid him good day. He made it to the corridor before his anger showed itself. He kicked the wall and cursed Robert for his false promises. He had needed that post, not an estate out in the damned country. Not that the house would not be an asset and it was generous of the earl, he admitted, but… Francis heard footsteps and turned to see his cousin, Cecil, walking towards him. *Damn,* he thought, *had he seen my little display of anger?*

'Cousin,' Cecil said, nodding a greeting and passing on by.

Francis hurried after him. 'Cousin Robert, may I have a word with you?'

'I cannot tarry, cousin.'

'I shan't detain you, but I was wondering if there was anything you could do for me?'

'Do for you?' Cecil repeated. 'I thought you were attached to the Earl of Essex.'

'Not attached, cousin. And we are family, after all.'

Cecil halted. 'Indeed we are, cousin, but I cannot help but think you chose to follow the Earl of Essex because you believed richer rewards lay in that direction.'

'Cousin—'

'I suggest you stay close to the earl, for he does indeed possess the favour of the Queen, and I am sure he can obtain for you all you desire. But Francis, a word of warning. The earl is, no doubt, a man of great charm and understanding, but I fear he would not look too kindly on one who would switch allegiance so easily. It would do you no good were he to hear of it. Good day to you.'

Francis watched his cousin limp away, annoyed with himself for his foolishness. By exposing his dissatisfaction with the earl, he had put himself in a dangerous place. His cousin would not help him, that much was clear, so it seemed Francis was tied to the Devereux star. He would need to make sure it did not fall.

XIX

Essex House, 1594

'Shall we go to the playhouse tonight, Robert?' Henry Wriothesley asked, his feet up on a stool, a cup of wine in one hand and a book of poems in another. He was always ready to make himself at home in any of Robert's houses.

'If you wish it, Henry,' Robert replied distractedly, intent on the letter he was reading.

'Do you want to hear my poem?'

Robert declined, saying that he had other things on his mind, and Henry, surprised, demanded to know what they were, what all the paperwork was that Robert was sorting through. When Robert told him it was intelligence, Henry snorted and joked that he doubted it was Robert's own.

Robert smiled at the playful insult and told him that the intelligence came from Anthony Bacon, Francis' brother, who, Robert had discovered, had an astonishing network of contacts, as good as any network Walsingham had created as Elizabeth's spymaster. Henry protested that Robert could not know of such a matter, that as so much of Walsingham's business had been conducted in secret it was impossible to know how deep or how extensive his spy network had been. But Robert was insistent and not a little annoyed that Henry should think so little of him. He reminded Henry he was a Privy Counsellor and had access to state papers. Henry raised both eyebrows and said he thought it odd that Cecil would let Robert anywhere near such sensitive documents, causing Robert to retort proudly that Cecil could not legally stop him.

'And I do know Anthony's network is good,' Robert persisted. 'You will not believe me, will you? I'll prove it to you.' Robert held up the letter he had been reading. 'This is from Anthony Bacon. A man called Esteban Ferrara da Gama, a Portuguese, is corresponding with highly placed officials in Spain. This same da Gama is currently here in London and staying at the home of Doctor Roderigo Lopez.'

Henry, intrigued, moved his feet to the floor and sat up. 'Lopez? The Queen's doctor?'

'The very same. So, what does the Queen's doctor have in common with a Spanish intelligencer?'

'Tell me,' Henry demanded eagerly.

Robert coloured a little. 'Well, I do not know yet, but it is suspicious, would you not say?'

Disappointed that Robert did not have any firm evidence he could read, Henry flicked his hand at him. 'They may just be friends, Rob.'

'Well, yes, they may,' Robert admitted, 'but it is also conceivable that this da Gama is sending information to King Philip of Spain. Court gossip that Lopez tells him over dinner or during quiet fireside conversations.'

'Very well, Robert, suppose he is doing that. What of it? I suspect if you made enquiries, you'd discover that a quarter of the court receives a pension from Spain for the very same thing. I even heard tell of one courtier, years ago, who was approached by a Spanish agent to spy on the Queen. The courtier agreed, took the agent's money, and then told him that he just needed to get the Queen's permission first. Such arrangements are accepted. They are just another means that Elizabeth can get away with not paying her ministers.'

'You are not thinking, Henry,' Robert snapped. 'I agree, there is nothing in it if da Gama is just a spy, but what if Lopez is involved? Lopez is constantly at court. He attends many of the highest people in the country. He has even attended on me. Through Lopez, da Gama could hear so many secrets. And Lopez has access to the Queen. He gives her tonics for her health, ointments for cuts and other ailments. What is to stop da Gama from putting a poison in one of those?'

Henry nodded, succumbing to Robert's ideas. 'Very well, you are right, this da Gama appears to be a danger, but what will you do about it?'

'Not do, Henry. Done,' Robert grinned at him. 'I have already ordered da Gama's arrest.'

Robert had returned to Essex House. Anthony Bacon, back in England, had sent a message to the court with the news that da Gama had been arrested and placed in a room awaiting interrogation. Robert did not delay in instructing his bargemen to take him home. Robert wanted to interrogate the prisoner da Gama personally.

'In here, my lord.' Anthony led the way to a small room at the end of the corridor and Robert followed, his heart beating fast in anticipation of what he would find inside.

Da Gama was sitting at a table in the centre of the

room. His black, bloodshot eyes widened in fear as Robert, Francis and Anthony entered. His whole body was rigid and he did not rise, just watched his visitors and swallowed uneasily as the door was shut behind them.

Anthony nodded at his brother, who sat down at the table, opened up his leather folder and placed an inkpot and pen upon the surface. He drew out some paper, dipped the pen in the ink and waited.

Now that he was here, Robert was unsure how to begin. But everyone was waiting on him. He had to speak.

'You are Ferrara da Gama of Portugal and you have been staying in Holborn at the home of Dr Roderigo Lopez,' Robert began. 'What is your exact relationship with Lopez?'

'We are friends,' de Gama said, his Portuguese accent strong.

'But you are in the pay of Spain?'

'I have business in Spain.'

'Does that business include passing intelligence to King Philip's ministers?'

'I do not understand.'

'You do not?' Robert glanced at Anthony. 'Yet I am told you understand English very well. And you seem to have very little difficulty in speaking it.'

Da Gama made no answer.

'Is Doctor Lopez also in the pay of Spain?' Robert continued.

'My friend has no business in Spain.'

'But he has a position here. A very good, a very elevated position. I find it hard to believe that Spain would make no effort to secure the services of one so close to the Queen of England. I find it very hard to believe that they would not employ you to persuade Dr Lopez to act in the interests of the King of Spain.'

Da Gama remained silent. The only sound was the scratching of Francis's pen as it recorded Robert's words.

'Senôr?' Robert asked loudly, insistently, worried that he was going to get nothing out of the interrogation, 'what have you been plotting?'

'I make no plot, my lord.'

'There is no point in lying, senôr. Why else would you be here, in the home of Doctor Lopez, if you did not want to get close to the English court? Have you tried to secure the allegiance of Lopez? He is a Jew. I am sure you could buy him for thirty pieces of silver.' Robert laughed and looked around at Francis and Anthony, who smiled loyally back.

'I make no plot. I am friend to Dr Lopez. No plot.'

Da Gama began to cry. Anthony stepped up to Robert and murmured that he was unlikely to get anything else out of him. Robert nodded an agreement. Francis collected his writing things and all three left the room, leaving da Gama still sobbing.

'My lord,' Anthony said, locking the door, 'I suggest we send an instruction to the ports of Rye, Southampton and Dover to intercept any letters from Portugal and have them sent on to Essex House for examination.'

'Yes, see to it, Anthony,' Robert agreed. 'We have the makings of a conspiracy here, I am sure of it. People may be in danger and I must do all I can to see no one comes to any harm.'

XX

Cecil trudged along the corridor towards Robert's apartments. He had been summoned and was irritated, but the summons was impossible to ignore or refuse. He knocked on the door and was greeted by Gelly Meyricke, who bade him enter.

'Ah Cecil, there you are,' Robert said, rising from his chair. 'You have kept me waiting.'

Cecil pursed his lips to bite back an uncivil retort. 'I had business that could not be delayed, my lord.'

'Well, you are here now.' Robert handed Cecil a paper. 'Read that. You will see that I did not ask you to attend on me for no trivial reason.'

Cecil read the paper quickly. 'You have proof that this da Gama is working for the Spanish?'

Robert had not given up on his idea of da Gama being guilty. He had given instructions that da Gama be interrogated again and again until he revealed his secrets. Kept confined, half-starved and terrified, da Gama had spoken at last. 'He has admitted it, Cecil. Francis Bacon is working on a full report of his confession. Da Gama has also admitted that he was engaged in a plot to assassinate Don Antonio.'

Don Antonio had once been the King of Portugal, but he was a bastard and King Philip of Spain had a legitimate claim to the Portuguese throne through his mother's bloodline. Don Antonio had been usurped from the Portuguese throne and forced into exile, persuading Elizabeth to give him a home in England while he worked to regain his kingdom. Elizabeth had agreed because if he were successful England would have a friend in Portugal. For eight years, Don Antonio had haunted the English court, but Elizabeth found him amusing and was, unusually, prepared to accept the cost of his keeping.

'Don Antonio's death would certainly be in the interests of the King of Spain,' Cecil agreed.

'Exactly so.' Robert snapped his fingers triumphantly.

'And you say da Gama has confessed this plot?' Cecil asked, wondering how on earth he could have missed such a plan.

'He has, and,' Robert paused to make Cecil look up at him, 'he has implicated Lopez.'

'Doctor Lopez? The Queen's physician?'

'Yes.'

'He has the trust of everyone at court. You yourself have employed Doctor Lopez, my lord.'

'Yes, I have, and what a damn fool I was to have done so.' Robert snatched the paper from Cecil. He had been examined by Doctor Lopez on several occasions during the previous year when his penis had developed some worrying lesions. Doctor Lopez had prodded and poked him, asked some impertinent questions, and charged Robert a fortune for ointment. The ointment had worked, Robert conceded, but the gossiping Jew had spread it around the court that Robert had suffered a disease of Venus. 'I have ordered the arrest of Dr Lopez and his home is being searched at this very moment.'

'My lord Essex,' Cecil folded the paper with vigour, wishing he could tear it up instead, 'why have you not informed the Council of any of this?'

Robert drew himself up. 'Why should I do so? *I* discovered this conspiracy, Cecil, I. Had I left it to you, the matter would have gone unnoticed and Don Antonio would have been unprotected.'

'That is a slander, my lord.'

'It is the truth.'

Cecil headed for the door. 'I and my father will also examine da Gama, but I cannot believe this plot to be true.'

'The evidence is being gathered, Cecil. Do feel free to interrogate the man yourself and you shall see.'

'Indeed I shall, my lord.' Cecil slammed his hand down on the door handle and left, forgetting to bow.

Burghley and Cecil were on the river, returning home after visiting da Gama at Essex House. Burghley settled heavily onto the cushioned seat of the family barge and tugged a fur blanket over his legs. 'So, my boy, what do you think?'

Cecil sat down next to him, clutching his folder of notes to his chest. 'It's a nonsense. Essex found no evidence of a plot in his search of Lopez's home and Lopez admits nothing. His account of his dealings with da Gama seems entirely plausible, do you not agree, Father?'

'I do. I feel sorely for Doctor Lopez that he has to suffer such treatment.'

'I do not like you being out on the river in this weather,' Cecil said, adjusting his father's blanket. 'I curse the earl for putting you through this.'

'It is not so much the matter itself but the reason why

Essex has begun this action that concerns me.'

'He has done this to curry favour with the Queen,' Cecil said. 'To show how statesmanlike he is.'

'But that is not all. He wants to discredit *us*, my boy.' Burghley breathed deeply, prompting a coughing fit. When it subsided, he continued. 'I think it best that you go to the Queen and tell her of this affair before the earl does. Leave early for Hampton Court in the morning and be sure to mention to her that the earl did not share any of his intelligence information with the Council until he had already proceeded far in the matter. That should tarnish his image a little.'

Cecil settled back into the seat, hoping that his father was right.

The horse was sweating, flecks of white spittle spilling from its mouth, but still Robert pricked its sides and urged it on ever faster.

He reached the stable yard of Hampton Court and abandoned his horse to the ostlers. Hurrying into the palace, he ignored the stares of courtiers and servants who looked after the dishevelled earl in bewilderment. He had no time to waste making himself presentable. He had to get to the Queen.

Elizabeth was reading in her chamber when Robert burst in and demanded to speak with her. He closed the doors behind him, wanting no witnesses to the interview.

Elizabeth looked him over. Her nose wrinkled. 'Could you not have washed before presenting yourself?'

'There was no time. Has Cecil been here? Tell me.'

Elizabeth shut her book, closing her eyes in exasperation. 'Yes, Cecil has been to see me this morning.'

'What has he said to you?'

'Do you make demands of me, sir?'

'He defames me, Bess.'

'Does he, indeed?'

'You cannot believe a word that man says. He hates me.'

'Oh, do not be so melodramatic, Robin. Of course, Cecil does not hate you.'

'He does, I tell you. He seeks to undermine me at every turn.' He paused to catch his breath.

Elizabeth studied him. 'What is it you imagine Cecil has said to me, Robin? What secrets do you think he has told me?'

Robert heard the contempt in her voice and, knowing that he was already on dangerous ground, bit back the anger that had been fomenting inside him. 'I presume matters concerning Don Antonio?'

'You presume rightly, Robin,' Elizabeth nodded. 'He tells me that you believe you have uncovered a plot on Don Antonio's life. One that may involve my own doctor.'

'Yes, I have and—'

'And he also tells me that there is no evidence to support your claim.'

'That is a lie, Bess,' Robert said, unthinkingly pointing a finger at her. 'His associate has confessed his involvement.'

'I am satisfied with the opinion of Lord Burghley and Sir Robert Cecil.'

'They have blinded you to the truth, Bess.'

'ENOUGH,' Elizabeth roared, her patience suddenly exhausted. 'You are a fool, rushing into matters of which you have no experience and little judgement.'

'Bess!'

'You dare to accuse my personal physician of treason

without any true evidence. Oh, and now I remember more. You do all this, make arrests, examine and accuse, without informing any of your colleagues on the Council about it.'

'I… I wanted to be sure,' Robert stammered, looking away.

'Oh no you didn't,' Elizabeth said, striding towards him and wagging her finger, 'you wanted all the glory. You wanted everyone to look at you and see how clever you are. Well, I will not have it, you hear? My court is no place for empty-headed braggarts. Not here in my court. Be gone from here. Get out of my sight.'

'You cannot mean it,' Robert begged. *Not again. Not banishment again.*

Elizabeth's eyes narrowed and she became very still. She had assumed her regal pose of aloofness, of untouchability, and even Robert, despite his anger, knew not to argue with it. 'I do mean it, my lord. I am quite sick of you. You will not come into my presence. I will not see you. Leave now.'

✽ ✽ ✽

Robert arrived back at Essex House, his poor exhausted horse nearly collapsing beneath him. He ignored the worried calls of his servants, the questions they fired at him, the wary looks from the waiting petitioners.

He wanted to be alone. Elizabeth had humiliated him again, talked down to him as if he were a child. He was tired, dejected. He had pain in his temples and black spots were floating before his eyes. He strode quickly to his apartments, barked at his page to get out, then slammed the doors shut and locked himself inside.

✽ ✽ ✽

Robert picked up the soiled napkin and wiped his forehead. His head felt tight, as though an iron band was wrapped around his skull, and he became dizzy when he moved. He recognised the symptoms and knew he was making himself ill. *No, I am not*, he corrected himself angrily. *Elizabeth and Cecil are making me ill with their accusations and unkindness. They would celebrate with a feast and dancing were I to die.*

I cannot be wrong about da Gama and Lopez, I cannot be wrong about their plot. Can I? Da Gama and Lopez had been plotting, da Gama confessed it. It has to be true.

Robert scanned Francis's record of the interrogations. There had to be something in the record that proved he wasn't the fool Elizabeth and Cecil thought him to be.

A sentence caught his eye. 'Lopez was in the presence of the Queen daily.'

Why mention the Queen? Robert wondered. *If the plan was to assassinate Don Antonio, why mention the Queen at all?*

His head fit to bursting, Robert began to frantically re-read all of the reports until he had found the answer to this question.

He unlocked the door and threw it open. He bellowed into the darkened corridor. 'Anthony!'

Burghley shuffled into the Council chamber and frowned down at his son who was sitting at the table. 'I was waiting for you in my rooms. You missed supper.'

'Forgive me,' Cecil said, rising and pulling out a chair for his father. 'This arrived an hour ago from Essex House.'

Burghley groaned. 'Oh no, not more nonsense. Read it

to me.'

'I shall not bother you with most of it. There are just a few sentences we need concern ourselves with.' Cecil ran his finger down the page. 'Here. *"I have discovered a most dangerous and desperate treason. The focus of the conspiracy was not Don Antonio but Elizabeth. The executioner was to have been Dr Lopez. The manner, poison."'*

Burghley's rheumy eyes widened. 'Is he trying to make out that Dr Lopez was planning to assassinate the Queen?'

Cecil nodded. 'Essex has discovered this so-called conspiracy after spending two days locked in his room. Father, I have read the same reports that Essex has and there is nothing to support this new fantasy.'

'Yet, I sense there is something more you have to tell me, Robert.'

Cecil sighed. 'I have also had reports from the Master of the Revels. Marlowe's new play, *The Jew of Malta*, is proving to be very popular at the playhouse. There is a great deal of anti-Jewish feeling in the city, and I fear that when this new idea of Essex's spreads – and it will spread, he will make sure of that, it is just the sort of employment he will give to our Bacon cousins – there will be no good in us defending a Jew who, if it can be proved, has nefarious associations with Portugal and Spain. The earl has interrogated da Gama again, I suspect under threat of the rack, and he now claims that he was tasked with persuading Lopez to poison the Queen.'

'Men will say anything in such circumstances.'

'I know, Father, but the earl has chosen to believe it and I expect that our cousins are circulating the confessions around the city even as we speak.'

Burghley thumped the table in anger. 'That I should be troubled with such a creature as the Earl of Essex at my time of life.' He sighed. 'He has given us no choice. We will have to arrest Doctor Lopez.'

Cecil placed a paper beneath his father's nose and Burghley unhappily read the warrant that his son had already made out.

'An innocent man, my boy, I am sure of it.'

'I agree, Father.'

Burghley passed the warrant back to his son. 'Have it dispatched as soon as the Queen has signed this.'

'And if the Queen will not sign it?'

'Tell her she must,' Burghley grew emphatic. 'Even though we believe Doctor Lopez is innocent, the formalities must be observed.'

Elizabeth's throat was tight and a pulse throbbed painfully at her temple. Ever since this business had begun, ever since Essex had stuck his nose into business that did not concern him, she had been plagued with pains. She did not want to be present, did not want to hear what she knew Burghley and Cecil were about to tell her of Lopez's trial.

Burghley spoke first. 'Dr Lopez claimed he only confessed under torture, but I am afraid his words were ignored. He was sentenced to death. The spectators applauded, very enthusiastically, the report says. Our agents have already recovered ballads from the city that speak of Jewish villainy and the talk in the taverns is that the people of London are looking forward to the execution.'

'The ballads,' Elizabeth said sourly. 'Was anyone else mentioned?'

Burghley and Cecil exchanged a glance. 'The ballads,' Cecil said, 'praise the Earl of Essex for discovering the plot, for preventing your assassination, and for delivering justice on a murderous Jew.'

Elizabeth winced. A murderous Jew? Doctor Lopez? A man she had trusted with her very life, whom she had seen daily, who had talked with her, comforted her, proved himself to be nothing but her trusted servant. Oh, that cruel boy, Essex. What was it in his nature that made him so spiteful? She closed her eyes and rested her head on her hand. 'If only they truly knew him.'

'Your Majesty?' Cecil leant forward, struggling to hear.

'The people, Pygmy. All they see is a hero, a shining boy. They do not see him as we see him, do they?'

'I am sure the earl is greatly endowed with all the virtues,' Cecil said carefully, seeing his father out of the corner of his eye nod in agreement with his caution.

'That's generous of you, Pygmy,' Elizabeth said. 'So, even though we three know Doctor Lopez is guilty of nothing more than having a suspicious and cowardly companion, I must throw him to the dogs to satiate the earl's bloodlust. Very well, let it be done. I do not want to hear any more of this matter. I do not want to hear of the execution, the manner of it, how the people cheered. Nothing.'

'Understood, Your Majesty,' Cecil said.

Elizabeth rose slowly, suddenly feeling the weight of her dress with all its layers and jewels. 'And I suppose that as the Earl of Essex is so lauded throughout my capital, I had better welcome him back to court.'

'It would be wise, Your Majesty,' Burghley agreed. 'There is no sense in stirring up anger over the earl's treatment.'

Elizabeth nodded, pursing her lips. 'Write to Essex, Pygmy. Tell him he may return.'

XXI

1596

England was in trouble. The weather that had been so much in England's favour in 1588 and dashed the Spanish galleons against her coasts and rocks now drowned her fields. Crops rotted, people starved, disease spread, and rebellion threatened.

Young men at Elizabeth's court, many of them friends and acquaintances of the Earl of Essex, who had too much time on their hands and an excess of testosterone that could not be spent on foreign battlefields, was spent on bloody quarrels at home. All was now faction at Elizabeth's court.

Gloriana did not shine as brightly as she once did; Cynthia the silvery moon, as Ralegh had once called Elizabeth, was demanding too much of her followers and was on the wane. The virgin star of Elizabeth was being eclipsed and the celestial sphere that was moving into her orbit was young, it was dazzling, illuminating the lives of all it shone upon, who, because they were dazzled by its brightness, could not see its false fire. The new star was shining brighter and brighter, and Gloriana looked old and dull by comparison.

Lettice checked her appearance in the mirror on her dressing table and decided to apply a little more colour. 'I am telling you, Robert, this is your moment. The whole country is tired of Elizabeth. That book proved it.'

'Mother,' Robert said reproachfully, but unable to hide his pleasure at her words. He had returned to Drayton Bassett to visit his mother, confident after his success in the Lopez affair that he could afford to leave the court without his reputation being besmirched in his absence. As Francis Bacon told him, who would dare criticise the hero who had saved the life of the Queen?

'Do not 'Mother' me,' Lettice snapped. 'That book that was published was dedicated to you and all it spoke about was who was to succeed to the throne when Elizabeth dies. And the writer said that you would have the greatest say in the matter. Do you know what you should be doing?'

Robert sighed, tired of being told what to do, who to acquaint himself with, what to say, and waited for his mother to continue. He knew she would. She was indefatigable.

'You should be making yourself agreeable to King James. You should be writing to him—'

'Mother—'

'You should—'

'Mother!'

'What, my darling?'

'I am already writing to King James.'

'You are?' Lettice cooed. 'Oh, you clever boy. You should meet with him, too.'

Robert shook his head and told her that visiting the

King of Scotland could be dangerous, for Elizabeth would not like it. She never liked to talk of the succession, was never willing to discuss who would come after her. Lettice pooh-poohed him, saying that as James Stuart was undoubtedly going to be England's king one day, it would be perfectly natural to pay him a visit. But Robert was convinced it was a bad idea and told her of a story he had heard from Francis Bacon. Bacon said Elizabeth had been heard comparing herself to King Richard II, the unfortunate English king, who had been usurped by one of his own cousins and murdered. Robert realised that by comparing herself to Richard, Elizabeth was implying that one of her own subjects could be another Bolingbroke. And Robert was the prime candidate.

Lettice's painted face lost its carefree expression. 'You do not mean that?'

Robert shrugged. 'It is what Francis said.'

'But, oh, my darling boy, if she has said that, then you could be in danger. She is such a suspicious old hag. If she thinks you are acting against her—'

'I will be careful, Mother,' Robert assured her. 'Francis Bacon looks after me in that regard.'

Lettice made a face. 'There is something very unpleasant about that man. Tell me, are the rumours about him being a sodomite true?'

Robert laughed and confirmed that the rumours were indeed true.

'He has not tried…' Lettice opened her eyes wider and nodded in his direction.

'No, Mother, certainly not.'

'So,' she smiled teasingly, 'if not Francis Bacon, who is keeping your bed warm these days? Not your wife, I know that.'

'I do perform my conjugal duty now and then.'

'I know that. The children do keep coming from her

and she is such a little mouse I do not suppose she would cuckold you.'

'Mother, must you?'

But there are others?' Lettice persisted. 'Please tell me you are not wasting all your time and manhood on Elizabeth.'

Robert, taking and kissing her hands, assured his mother there were other women, plenty of them in fact, but that none were important to him.

Lettice was pleased to hear it and began talking of another subject that had been very much on her mind of late: her exile from court. She asked if he were still in favour with Elizabeth and Robert, surprised, assured her he was.

'Then why am I still not allowed at court?' she demanded shrilly. 'Do not look at me like that. Elizabeth has never allowed me to come to court ever since I married Leicester, and I am heartily sick of it. If you are so much in favour, you can persuade Elizabeth to receive me. Can you not?'

'I can try, Mother,' Robert promised half-heartedly. But it was true, he reflected. How dare Elizabeth continue to keep his mother in exile? What had his mother done but marry the man she loved? He would speak to Elizabeth and demand that she receive Lettice.

'How can she refuse you anything, my darling? Are you not Great England's Glory and the world's wide wonder?'

'You have been reading Spenser,' Robert said, blushing in recognition of the quotation.

'Of course, I have, we all have.'

'Do you think it's true, what he calls me?' Robert asked quietly, hardly daring to believe.

Lettice noticed the change in her son's mood and moved to sit by his side. 'It is true, my darling. You are the hope of the age. You should see and hear what I do. When I go out in my carriage, I am cheered just for giving birth to you. You are loved, Robert, and not just by your family and friends. I tell you, Elizabeth should fear you because you are everything she is not – young, courageous, noble – and, believe me, my darling, the country knows it.'

XXII

Spain was continuing to be a thorn in England's side. The old sea dogs, Drake and Hawkins, had been almost constantly at sea since 1589, attempting to keep the seaways clear of Spanish ships and rob them of their treasures. Where this had worked in the past, the two men had been forced to discover that times had changed and they had not noticed. Gone were the heavy, cumbersome Spanish galleons that had proved so ineffectual in the Spanish armada of 1588, ships so large that they had not been able to turn quickly enough to see off the small English ships that darted in and out between them. But it seemed Spain had learnt her lesson. The ships they were now building were small frigates, ideally suited for sailing rings around any English ship. Emboldened by successes against Elizabeth's merchant adventurers, King Philip of Spain was preparing to launch another armada, one that would be faster, more manoeuvrable and ultimately more successful than any England had been threatened with yet.

Always aware of England's vulnerability, and kept informed by the Bacon brothers' spy network, Robert saw the danger from Spain. And he was not alone. Walter Ralegh, released from the Tower and trying to claw his way back into favour, warned of the dangers of not meeting the Spanish problem head on. Elizabeth would only approve small raids against the Spanish, but such endeavours, Ralegh warned, only taught the Spanish what to expect from the English and made them better prepared for the next battle. What was needed was one large, decisive action against the Spaniards. Robert voiced his support for such an action, not caring that he was siding with Ralegh. To Robert's surprise, Lord Burghley, long an advocate of not engaging in expensive military affairs, seconded him. Spain would have to be dealt with and soon, he said, adding that it would be far cheaper in the long run, a comment guaranteed to raise Elizabeth's interest. With Burghley's support, the Privy Council concluded that a major offensive should be launched against Spain. All they needed was Elizabeth to agree.

She did, at first. Elizabeth agreed to the putting together of a fleet of fifteen ships to be commanded by four commanders. These commanders were to be the Earl of Essex, Sir Walter Ralegh, the Lord Admiral Charles Howard and his brother, Lord Thomas Howard. But then news came that the Protestant King Henri of France had converted to Roman Catholicism in order to gain full control over his country and appease the Spanish. The Spanish were not convinced by this sudden conversion and decided to seize hold of Calais, the French port nearest to the England mainland.

King Henri appealed to Elizabeth for help to keep control and Elizabeth knew that England's trade would be severely hampered, even damaged, if Calais were to become controlled by Spain. So, the fleet that had been gathering to attack Cadiz, the largest and strongest Spanish port, was split in half, with Robert and the Lord

Admiral tasked with ensuring the Spanish were not successful at Calais. But Elizabeth also wanted assurances from King Henri that once Calais was under his control, the English would still be allowed to trade from it. Robert continued to make preparations for Calais, but with no assurance coming from the French, Elizabeth cancelled the expedition. The Privy Council were astonished and dismayed at Elizabeth's decision, and even Burghley allowed his irritation with her to show. But Elizabeth was resolute. She was not going to spend money on a venture that would only benefit the French.

Robert began a journey back to court, furious with Elizabeth for changing her mind. Halfway back to London, he received another message from the Privy Council, stating that Elizabeth had decided to recommence with the expedition to Calais, for she had received news that the Spanish were not so secure in the port as she had been led to believe. Calais, it seemed, was still available for the taking. Overjoyed, Robert turned his horse around and headed back to the coast.

But Elizabeth's changes of mind had cost the English force dear. As Robert's fleet sailed across the Channel, there was no sound of gunfire coming from the French port that would signal battles being fought. The Spanish had made good ground and taken the port of Calais, wresting it from the French. Calais was now in Spanish hands and England had lost her only trading port in France. There was nothing left to fight for in Calais. It was best for Robert and the Lord Admiral to rejoin the fleet at Dover and attack Cadiz.

But when they arrived at Dover, they found chaos. No administrative system had been put in place and arms and men were arriving daily without any official to tell them where they should be put or who to report to. Robert proved himself an adept at administration, arranging men into companies and for supplies to be properly distributed. Which made it even more galling when he received a letter from Elizabeth complaining about his lack of action against the enemy. Robert railed and asked his fellows what more he could do? They all agreed with him. The Queen was being unreasonable. As if he needed more proof of this, Elizabeth suddenly recalled Robert to London, worried that an expedition to Cadiz would prove just as futile as the one to Calais.

Robert lost his temper. From Dover, he wrote to the Privy Council, pleading with them to make Elizabeth see reason. He did not know it, but the whole of the Council sympathised with him, for they too were exasperated by Elizabeth's frequent and irrational changes of mind. Against all his inclinations, Cecil presented an argument to the Queen of the absurdity of pulling out of the Cadiz expedition at such a late stage. Essex was poised, he argued, ready to do the Spanish a great hurt and all for love of her. And what of the money that had already been spent? he asked, appealing to her parsimony. Was that all to be wasted?

This question hit home and Elizabeth was at last persuaded to allow the fleet to set sail. Robert, wondering what the hell was happening in London, received a letter from Elizabeth that contained his commission to depart and attack Cadiz. She also wrote of her prayers that he, Robert, would return to her unharmed to the great joy of her heart.

Robert didn't give a damn about Elizabeth's heart. He was off to war.

XXIII

Robert had command of the *Due Repulse*, a ship newly built and still smelling of freshly cut timber and tar. Robert walked the deck proudly, pleased to be away from court, and especially pleased to be away from Elizabeth, whose prevarication and constant mind-changing had driven him and his fellow counsellors to the limits of their wits. Not only that, but Elizabeth had grown cloying, demanding his presence at all hours and laying her hands upon him at every opportunity as if to prove he belonged to her. He shuddered at the memory of those deathly white clawing hands. He endured her touch, as he had always done, but the scales had fallen from his eyes of late and she was no longer a magnificent royal creature, but simply an old woman who wore magnificent clothes and covered herself in white lead paste to hide her wrinkled and sagging skin.

A Council meeting, held that morning on the Lord Admiral's ship, the *Ark Royal*, had concluded that the Earl of Essex should lead the attack on the city of Cadiz. Robert had been exhilarated by the decision. What a glorious challenge! He had hurried back to the *Due Repulse* and given his orders. The wind had come up, the sails were full-bellied and the ship was heading for Cadiz with a plan to launch a surprise attack on the city.

It was near noon when the city came into view on the horizon. Robert's heart began to beat faster, the blood rushing in his ears indistinguishable from the water breaking against the ship's bows. This was what he had been born for: battle, not bowing.

The *Due Repulse* reached the nearest safe point and Robert ordered his men into the boats. Sitting proudly at the stern of the lead boat, Robert heard the clanging of the town's church bells, alerting the citizens to the attack that was approaching. The wind picked up. The wind that had aided their journey to the Spanish port now threatened the small English boats and barges. Each boat in the small flotilla began rocking from side to side, water spilling over the gunwales. Robert watched in horror as two of his boats capsized and the men, dressed in heavy steel armour, sunk quickly beneath the water. In less than a minute, fifteen men had been lost. Robert would remember their screams for the rest of his life.

Robert saw the Spanish troops mustering on the shore, taking up positions behind barrels, while their galleons bobbed on the sea some distance behind the English ships.

The thousand men in the English boats landed and, surprising the Spanish with their speed, overcame the soldiers and headed straight for the citadel. The citadel walls were already in a state of disrepair and Robert led a company of men through a breach in one of the stone walls, hacking down anyone who stood in his way and so on through to the centre of town. Skirmishes throughout the town were dealt with by men from the other ships and by the next morning, Cadiz was in English hands.

Knowing the frenzy and lust that soldiers were prone to in battle, Robert issued orders that the churches were not to be violated and that all the churchmen and women in the town were allowed to be evacuated to safety. But he also knew the city offered riches and he made no attempt to stop the English troops from plundering. It was their due, after all, as the spoils of war. The English soldiers pocketed a great deal of wealth, but they did not realise how much more of it was safe in the holds of the Spanish merchant ships that had been anchored in the bay. Unable to sail these ships past the English fleet, the Spanish fleet commander decided it were better the sea had his treasure rather than the English, and he ordered the ships to be torched. Twelve million ducats worth of cargo either went up in smoke or sank to the seabed.

Cadiz had been captured, but the fortune Elizabeth had been promised, and which had finally persuaded her to set her men upon the Spanish, was lying at the bottom of the sea, irretrievable. It was a blow, the four commanders knew, but Robert reminded them of the brave action they had just fought, and to reward the troops, knighted many of the officers and men. So, dear Gelly Meyricke became a knight thanks to Robert, as did Charles Blount, he of the golden chess piece, all former enmity forgotten. Robert had knighted men before, but he had forgotten, or chosen to ignore, Elizabeth's fury at his presumption in doing so. In Elizabeth's England, a man had to earn a knighthood through years of devoted service: to *her*, not to her nobles.

Meanwhile, the four commanders, troubled by the loss of the Spanish fortune, sought a remedy. There was a Spanish fleet sailing for Cadiz and this fleet carried more treasure than the one that had been lost. The best thing for the English, Robert insisted, would be to wait at Cadiz for the ships to turn up and then simply plunder them. He proposed the setting up of a permanent English base with himself as governor, but his co-commanders shook their heads. His commission from the Queen did not allow for such a position and they would not ratify it. Besides, the English army was growing thin as men deserted, their pockets filled with Spanish gold.

The question was, what to do with the men who were left? The other commanders suggested that they sail the fleet around the coast and raid a few more Spanish ports and grow rich that way. Overruled, Robert had no choice but to consent and gave orders that Cadiz was to be destroyed, making it useless as a port for the Spanish. Robert watched as the smoke rose over the town, and climbed into the last boat with a heavy heart, not at all certain that he had done the right thing in letting the other commanders tell him what to do.

Back at sea, matters were no better. The other commanders appeared to be sailing aimlessly around the Spanish coast, trying to find the Spanish treasure fleet. They passed Portugal, many of whose ports were in Spanish hands, and decided to raid the town of Faro in an attempt to line their pockets. But the inhabitants of Faro had heard of the English raiders and had taken themselves and their goods into the mountains so that there was nothing left for the English to plunder. Frustrated, the English set fire to the town and were pleased to watch it burn.

Once more on their ships, Robert tried to persuade the other commanders to sail to the Azores where the Spanish treasure fleet was certain to have landed, but the others were tired of fighting and refused and turned their ships homeward. They passed Lisbon on the way, and once again Robert appealed to Ralegh and the two Howards to attack the town, but he was shouted down. The commanders would have done better to listen to Robert. For, while they were arguing, the Spanish fleet had been only a few days' sail away, and had the army acted as

Robert wished and hidden amongst the hills to lay in wait for the Spanish, they would have been able to rob the fleet of its valuable cargoes of gold and silver, worth twenty million ducats.

Another fortune had eluded English hands, simply because the four commanders had been bickering over whether to continue the fight or to head home. Elizabeth would not be pleased.

St Paul's was always busy, serving as a thoroughfare for people who wanted to buy and those who wanted to sell. Amongst the wares on offer were books, pamphlets, play scripts, pies, fish, meat and sex. A church may not have seemed the most suitable place for any of these trades but the Londoners did not seem to mind. The tradesmen shouted their wares, the punks bared their breasts and the preachers shouted over the noise. Some days they were listened to, some days they were not.

But everyone listened to the sermon on the day following the Earl of Essex's return to London, for the preacher in the pulpit was not talking of God or sins or hell; he was talking about greatness and giving thanks for the hero of Cadiz.

The Earl of Essex, the preacher said, had shown extraordinary military skill and unparalleled bravery in his command of the English forces, reminiscent of that other great English hero, Henry V. The congregation had agreed wholeheartedly with the sentiments being expressed and delivered a rapturous round of applause at the conclusion of the preacher's sermon. The applause echoed throughout the building and rumbled out of the doors, attracting the attention of those in the narrow London streets. It also attracted the attention of one of

Burghley's men, who wrote a letter to inform the chief minister of the incident.

The letter was passed to Lord Burghley as a doctor unwrapped the bandage around his gouty foot. He put on his spectacles, but gave up trying to read it and instead, passed it to his son who was supervising the doctor's treatment. Cecil read it through to himself first, then aloud to his father, who at the conclusion, said simply, 'The Queen will not like that.'

Agreeing, Cecil resolved to make sure Elizabeth heard about it.

'There are to be no more sermons about the Earl of Essex or the attack on Cadiz. Is that understood?'

Burghley winced at the tone of Elizabeth's voice – cold, chilling even, the same tone she had spoken in when told of the Babington plot years earlier, when six of her subjects had plotted to assassinate her and put her cousin, Mary Stuart, on the throne in her place. Elizabeth had demanded that the six conspirators' executions be prolonged, so that they endured unimaginable agony, using all the skill of the executioner. The Queen could be cruel, Burghley had learnt that day. She could be very cruel indeed.

'No, Your Majesty,' his weary voice had answered. He wanted to leave, to go back to his rooms and lie down, to not have to bother anymore with the Earl of Essex, but he had to consider his son. For Cecil to rise, Essex had to fall. 'Especially in light of the report I have heard.'

Elizabeth's ears pricked and she gave him a sharp, questioning look.

He continued. 'That the plan for the campaign at Cadiz was not, in fact, of the earl's devising but Sir

Walter Ralegh's. The Earl of Essex did have a plan of attack but it was a highly risky venture, reckless one might even say, and had he not been dissuaded from it by the other commanders, the outcome might have been different. Yes, very different indeed.'

He watched Elizabeth, her expression stony. She said nothing, merely turned her head away from him towards the window, raised an arm and waved her hand limply at him, telling him to go. He backed out of the room into the corridor.

'Did you tell her, Father?' Cecil's face was eager, his colour heightened.

'Yes, my boy. I told her.'

'What did she say?'

'Nothing,' he shrugged his bent shoulders and began walking.

'She said nothing?' Cecil, following after his father, was incredulous.

'What were you expecting?'

'I don't know. A rebuke, outrage.'

'My boy,' Burghley came to a grateful stop, for the pressure in his left foot was almost unbearable. 'The seed of distrust of Essex has been sown. It will take root and who knows what will grow. Be patient.'

Robert returned to London to cries of adulation and admiration, but if he had hoped for a warm welcome from Elizabeth, he was to be disappointed. He arrived at Whitehall Palace, and instead of being allowed through to Elizabeth's private apartments, was shown into the Presence Chamber where Elizabeth and the rest of the court awaited him.

He had ordered a new suit of clothing for his

triumphant return and there was no missing Robert as he entered the chamber for he glittered with gold thread and jewels. He was surprised that no courtier stepped forward to greet him, that none offered their congratulations. No one even smiled at him.

Robert headed for the dais at the opposite end of the chamber where Elizabeth sat. As he drew nearer, he saw her unwelcoming expression and he felt sweat prickling on his top lip beneath his newly-grown beard.

'Your Majesty,' he bowed low.

'Lord Essex,' she replied coldly, 'you dare show yourself at my court?'

There was a hush and courtiers glanced at one another beneath lowered lids.

'Dare?' Robert queried. 'I do not understand. Our mission was a success. Do you not hear the church bells? London rejoices in my triumph.'

'My people are ignorant of the true state of affairs,' Elizabeth sneered. 'Are you aware of how much your escapade has cost me? How much of my money has been wasted on a fruitless venture?'

'Hardly fruitless, Your Majesty,' Robert protested. 'Cadiz was taken.'

'What of it?' Elizabeth demanded. 'What good does that do me? The bulk of the Spanish fortune, which I was promised would be mine, lies at the bottom of the sea, and what wealth was brought back to these shores has been stolen from me at the dockside by your officers.'

'I am not to blame for their actions.'

'But you are to blame for bestowing knighthoods on such creatures, an act I expressly forbade you to do.'

'Those men deserved to be rewarded.'

'I choose my own knights, sir. I will not have them chosen for me by a rash, vainglorious youth.'

'I protest I am none such.'

'Indeed you are, sir.'

'Could you have done better than I?' he retorted, furious and indignant. 'Were you a man, you could go into battle yourself and see and experience the trials of command. Had you seen their courage, you would have knighted such men yourself.'

Elizabeth's eyes blazed. How dare he remind her that she was not a man? How dare he speak of her deficiency? Was he implying that she was unfit for rule? She did not trust herself to speak further, conscious of the hundreds of eyes that were upon her. She stepped down from the dais, and with a cruel cold stare at Robert, disappeared through the door that led to her private apartments.

A moment after Elizabeth's last lady had followed her, the silence in the room was broken and Robert found himself surrounded. He accepted gratefully their thanks and welcome, but his sensitive heart went out most to Henry Wriothesley, who took his arm and drew him aside.

'My dear fellow,' Henry said, embracing him, 'what a welcome.'

'She knows I speak the truth, Henry,' Robert said, his throat tight with impotent anger. 'How dare she treat me like this? How dare she subject me to such public humiliation?'

'She is a bitter old woman,' Henry said, lowering his voice, 'pay her no heed. Did you know that the Archbishop of Canterbury ordered a service of thanksgiving for your victory, and Elizabeth said it could only take place in London? The rest of the country has not been allowed to celebrate your achievement. She is frightened of you, Robert, and that is the truth. She knows that the people have grown tired of her and are just waiting for her to die.'

'Be careful, Henry,' Robert said, drawing his friend

closer. 'You could lose your head for even thinking those words you just uttered.'

'Oh hell, I am sick of bending my knee to an old woman, Rob, and I tell you, I am not the only one.'

'Hush, Henry, hush.'

'You would not bid me be quiet if you only knew of her treachery towards you,' Henry said savagely.

'What do you mean? What treachery?'

'Burghley has retired. As soon as you left the country, she made Cecil her principal secretary. The hobgoblin clerk now holds one of the highest offices in the country and is very well placed to do you mischief.'

Robert shook his head in disbelief. 'She ignores and humiliates her nobles and raises a commoner to those offices which are rightfully ours, Henry.' He laughed without humour. 'But then, I should not be surprised. What is the Tudor stock, eh? Nothing but the offspring of a Welsh steward. And before you say it, Henry, I know my mother comes of the same stock, but my father was a Devereux. My ancestors came over with William the Conqueror.'

'Exactly my point,' Henry thumped Robert on the arm. 'With such an ancestry, what can you not do?'

XXIV

'I *am* going to write to him, Anthony,' Francis insisted.

Anthony snatched the pen out of his brother's hand. 'It is not your place to do this.'

'We are his advisers, Anthony. If we do nothing to curb his words and his actions, he may undo us all. Now, give me the pen.'

A moment passed while the brothers stared at one another, then reluctantly, Anthony gave the quill back and watched as Francis dipped it in the inkpot and began to write. 'What are you going to say?'

'I am going to tell him that he is a great nobleman, but that he has some qualities that anger the Queen.'

'You should name them so that he cannot be ignorant of what they are.'

'I will. Listen. He is unruly in his temper, he shows no obvious sign of the great intelligence he possesses, nor does he have the wealth to support his noble station. He has a martial spirit, which the Queen never admires. And most importantly, he has the affection of the people and courts it openly, which displeases the Queen even more.'

Anthony, still unconvinced at the rightness of the action, winced at the words. 'Francis, do you not think he will judge us impertinent?'

'If we do not check him—'

'Yes, yes,' Anthony waved him quiet, 'you are right. Continue.'

Francis wrote the letter and then passed it to his brother. Anthony read.

'Your lordship must hold his tongue and not complain so noisily nor so frequently of the wrongs committed by the Queen against your person. You should try to compliment the Queen as you once did, for your flattery has of late become insincere and inconsistent. Although contrary to your generous and open nature, your lordship must act as other courtiers do and mould your behaviour to please the Queen. As an example, you could announce an intention to visit your estate in Wales, a plan that would necessitate a prolonged absence from court, and then, if the Queen expressed displeasure at such an intention, cancel it, to prove that you conform yourself to her wishes. To this end, I can but only recommend you read *The Prince* and become a true disciple of Machiavelli.'

Anthony finished reading and nibbled on his bottom lip for a few moments, then nodded his agreement and told Francis to send the letter, quickly before he changed his mind.

Francis folded the letter, poured hot wax upon the fold and pressed his signet ring into it to form a seal.

'I fear we are wasting our time though,' Anthony said, running his fingers through his thinning hair. 'The earl is not capable of such subtlety and double-dealing.'

'I know,' Francis said, putting the letter aside and picking up another sheet of paper, 'but I am making a copy and it will at least show that we tried to restrain him.

I do not want to be accused of treason at a trial if and when the earl decides to act.'

XXV

1597

Cecil was in his office at Whitehall Palace, reading the latest correspondence from his informants in Spain. The Spanish fleet had mobilised. King Philip, smarting from the English attack on Cadiz, had ordered his armada to set sail. Robert had once more been given command of the *Due Repulse* and, for some reason best known to himself, had announced that the Spanish had been sighted approaching the English coast, then that they were also making for Ireland, playing on the Queen's fear that the Spanish would use that country and the Catholic Irish to launch a two-pronged invasion on England.

Neither of these claims, Cecil's intelligencers reported, were remotely true. Nevertheless, as a precaution, Cecil had Elizabeth confirm Robert in his role as commander, but Elizabeth had insisted on telling Robert that he must stay around the English coast and not think of sailing off to Ireland on a wild goose chase, leaving England vulnerable to attack.

Robert, in Cecil's opinion, was better away from court than in it. He could do less damage at sea.

As it turned out, God still favoured the English, for He arranged for a storm, just like the one that destroyed the Spanish fleet in 1588, to blow up and the Spanish ships were forced to sail home.

Robert returned to court, only to be met with yet more complaints from Elizabeth, and to discover that in his absence, the Lord Admiral, Charles Howard of Effingham, had been raised to the earldom of Nottingham. Ostensibly, the elevation was in recognition of Howard's past service, but Robert in his present mood was unable to view it as anything other than a snub against himself. The news was made worse by the making of Howard the Lord Steward of Parliament. Such a position meant that Robert would have to walk behind Howard in any and all official processions.

This was too much to bear. Robert was furious and he let his anger show, continuously sulking and rebuking Elizabeth for her blatant efforts to undermine him. But Elizabeth refused to acknowledge her errors or insults, and Robert decided he had to get away, he had to leave court, for his own sanity, if nothing else.

He gave out that he was ill and retired to his house at Wanstead, locking himself in his bedchamber and refusing all company.

⁂

'Is he ill?' Elizabeth asked as she tried on another dress, her fourth that morning. Her ladies tried to hide their irritation at her indecisiveness. 'I heard that he is ill.'

Cecil, hidden behind a screen for decency's sake, scratched his nose and sniffed. 'Francis Bacon writes that the earl is ill, if locking himself up in his room and wrapping himself in blankets can be accounted an illness.'

'I pity him. Perhaps I have been a little harsh. I know the past few months cannot have been easy for him.'

Cecil suppressed a sigh. It had been pleasant in the earl's absence; there had been no outbursts of petulance, no ridiculous claims or demands made in the Privy Council meetings.

'I think I shall write to the earl,' Elizabeth was saying, 'and assure him of my affection.'

'If you think that wise.'

'You think it unwise, Pygmy?'

'Indeed, madam, I can think of nothing more restorative to the earl's health than your avowal of affection.'

Elizabeth pursed her lips, amused by Cecil's sarcastic rejoinder. 'It would be helpful though, would it not, Pygmy, to have the earl attending Council meetings once more? Especially in view of the French who are intent on paying us a visit.'

'It is true that the French king considers the earl a friend,' Cecil allowed carefully.

'And we would do well to present a united front to the ambassador. You know how keen the French are to make capital out of English divisions.'

'You are correct, as always, Your Majesty.'

'And indeed, I hear that Robert has been somewhat maligned. His conduct at Cadiz was not as foolhardy as I had been led to believe.'

Cecil looked at her quizzically. 'From whom have you received such information, Your Majesty? If I may ask?'

'You may ask, Pygmy. From Sir Francis Vere. He told me certain things and when I cross-examined that rogue Ralegh on the points, he was unable to answer to my satisfaction.'

'Indeed?'

'Indeed, Pygmy. So you see, Robert may have some justification in acting as he does.'

'His behaviour, if I may, does not befit a grown man but a child.'

'Oh,' Elizabeth wafted her handkerchief at him, 'let him have his sulks, Pygmy. What harm can it do? No, I am minded to have him back at court.'

'And if he will not come? The notion of the new earl of Nottingham having precedence over him seems to be a major point of contention with the earl.'

'Hmm.' Elizabeth tapped her finger on the table, pointing as she considered. 'Well, I can make Robin Earl Marshal of England. That way, Nottingham will have to walk behind Robert once again and poor Robin's wounded pride shall be salved. Make a note to that effect, Pygmy.'

Reluctantly, Cecil made a note, wondering why Elizabeth was being so considerate towards Essex. Was it some new stratagem, or was she simply being a woman?

Lettice smoothed her son's auburn curls, now flecked through with grey, and leant down to kiss his forehead. 'My clever boy,' she purred, squeezing him tighter.

'You see, Mother, this is power,' Robert said, his face glowing with pride. He held Elizabeth's letter under her nose, making her read it again. 'To gain such a title as Earl Marshal of England, and I had to do nothing, save retire to my house and refuse to attend court.'

'Yes, I know,' Lettice said musingly. 'Elizabeth must be growing soft in her old age. I doubt if even Leicester could have pulled off such a trick.'

'Do not call it a trick, Mother,' Robert scolded,

carefully refolding the letter as though it were something sacred. 'It was a stratagem.'

'Whatever you say, my darling.'

'She needs me, you see, Mother,' Robert said assuredly. 'She has realised I am not just a plaything as Leicester was, someone to keep her amused. Leicester was never loved by the people. But the people do love me and Elizabeth dare not put me down for fear that the people will rise against her.'

XXVI

1598

His father was in bed when Cecil arrived home at Burghley House. He handed his cloak and gloves to a servant and then made his halting way up the oak staircase. He knocked before entering his father's bedchamber in case the old man was asleep, but Burghley's croaky voice called for him to enter.

'How are you, Father?' Cecil asked, kissing his father's cheek.

Burghley pointed at his foot and informed Cecil that it was agony. Cecil cast a reproachful look at the swaddled foot, knowing that nothing could be done to ease the pain.

'What news today, my boy?'

Cecil sat down on the stool kept by the bed. 'I am to go to France to continue negotiations with King Henri. I wish I did not have to go, Father. I will be away some months and I hate to leave you.'

'Oh,' Burghley patted his son's cheek with a cold hand, 'you must not worry about me. It is an honour for you to be sent. A demonstration of Elizabeth's trust in you.'

'I know I should view it as such,' Cecil bowed his head, 'but much could happen in my absence. The Earl of Essex—'

'I wish you would not concern yourself with the earl, Robert.'

'I have to, Father, he has all the advantages I lack.'

'That is not true,' Burghley thumped the bedclothes with as much indignation as he could muster.

'It *is* true, Father. I know what I am. I can never fight in battle or woo the Queen. All I have are my wits to recommend me. Out of sight will be out of mind with the Queen, and you can guarantee that Essex will take advantage of my absence.'

'I think you credit that young man with too much intelligence, Robert. All you need to do is prepare the ground before you go.'

'How do I do that?'

'Make yourself a friend to the earl. Invite him to dine with you. Put him under obligations to you. Speak well of him to the Queen. He is always short of money. So, see that he gets some.'

'The Queen granted him the monopoly on the farm of sweet wines years ago. That brings him a tidy sum.'

'He has expensive tastes, my boy. The money he gets from the sweet wines is not enough. Those papers you left me this morning about imported goods. There are cargoes due shortly of cochineal and indigo. Let the earl buy them cheaply. That will make him a good profit.'

'Will he not wonder why I am suddenly such a good friend to him?' Cecil asked wryly.

'Tell him the truth. Let him know that you do not want him poisoning Elizabeth's mind against you and make him promise that he will not. I know that young man. I know how he thinks. He will not only feel grateful to you for letting him make money, he will also feel honour-bound to promise he will not act against you.'

Cecil shook his head. 'It will pain me to benefit him in any way.'

Burghley smiled. 'You do not have to like it, Robert, just to do it. Trust me, my boy.'

At Essex House, Lettice fingered her pearl earring and angled her head to see her reflection in one of the gold plates mounted on the cupboard. The image was a distortion, she knew, but she looked well enough to her eyes. She wondered how Elizabeth would look. It had been more than a decade since they had last been face to face and Elizabeth had already begun to paint then. Of course, Lettice painted, too. Elizabeth had made it fashionable to wear the white lead makeup over the skin and cover thinning grey hair with lustrous red wigs, but Lettice had the advantage of years, being several years younger than her cousin. She hoped she looked better than Elizabeth. That would be thumbing her nose at the bitter old crow.

'You look fine, Mother, stop worrying,' Robert said, coming into the chamber. He had finally persuaded Elizabeth to receive his mother back at court and this was to be their first meeting. He knew that Lettice was anxious and was determined to calm her.

'I'm not worrying,' Lettice protested, moving away from the plate. 'Do you have my gift?'

Robert dipped his hand into his purse and pulled out a velvet pouch. He passed it to her and Lettice checked the contents, an emerald that had made a huge hole in her finances. But Elizabeth liked expensive presents and

Lettice deemed it a price worth paying to be allowed back at court.

'What time is it?'

'I heard the clock strike twelve,' Robert said.

'Then she should be here,' Lettice exclaimed. She hurried to the window, scanning the river for a sight of the royal barge. 'I can't see her.'

'She will be here,' Robert said, moving to his mother, placing his hands on her shoulders and kissing her cheek. 'She promised me.'

But when another hour had passed and Elizabeth did not arrive, even Robert had to admit that she had broken her promise. Lettice fumed and spat out curses against her while Robert quietly seethed. She had once again made a fool and liar of him, and not only him but his mother, too. He left Lettice consoling herself with a jug of his finest wine and took his barge back to Whitehall Palace. He demanded an audience with Elizabeth, who eyed him coolly as he spoke of his wrongs and her unkind treatment of him.

When he had run out of breath and self-pity, Elizabeth had stepped up to him, her face, the white paint cracked and flaking, mere inches from his. She had sighed, her breath, tainted by decay, wafted over him and his nostrils tightened in revulsion. She reminded him that she was queen and his mother little better than a whore, and if she chose to remain unreconciled with the woman who had seduced and deceived as good a man as the Earl of Leicester, then she was quite at liberty to do so.

Robert found himself unable to answer, stung, hurt, chastened by the hate directed towards his beloved mother. Elizabeth, victorious at silencing Robert, had smiled a crooked smile and joined the company in the next room who were settling to watch a play.

Robert had been left to consider the kind of life he was

leading, in thrall to, as his mother had quite rightly called her and he could agree with her now, a bitter old hag.

XXVII

Henry helped himself to a cup of wine and put his feet up on the table. Francis Bacon looked at the booted feet with envy, admiring the soft leather and quality cut that only an earl could afford. They made him think of his own shoes, made for him by a second-rate cobbler and which rubbed both little toes every time he moved. *I am a martyr to blisters*, he thought.

'My only consolation,' Robert was saying from the window embrasure where he watched the wherries with their swinging lanterns on the river, 'is that Cecil achieved nothing in France. All the while he was there, King Henri was making a secret alliance with the Spanish.'

'Are we always to have the Spanish as enemies, do you think?' Henry asked, flicking his long hair back over his shoulder.

'If we pursue Cecil's inept policy of suing for peace, we are,' Robert muttered.

'But surely, the failure of the French alliance means that you can now pursue an anti-Spanish policy in Council, no?' Henry asked.

'I wish I could,' Robert shook his head. 'Burghley and Cecil are still advocating peace with Spain and the Queen listens to them because she does not want to spend money on war.'

'And I thought Burghley had retired,' Henry muttered into his cup.

'There is little money available for war, my lord,' Francis said, feeling the need to point out this small fact.

'Money can always be found, Francis,' Robert said. 'And, my God,' he said, his manner growing heated, 'I tell the Council, I do not know how often, that England should not even contemplate making a peace treaty with a Popish country, but do they listen? You cannot trust the word of a Papist, can you, Henry?'

'Certainly not,' Henry replied on cue with all the vehemence he could muster.

'I have to do something. I have to try to convince the Council and the Queen that we should not sue for peace with Spain.'

'I have an idea,' Henry said after a moment's thought. 'Write a letter.'

'To whom?' Robert asked sulkily, wondering how a letter could help him.

'Well, ostensibly to Francis's brother, but in reality, it will be made public. In it, you make a reasonable and well-judged argument both for and against peace, but come down on the side of the virtues of going to war with Spain. And then, of course, we get his brother to circulate it, anonymously. The power of the written word, Rob, it should not be underestimated.'

Robert glanced at Francis, who sat tight-lipped, his eyes fixed on his knees. 'What do you think, Francis?'

Not wanting to earn the scorn and derision of Wriothesley, who once he found a weakness in a person would continually work upon it, Francis agreed that it was worth considering but he carefully stopped short of saying it was a good idea. Robert may have asked for his opinion but Francis was becoming accustomed to his advice going unheeded.

'I will do what you say, Henry,' Robert said and began to pace the room. 'I shall be moderate, judicious, all the things Cecil thinks I am not. My arguments will be so damn persuasive that the Council will have to listen. I will beat that damn Pygmy yet.'

Elizabeth had decided to attend the Privy Council meeting, curious to see how matters were between her rash youth, *although*, she reflected, *he is not so young these days,* and her Pygmy. She had heard reports of their disagreements, their seeming reconciliations, even of Robert's sometimes disconcerting behaviour, and wanted to see for herself.

Now, Ireland was causing trouble. Encouraged by their fellow religionists in Spain, the Irish were denying their English masters and rebelling against them. Ireland needed a new English governor and the Privy Council were trying to reach a consensus as to who that should be.

It became apparent to Elizabeth during the course of the meeting that none of her subjects wanted to be Lord Deputy of Ireland. Perhaps it was not surprising. Ireland had defeated many English governors, Robert's father, Walter Devereux, included. But the post could not remain vacant and Elizabeth demanded names.

'Sir George Carew,' Robert offered.

Elizabeth glanced at Cecil. 'What think you of Carew, Pygmy?'

'I think not, madam,' Cecil said, too annoyed to elaborate his reason.

But Elizabeth knew his reason. She knew that Carew was a friend to Cecil and an enemy to Robert and that Robert thought the best place for such a man was a country as unpleasant as Ireland. She laughed. 'Oh, Robert, what a suggestion. Name another.'

Robert frowned at her. 'Why do you laugh, madam? I name Sir George Carew as the most suitable man for the post. I see no cause for merriment.'

'Do you not indeed?' Elizabeth said, her voice taking on a steely edge. He was defying her. Again.

'I cannot believe the earl is serious,' Cecil said, smiling at the Queen, sensing her anger.

'I am perfectly serious, Master Secretary,' Robert said through gritted teeth. 'And you had better take care how you mock me.'

'Be careful who you threaten, my lord,' Elizabeth said. 'Now, name another.'

'Sir George Carew,' Robert repeated doggedly.

'God's Death,' Elizabeth growled. She squeezed her eyes shut and clenched her fist. 'I will hear no more of your ridiculous chatter. Be quiet.'

'I will not be quiet,' Robert jumped up from his seat, his eyes blazing at her.

'You will be quiet, sir,' Elizabeth retorted, rising to match him, 'or you will suffer for it.'

As one, the counsellors rose, for it would not do to remain seated while the Queen stood. Robert opened his mouth to reply but he could think of nothing that would serve as a suitable rejoinder, nothing that would shut her up. He turned his back on her instead.

No one had ever turned their back on Elizabeth. It was unthinkable that anyone would dare show such disrespect. She stared at Robert's broad shoulders for a moment in astonishment before stretching out her arm and striking him savagely across the back of the head.

The blow stinging, Robert whirled around, his face red with rage. His right hand flew to the sword that hung on his left hip, and he had drawn it at least four inches from the scabbard before the Earl of Nottingham stepped between him and the Queen.

His hand stayed, Robert found his voice and it trembled with fury. 'I will not endure this insult. I would not have taken it from your father. I'll be damned if I'll take it from you.'

Robert pushed Nottingham out of his way and exited the Council chamber, leaving behind stunned counsellors and a shaken and silent Elizabeth.

Robert, to everyone's surprise, had not been arrested after the incident in the Council chamber, nor had he even been dismissed from the court, despite the counsellors' pleas for the earl to be publicly punished. Elizabeth had seemed shocked into inaction by Robert's assault, and had said nothing, done nothing, but retired to her private apartments and resumed her reading.

Robert had decided to remove himself from court, instructing Francis to spread the gossip that such discourtesy from the Queen and her ministers had made him unwell and he was retiring to his house in the country at Wanstead to recover. Lord Keeper Egerton, who had long been a friend to Robert, had followed him there.

'You've used this stratagem before, my lord,' Sir Thomas Egerton said, warming his backside before the fire. 'You should be careful it does not grow stale.'

'I will not stay at court to be abused,' Robert said stubbornly, resting his chin on his hand and staring into the dancing flames.

'Self-imposed exile gives your enemies at court the

opportunity to move against you without hindrance, do you not see that?' Egerton pleaded.

'I have had enough of court intrigue,' Robert snapped. 'I am no Machiavelli, Egerton, I am not cunning enough for court. Do you know, Francis Bacon sent me a letter telling me I need to act like a true courtier and be cunning and sly? I cannot, no, I will not do it.'

'The Queen herself wants you at court. She is not angry, I assure you, despite all.'

Robert turned on him. 'Why should *she* be angry? It was I who was insulted, Egerton. She struck me as if I were a child who had misbehaved.'

Egerton held up his hands. 'She is the Queen, my lord.'

'What of it?' Robert spat. 'Cannot princes err? And cannot subjects receive wrong? Is an earthly power or authority infinite? Pardon me, pardon me, my good lord, I can never subscribe to these principles.'

Egerton was aghast. 'My lord, it is treason you speak.'

'Treason? To speak the truth? I am no snivelling child, Egerton. I do not cower when the Queen snaps her fingers. I will return to court only when she apologises for her behaviour to me.'

'Well, what did the wretch say?'

It was morning, past nine o'clock, and Elizabeth was sitting up in her bed, still dressed in her night attire. She was not feeling well. She had a terrible headache that was causing black spots in her vision. She had still had her ladies make up her face, however. She was not prepared for any man to see her so naked.

Egerton returned to court, was aware that Cecil had spies in every noble's household and not wanting to be implicated in treason, gave Elizabeth a true account of his meeting with the earl: how he looked, how he acted, and what he said.

Cecil, standing at the other side of the bed, snorted. ‘He demands an apology from Her Majesty? Is the man right in the head?’

‘In truth, Sir Robert,’ Egerton said unhappily, ‘I do not know. He is certainly changeable. In deep contemplation and melancholy one moment, choleric and enraged the next.’

‘So, no change there, then,’ Cecil muttered under his breath. He looked down at Elizabeth. ‘An apology will not be necessary, Your Majesty. I have had a report this morning that the earl is already making preparations to return to court. He has heard of your favour towards Lord Grey and is determined to stop it. I believe he will be at the palace gates by the end of tomorrow.’

‘Oh, how fortunate I do not need to apologise,’ Elizabeth said with a tight smile, keeping her eyes closed.

‘I was not suggesting that you did,’ Cecil said, shuffling his feet.

‘I know, Pygmy. It is just like Robin to cause trouble at such a time when your father is so ill. Does the wretch not know how greatly I am distressed by it?’

Cecil wanted to say that it was *his* father who was dying and he had every right and reason to be more distressed than Elizabeth, but he kept his feelings to himself. ‘My father will be gratified by your concern, Your Majesty.’

‘Indeed,’ Elizabeth nodded. ‘What is my headache and indisposition compared to his suffering? I shall rise from my sickbed and visit him today. I will not let my dear old servant think he is neglected by his queen.’

‘And what of the earl, Your Majesty?’ Egerton asked tentatively. ‘Will you allow him to enter the court?’

Elizabeth sighed. 'I cannot have such discord within my Council. Yes, he may return to court. I will receive him. And neither of us will have to apologise to the other.'

ᘓ ᘓ ᘓ

The sun shone bright and warm through the window, but the hand Cecil held was already growing cold.

Lord Burghley was dead.

Cecil's mother, Mildred, and his wife, Elizabeth, were clustered around the old man's bed in Burghley House. Elizabeth, he blessed her kind heart, was crying. Mildred was stony-faced, not trusting herself to give way to her feelings. Cecil did not even realise he wept too and only became aware of it when the dried tear tracks tightened his cheeks.

He had lost a great love with his father's passing. His wife loved him, it was true, but his mother had only a regard for him as flesh of her flesh, bone of her bone. She had always loved his brother more. His father, though, had loved him deeply, felt his pain and resented his bodily misfortunes, perhaps more so than Cecil himself.

Cecil had an unpleasant suspicion that his own heart was hard, that without his father he would view the world as cold and unforgiving and treat all who were in it as such. He was what his father had made him in regard to his brain and his abilities, but his father had not been able to make him compassionate. The world regarded him as a freakish thing, so the world would have to be fashioned to dance to his tune.

Cecil stayed with his father, even when Mildred and Elizabeth had left to seek the warmth of their private apartments and the comfort of hot food and warm wine. Left alone, the force of his grief lessened and he was able to reflect. His father had never quite recovered from the shock of Robert's behaviour at that damned Council meeting when he had almost drawn his sword on the Queen. Burghley's last few weeks had been consumed with concern for Elizabeth and Cecil was convinced that it had hastened his father's death. Cecil knew that Robert was to blame.

XXVIII

In the weeks that had passed, the Irish problem had not gone away. The Irish rebels, led by a man called Tyrone, massacred two thousand English soldiers. News of the Irish victory soon spread, and the rebels moved through Ulster and Leinster and reached the walls of Dublin. The English colonists, those who escaped the slaughter, watched as their homes were destroyed by the rebels and were forced to flee, desperate to reach one of the few remaining English strongholds in Ireland.

Tyrone had achieved almost all of what he desired through rebellion. To all intents and purposes, he had made himself king of all Ireland.

‘Those poor people,’ Elizabeth said when Cecil had finished giving her the news. ‘What miseries they have suffered at the hands of those animals. And why has this been allowed to happen? Because my Council have refused to name a suitable governor to take charge of Ireland.’

The counsellors looked shamefacedly at one another. One spoke up. 'We would have been able to agree on an appointment were it not for the Earl of Essex, madam.'

Elizabeth grunted and looked around the table. 'Well, where is he? Why is Essex not here at this meeting? I know he is at court.'

'I believe the earl is ill,' Cecil said, adding, 'truthfully, this time.'

'Then send my doctor to him,' Elizabeth said, her tone peremptory. 'Tell him that as soon as he is well, he must attend the Council. We need to appoint a Lord Deputy for Ireland.'

Another of her counsellors spoke up. 'But the earl rejects all of the names proposed, Your Majesty. He claims none of them is able.'

Elizabeth gnawed at her bottom lip and then looked up at Cecil. 'Then who would be able in his lordship's eye?' she wondered. 'A man of proven military ability? A man who can command affection and loyalty?'

Cecil held her gaze. 'Someone very like the earl, in fact.'

'Just so,' she agreed, the corners of her thin lips turning up.

'However, I may be wrong to voice this,' Cecil said warily, 'but is it wise to give such an important command to the earl? He would, after all, have a considerable army at his disposal.'

'I am not sure I understand you, Pygmy,' Elizabeth countered. 'Are you suggesting the earl would betray me?'

Concerned he had misread Elizabeth, Cecil shook his head. 'No, Your Majesty. I am sure the earl can be trusted.'

'Then I shall appoint the Earl of Essex as Lord Deputy of Ireland. What say you, gentlemen?'

Her decision was met with a chorus of agreement and not a little relief. None of the counsellors had ever been comfortable when Essex was in their midst and it would be pleasant to have him out of the country so that their meetings could return to a semblance of normality.

Elizabeth decided she had spent long enough at the meeting. She rose and a secretary pulled her chair away to aid her exit. She touched Cecil on the shoulder. 'Do not worry, Cecil. He will have his hands full in Ireland and he will not have time to cause any trouble. That country has broken far better men than he. He will see his appointment as Lord Deputy as an honour, a confirmation of my faith in him. If he succeeds, he will be a hero. The people will champion him as the saviour of Ireland. The prospect of that is too great for him to refuse the post.'

'I wish I had your insight into his character, madam,' Cecil said.

She laughed. 'I have been looking into men's hearts for almost forty years, Pygmy. There is no mystery in them.'

It was a sombre dinner at Essex House. Robert had visited the court briefly upon Elizabeth's summons and had been told of his new commission. Stunned by the news, unsure whether it was good or bad, he had found himself thanking Elizabeth, making a few requests regarding the appointment, and leaving as quickly as he could.

'So, you are going to Ireland,' Henry said, wiping his fingers on the napkin laid over his left shoulder.

'Yes,' Robert nodded unhappily, pushing the remnants of his food around his plate with a knife. 'The Queen decreed it, the Council urged me to accept, and the people think I am the right man to go.'

'It is unfortunate. You will be away from court for a long time. Cecil will take advantage of that.'

'You do not need to tell me, Henry. But what can I do? If I refuse to go to Ireland, I disobey the Queen, and she may send me to the Tower. And I will be seen by everyone as a coward if I do not accept the post. And, in truth, I think it may be better to command an army in Ireland than have to do battle at court.'

Henry drained his cup. 'You look tired, Robert.'

'I am not sleeping well,' Robert admitted. 'Not just because of this business with Ireland. Elizabeth is demanding I clear all my debts to her. My debts amount to ten thousand pounds and more, Henry. Where the devil am I supposed to find the money to pay her all that? She knows I do not have it. And she has also refused to make you Master of the Horse as you bid me ask because of your marriage.'

'Curse her bones,' Henry spat. 'I had to marry Mistress Vernon, she carries my child.'

'Of course, you had to, but Elizabeth has no sense of honour. And I asked to have Charles Blount on my Council when I go to Ireland and she has refused that, too. She ties my hands before I even get to the hellish country.' Robert gulped down his wine. 'And there is more. Another book has been published with a dedication to me. This one actually compares me to Bolingbroke.'

'You should be flattered, Robert. I would be.'

'It makes my position so difficult. You know how sensitive Elizabeth is about the succession.'

'I have said it before, Robert,' Henry said. 'If the people are seeing you as another Bolingbroke, then Elizabeth has every reason to fear you.'

Robert threw his knife onto his plate and turned to Henry. 'Oh hell, come with me to Ireland, Henry. I feel I am going to need my friends about me.'

'Oh, I suppose I may as well. There is nothing for me here. Indeed, I think it might be a good idea to get some soldiering practice in.'

Robert's face brightened. 'You will not mind leaving your wife? The child?'

Henry had easily forgotten about his new responsibilities. Perhaps he should stay with his new wife? But stay and do what? Sit at her side and watch her grow fat? There was no reason for him to stay at court, not with Robert in England and the Queen scowling every time she looked his way. He shook his head, assured Robert that his wife and child would be well looked after, and said to sound the drums, for he was, like Robert, for Ireland.

XXIX

March 1599

Robert had been wrong to worry about going to Ireland, he decided. It was an opportunity, not a punishment of sorts, and his reputation could only be strengthened by a military campaign. His popularity, it seemed, was growing ever stronger, if his departure was anything to go by. Prayers for his success and safety were said in all the churches, and as he and his friends who were joining him on the campaign made their way out of the city, the people of London thronged the streets to cheer him on his journey. For four miles his route was lined with well-wishers, their cheers only diminishing as the sky began to darken and rain began to fall. If Henry and Charles Blount, who rode by his side despite the fact that they had no official place on the campaign, for the Queen had not confirmed any of Robert's proposed appointments, considered the rain and hail to be an ill omen, they kept the thought to themselves.

The weather continued to be foul, so that by the time the party reached the disembarkation port at Beaumaris, their spirits were low, made worse by the stormy passage across the Irish sea that turned their stomachs and made them thank God when they stepped upon the solid earth of Ireland. Their stomachs settled and the weather more clement, Robert and his friends began to look forward once more to winning Ireland back for England. Robert was sworn into his office as Lord Deputy of Ireland, and soon he was being fêted and celebrated with feasts, pageants and jousts and Robert felt sure that his glorious destiny was soon to be realised.

But this feeling soon faded. His strategy for a land and sea attack was vetoed with the English officials who had spent many years in Ireland telling him it was not possible with the limited resources he had been provided with by the Council. It was also a poor idea, he was told, because there were rumours that Spain was preparing to launch another armada, and they might choose to attack from the Irish Sea. Then Robert received a letter from the Privy Council giving him his orders: he was to journey north and attack Ulster.

The leader of the rebels, Hugh O'Neill, Earl of Tyrone, was carrying out his own policy of stripping the land around the Pale of all its means of sustenance and travel so that the English forces found little food and no horses available to them. He was also encouraging formerly loyal nobles to the Queen to turn and join forces with him, so that soon, Robert and the English army were surrounded by enemies on all sides. It was hopeless, Robert decided, to carry on with the Council's policy of heading north. The only choice open to them was to go back the way they had come and try to secure the territory in the south.

When the Council received his letter, they were disappointed but Elizabeth was furious. Robert had had his instructions and was blatantly ignoring them. The more serious problem was not in the south of Ireland but the north, in fact, wherever Tyrone was. No one else in Ireland carried his authority or martial ability, and only by capturing Tyrone would the war turn in England's favour. What was Essex playing at? Elizabeth shouted at her Council as she paced behind their chairs, they keeping their heads down, not wanting to share in Essex's disfavour. But there was more. Even though Robert had been warned about dispensing knighthoods years before and had been expressly instructed that he was not to make any more knights on the Irish campaign, he was creating new knights by the dozen. Being a knight will no longer be thought of as an honour, Elizabeth snarled, if every raggle-taggle man in the army was made one.

Elizabeth had sat herself down at the Council table and bade Cecil take out his pen and commit to paper the words she spoke. So Cecil wrote that Robert must not create any new knights and that he must stop prevaricating, head north and attack O'Neill at once.

Robert tried to obey but the Irish rebels were too strong and had far more resources than he. Worse still, he fell ill and was confined to his bed for almost two weeks while his troops were either harried or killed by the stealthy attacks of the rebels, or were weakened by fever. The campaign dragged on and no gains were made. The spies the English lords in Ireland had cultivated were either returning useless information or disinformation, while the Irish spies in the English ranks were astonished at the free-talking English lords, who boasted and bragged openly of their strategies to subdue the enemy and who rushed to inform Tyrone so that he always seemed one step ahead of Robert.

But even Tyrone grew weary of fighting and, conscious of his own dwindling resources and not wanting to battle through winter, sought a means of bringing the fighting to an end, even a temporary one. Having heard of the unhappiness of the English Lord Deputy, he believed he would find the means quite easily.

The day was cold. Robert still felt ill, his body shivering not only from the cold but the fever he had contracted back in Dublin. He sat a little unsteadily on his horse, his legs encased in woollen hose, his chest swaddled with wool and a fur cloak around his shoulders, burying his face up to his cheekbones, which now stood out prominently on his pale and blotchy face. Henry Wriothesley had urged him not to get out of his cot bed, doubting his friend's ability to stand let alone sit his horse, but Robert was adamant. There had to be an end to the chaos and misery he found himself in, and the chief rebel, Hugh O'Neill, Earl of Tyrone, had offered him a way out.

'I think he is coming,' Henry said, astride his own horse alongside Robert.

Robert glanced at him, wincing at the pain in his neck muscles, to see where Henry was looking. He followed his gaze up to the ridge of the hill and saw a small party of horse against the grey sky, their pennants billowing in the wind.

'Robert, are you sure this is wise?' Henry asked. 'We don't know how many men are over that hill. This could be an ambush.'

'Tyrone's messenger says his master seeks the mercy of the Queen. He knows he cannot withstand our forces for much longer. He needs to make a peace.'

Henry sighed, wishing that Robert held a clearer picture of their situation. The truth was far from how Robert believed it to be. Robert's army had suffered setback after setback, their conventional warfare methods ineffective against the stealthy tactics used by the Irish rebels. Like Robert, the army had succumbed to the illnesses and diseases that beset the bog-ridden Irish country, and many had died from the flux or fever. Many had been ill and recovered but were still too weak to fight, while others, too many others, had deserted, no doubt fleeing back to the safety of England. Henry suspected that Robert was not truly unaware of how bad things were and was clutching at any straw that could save him. Henry wanted to get back to England too, but he was worried that by treating with Tyrone, they were engaging in a pact with the devil.

Henry and Robert watched as Tyrone came down the incline on his horse, leaving his escort behind. Robert gave Henry a look that seemed to say that he was right to trust Tyrone, else why would he risk a meeting alone? Henry nodded to concede the point and even managed a smile. They turned back to Tyrone, who was riding his horse into the ford, stopping in its midst where the water lapped at the belly of the mare.

'Stay here,' Robert said, and nudged his horse's sides, trotting to the ford and mirroring Tyrone's position.

Tyrone was a man in his late forties or early fifties, dark-haired and dark-eyed, and with a heavy black beard streaked with grey. His expression was cheerful and he greeted Robert heartily, almost familiarly. He noted Robert's gaunt appearance and saw confirmation of his spies' reports that the earl had been ill. His reports had also told of how dejected Robert had become and thought happily that the meeting would be easy.

'It is my honour to meet with the great Earl of Essex,' he said in good English but with a strong Irish accent.

'You do me too much honour, my lord,' Robert returned. 'I welcome the chance to resolve this matter.'

'Well now, I don't know about resolving,' Tyrone laughed. 'The problems of Ireland cannot be resolved in one merry meeting, my lord, but I hope that we can reach some agreement before the winter comes.'

'I too. What do you want to propose?'

So, he's going to leave it to me to decide, Tyrone thought and wondered at Elizabeth sending so poor a commander to fight her cause. *Well then, let's see what this man will agree to.*

'A truce,' he announced, 'to last for six weeks from today, and then six weeks after that, to give us both time to view the situation objectively.'

'I had thought you would rather fight,' Robert said, surprised.

Tyrone shook his head. 'I'm not a fine young man like yourself, my lord. I yearn for the comforts of home too much. And it pains me greatly to see Irishmen die because England cannot see that she would be better off leaving us alone.'

'The terms of the truce. You say for six weeks—'

'Renewable every six weeks, I said. And if either one of us feels like fighting, we need only give the other a sennight's notice and we can start bashing each other's brains out again.'

'And what else?'

'We've been quite successful in capturing our towns back from the English hands, I'm sure you'll agree, and as it took so much effort to get them, we'd like to keep them, if it's all the same to you. So, all our spoils of war are to stay in our hands. I'll also guarantee you and your army free passage to the English-held towns, and to the ports, for I hear you might be planning on returning to England.'

'How have you heard that?' Robert asked sharply, embarrassed by the insinuation.

'You have your means of information, my lord,' Tyrone winked, 'I have mine.'

Robert, dismayed to discover that he had Irish spies in his camp, looked down at the water that swirled around his horse's legs. But what did it matter? he decided. His battle here was over. He was sick, his men were deserting in droves, Elizabeth refused to send him reinforcements, nor the money or arms to equip the remaining troops properly. How could he fight a war without her support? The letters he received from her were full of nothing but criticisms, asking why he had not taken that town or this, why he remained where he was instead of leading assaults into the enemy territory. It was all very well for her, sitting there in safety and comfort in London. What did she know of battle, of trying to command an army? A truce, this truce that Tyrone was proposing, was the only way there could be some sort of peace in Ireland, the only way he could go home.

'I accept the truce,' Robert declared.

'That's grand of you,' Tyrone said, holding out his gloved hand to Robert. Robert took it, feeling the older man's strong grip almost crush his own weakened extremity. 'We must have it set down on paper, so you can see that it binds me.'

'I will not insist on that. I give you my word. I need no more than yours.'

'Well, that is a fine gesture, I must say, but I'd prefer it to be set down. I'll have it written immediately and send it to you.'

'I thank you and wish you good day.' Robert pulled on his reins and his horse turned smartly, eager to be out of the freezing water. It cantered up the hill back to Henry.

'Well?' Henry asked, one eye on Robert, the other on Tyrone riding back to his escort.

'I have agreed on a truce with Tyrone. Six weeks from

now and renewable.'

'A truce, Robert?'

'Yes, Henry. It was the only thing to do. It means peace. For a time, at least.'

'What else does it mean?' Henry asked, unsure whether Robert had made the right decision.

'It means we can go home,' Robert replied. 'And I mean to.'

Robert was cold. The fur cloak could not keep him from trembling and his head was just one great throbbing pain. He listened as Henry read the letter from the Council, growing more despondent at every word. Elizabeth and the Council had heard of his truce with Tyrone and were outraged.

'It seems I can do nothing right, does it not, Henry?' Robert said when Henry had finished.

'The Queen and Council do not understand the situation here, Robert,' Henry replied wearily. He too was feeling ill and wished for nothing more than to be allowed to go to his bed. 'I thought perhaps you had been rash in agreeing to the truce, but upon reflection, I do not see what else you could have done. Your army is decimated by the flux and our supplies are almost spent. I tell you, this is Cecil's doing. He moves against you, defames you and misrepresents your every act to the Queen. I swear he is in the pay of Spain. If only he could be got rid of.'

'I will not stay here, Henry,' Robert said, pulling his fur cloak tighter. 'This country killed my father. I will not allow it to kill me. I shall return to England as I planned.'

'But the Queen forbids it, Robert.'

'Damn the Queen. Let her try and forbid it when I march into London with an army at my back. I will go,

Henry.'

'What do you mean to do, Rob?'

'Talk to her. I can explain my actions if I can but see her, face to face. Surprise the Pygmy. Are you with me, Henry?'

'You know I am,' Henry assured him warmly, who had not enjoyed one moment of the campaign and was longing for the comforts of London and home. 'I wish I had never come to this bog hole. Let us march on London.'

XXX

Elizabeth sank her aching feet into the gold bowl of warm, rose-scented water with a moan of pleasure. She adored her clothes with all their finery and delighted in the impression they made, but as she had grown older and her frame more frail, she found the weight of all the silk, gold and silver thread and jewels almost too much to bear. Ashamed as she was of her thin, grey hair, she was even glad to have the tight red wig removed from her head.

She leant against the back of the chair, resting her head and closing her eyes, aware of the tense silence amongst her ladies. She had shouted at them earlier for pricking her with pins as they removed her sleeves and they were being careful not to attract her attention.

There came a clatter from the adjoining room and Elizabeth lifted her head. She heard protestations from the guards, the sound of a scuffle, and then the doors were yanked rudely open. Elizabeth gasped at the intrusion, aware that she wore only her shift and nightcap.

'Bess,' the person in the doorway declared loudly, and with rising alarm, Elizabeth recognised the voice of

Robert. He came nearer and at such close range, even her myopic eyes could read the shock of her appearance in his expression. Her blood rushed to the paper-thin skin of her cheeks, and she felt only a sudden and intense hatred for the man who had caught her looking so ordinary, so vulnerable.

'Robin,' she said, her voice trembling, 'what are you doing here?' She rose, stepping out of the bowl, her feet dripping water onto the floorboards.

'I had to come,' he said, recovering his equanimity quickly. 'I have to tell you the truth about Ireland.'

'What truth, Robin?' she said, signalling with her eyes for one of her ladies to fetch help.

'Cecil has been lying to you about me, Bess. The truce. I did what I thought best. You haven't been there. You don't know what I have suffered. Men dying by the dozen, deserting, and I know not what.'

'Oh, you poor man,' Elizabeth said, her bewildered mind trying to grasp what was happening. Cecil's words, spoken months before, about giving Robert an army came rushing back to her. *My God*, she thought, *has he come to depose me?* 'Did you come alone?' she asked, fearing the answer.

'I hurried on ahead. I had to get to you first, you see?'

'Ahead of who?'

'The army, Bess. I could not leave them in Ireland, could I? A commander does not desert his men, does he?'

So, he does have the army at his back, Elizabeth realised. *What is he planning? To march on the city, take it over? Kill me?* Her heart beat even faster.

'You must not worry now you are here, Robin. Look at the state of you, all muddy and wet. You need to wash and rest.'

Elizabeth almost cried out in relief as Cecil silently entered the room behind Robert, his clothes obviously thrown on in a hurry. He stared at Robert and Elizabeth knew he was thinking the same terrible thoughts as she. They exchanged a glance and Cecil understood that Elizabeth needed him to take charge of the situation.

'Good evening, my lord,' he said.

Robert jerked around and was dismayed to see Cecil. 'Bess,' he appealed. His long, perilous horse ride had taken all his strength and he, with great shame, felt tears course down his cheeks to soak his matted beard.

'It is all right, Robin,' she said, taking his arm to persuade him to rise. 'Cecil is concerned for you. See Cecil, does not the earl look tired?'

'Exceedingly so, Your Majesty. He must have had a hard journey.'

'Ladies,' Elizabeth called, 'have the earl taken to his apartments. See that he rests and has all he needs.'

Cecil and she stood side by side while Robert was led away. The guards closed her chamber doors, shamefaced because they had failed her, and Elizabeth said quietly, 'He has brought the army with him. I must be kind to him, Cecil. I must appear to listen. Reassure him of my affection.'

'Agreed, Your Majesty. We need to know his intentions.'

'I shall find them out,' she said vehemently.

'He has deserted his post, madam,' Cecil reminded her.

'I know he has,' she snapped. 'And when I have made sure that he does not come to depose me, he shall pay for it, I promise you.'

Robert was feeling better. He had fallen into his familiar and comfortable bed and sheer exhaustion had put him into a deep sleep. He had woken refreshed almost ten hours later, broken his fast and was eager for his meeting with Elizabeth. He was sure all he needed to do was explain and all would be well. He had said so to Henry and to those who travelled with him. If his companions had had any doubts, they had kept them to themselves.

Robert expected to have a private interview with Elizabeth, so was disconcerted to be told to present himself in the Presence Chamber. When he entered, he found Elizabeth sitting on the dais in the chair beneath her canopy of estate, erect, regal, so unlike the thin old woman he had encountered the night before. He found the change in her faintly amusing and had to stop himself from laughing. Was she trying to be magnificent still? He had seen her as she really was. She could not fool him any longer. He bowed and began by asking if their talk could not be held in private.

'I think it best we talk in public,' Elizabeth had answered coldly and her stern aspect knocked his confidence.

Before he could speak further, Elizabeth began questioning him. Why had he left his post? How did he explain his ineptitude at dealing with the Irish rebels? Why had he disobeyed her strict commands and bestowed knighthoods? One accusation followed another and Robert found himself stammering out answers, giving one reason and then contradicting it with another, blaming others for his misfortunes.

Elizabeth was unmoved and the events of the previous night still painful in her memory. 'I have heard enough of your excuses, my lord,' she said, her voice growing louder with each word. 'I never desire to see your face again.'

Robert was ushered, protesting, from the room and was taken to the Privy Council chamber. He was sat down at the end of the table while Cecil, Hunsdon, North, and his grandfather Knollys, sat at the other. Robert tried to appeal to his grandfather, but Knollys refused to meet his eye. So, he tried to explain what he had been through in Ireland. They did not understand, they did not even try to. Or refused to. They just took their damned notes and answered none of *his* questions.

Robert was returned to his chamber and told that he was not to leave it. The doors were closed upon him and Robert, with a sickening feeling, heard the key turn in the lock. To ensure he made no attempt to leave, two guards were posted outside Robert's door.

Alone in his room, Robert fell onto his bed and pummelled his pillows in frustration and despair. He had been tricked, by Elizabeth, by Cecil, by his friends who had spurred him on to this course of action. He had returned to England with an army at his heels. He had had an opportunity to make London his and only his sense of honour had stopped him. He had been a damned fool.

'Lord Keeper Egerton has removed the earl from the court and taken him to York House, Your Majesty,' Cecil informed Elizabeth a few days later.

'And what of his companions who returned with him from Ireland?' she asked. 'Southampton, Rutland and the others?'

'At liberty, madam. We have nothing to charge them with. They were never commissioned, so we cannot charge them with deserting their posts.'

'Are they not to be considered a danger then?'

'We think not. The earl is the figurehead. They are nothing without him.'

'I am glad to hear it.'

'The earl himself, Egerton reports, has fallen into a great melancholy, eating little, sleeping fitfully. And he appears to be afflicted with the flux. His friends have sued to visit him, but the earl says he will not see them unless they have your permission. So it seems he is becoming conformable, madam.'

'Well he has seemed so before, Pygmy,' Elizabeth said wryly. 'Let us wait and see.'

'Yes, madam,' Cecil said, happy that Elizabeth did not seem ready to forgive and forget just yet.

XXXI

'This cannot be an end to it,' Henry Wriothesley said to Lord Mountjoy, just as Julius Caesar was being warned to beware the ides of March on the stage of the Theatre.

'What option do we have?' Mountjoy retorted, his eyes on the play. 'Essex is under house arrest.'

'But look at the support he has, Mountjoy,' Henry persisted. 'Whenever men walk by York House, they cheer for Robert. And there are ballads being printed that laud his name and denounce Cecil as a Spanish agent. Essex is the people's champion and they are outraged at his treatment.'

'I have done what I can, Wriothesley. I have written to King James to assure him of Essex's fidelity. I wrote that in spite of what he may have heard, Essex has no designs on the English throne for himself and will support James's accession when Elizabeth dies.'

'Keep your voice down, man,' Henry hissed, looking about him uneasily. They were seated in the galleries rather than on the stage, pressed in on either side by fellow playgoers.

'Essex could always escape,' Mountjoy said,

undeterred. 'Journey to France. King Henri would welcome him, I am sure.'

'We should put it to Robert,' Henry said, joining in the applause almost absentmindedly. 'Once he agrees to let us visit him, of course.'

❧ ❧ ❧

'Ireland still needs a commander,' Cecil reminded Elizabeth.

They were in the music room and Elizabeth was playing on the virginals. She was very good, Cecil admitted, although he wished she would stop playing while he was talking to her.

'A commander who will obey commands this time, if you please, Pygmy.'

'Indeed, yes, madam. In fact, I do have a suggestion. Lord Mountjoy.'

'Mountjoy?' At last, Elizabeth stopped her playing, but only to frown at him. 'Are you mad? He is a friend to Essex.'

'Yes,' Cecil agreed, enjoying the look of surprise on Elizabeth's face, 'but he is also an able soldier. He already has experience of Ireland, he knows the situation there. And I do believe, removed from the earl's circle and influence, he will prove a most loyal commander.' *Divide and conquer,* Cecil thought. *It's a strategy that always triumphs.*

Elizabeth grunted and resumed her playing. 'If you say so, Pygmy. I trust your judgement.'

'Thank you, madam. Speaking of the earl's circle, I can inform you that the Earl of Southampton has visited the Earl of Essex and spoken with him at length about escaping to France. The earl replied that he would prefer to stay and risk his life in England than become a fugitive in France.'

'How noble of him,' Elizabeth snorted, not needing to ask Cecil how he obtained his information. She knew he had paid spies in every noble's household and had had good reason to be grateful for it.

'We must decide whether to take legal action against the earl or not. Public opinion is mounting in his favour. They think he is imprisoned unjustly in York House.'

'Proceed with the Star Chamber examination,' Elizabeth told him without hesitation. 'He will answer the charges against him and the people will know what he is guilty of.'

'And his punishment, madam?' Cecil asked, hardly daring to look at her. 'When he is found guilty?'

'I cannot be too severe, Pygmy,' Elizabeth said, her tone a little regretful. 'Not with the embassy from the Netherlands due. How would they react if I were to publicly disgrace a Protestant champion? One who has fought for them in their own country?'

'Very wise of you, madam, and I agree. What is his punishment to be then?'

Elizabeth rested her long fingers on the black and white keys. 'Exile. Let him retire to the country, never to come to court again.'

Cecil smiled behind her back. 'As you instruct, madam.'

XXXII

A year passed and still Robert languished in the country, moving from Chartley to Wanstead and back again to Essex House, in attempts to escape the ennui of banishment. His debts were mounting up and his money running desperately low. Away from the court, he had no access to funds. Again and again, he wrote to the Queen asking her to forgive his past indiscretions, assuring her he was sorry, that he knew he had acted badly, and asking to be allowed to return to court. Elizabeth ignored all his letters, for she knew the real reason behind them. The monopoly on sweet wines she had granted him ten years earlier, and which provided Robert with a handsome and regular income, was coming up for renewal. Without it, Robert's financial position would indeed be precarious.

Robert waited to hear about the monopoly, months of agitation and great concern. When the answer came, there was no consolation. Aware that the Commons were unhappy with her distribution of monopolies to court favourites, Elizabeth refused to renew his licence. In a stroke, Robert's chief source of income was gone.

His position as a man of influence and power had also melted away. No longer the favourite of the Queen, no one courted his good opinion or asked for him to act on their behalf. His reputation as a soldier had also been damaged, for his friend, Mountjoy, had accepted the post of Lord Deputy of Ireland and was ably suppressing the rebels, succeeding where Robert had failed.

Robert's desperate situation began to affect his mind. He railed at those about him, decrying his enemies, who, to his mind at least, had become legion. Lettice joined him in his exile at Wanstead House, worried over the decline in her son. Grown too old to have any fight left in her, she begged Robert to give up all thoughts of returning to court. Such a desire would only lead to disappointment, she told him, especially as Cecil was in command of so much power, but Lettice soon found that any mention of the hunchback Cecil only inflamed her son's anger and made him more distracted and his behaviour unsettling.

Cecil, Robert was convinced, was to blame for everything. If only Elizabeth could be made to see it.

'I am glad I can still count you as a friend, Henry,' Robert said, grabbing Wriothesley's hand with both of his own. 'I fear I have so few.'

'You must not think like that, Robert,' Henry said, concerned at the appearance of his old friend. Robert had lost a great deal of weight, his auburn hair was heavily shot through with grey and his skin was blotchy with small patches of dry, flaky skin. He was glad that Robert had, at last, agreed to see his friends, and so he and Sir Charles Danvers, a friend from the days of the Irish campaign, had paid Robert a visit. 'Cecil is not greatly liked at court and hated throughout the country. I am sure he is in league with the Spanish. He still counsels the Queen to make peace with them.'

'But what of King James?' Robert asked. 'Does he know of my situation?'

'I have kept in contact with him, never fear.'

Danvers poked Henry in the arm. 'Tell Robert what you told King James.'

'Very well, Danvers,' Henry said, shaking him off. 'I have written in my letters that Cecil is no friend to King James and that he is making overtures to the King of Spain because he wants to put his daughter on the throne after Elizabeth. I did say that you, Rob, know this to be true. I thought your name would carry more weight and I implied that King James needs to make himself your friend and not Cecil if he has hopes of the English throne. Was I right to do so?'

'Admirable, Henry, I commend you,' Roberts said, grasping him by the shoulders. 'I am convinced my future lies with King James. Elizabeth has abandoned me.'

'Mountjoy too,' Danvers said. 'We wrote to him, asking him to write to you a letter complaining of the way Cecil and his faction had taken control of the government, and that you are needed to set things right. We would then make sure the letter was read around court.'

'Anthony will help with that,' Robert said eagerly.

'Bacon?' Henry said doubtfully. 'I do not think we should involve him. He is loyal to the Queen. His brother, too.'

'Not to me?' Robert asked, aghast.

Henry shook his head. 'Not anymore. But it does not matter anyway. Mountjoy refused to write the letter. He says he is the Queen's servant, not yours.'

'The traitorous dog! After all, I've done for him.' Robert turned away, shaking his head unhappily.

Francis, Anthony, Mountjoy. All gone, all turned away from him and towards the Queen and Cecil. His worst fears had been confirmed. He had been deserted.

❧ ❧ ❧

In the heated atmosphere of Essex House, isolated from the court and surrounded by resentful friends who whispered in his ear against the Queen and her ministers, Robert grew ever more convinced that Cecil was growing in influence and developing policies that were determined to ruin both Robert and the country.

Robert's friends, those who felt they had been overlooked by the Queen and disadvantaged by Cecil, were looking to him to help turn their fortunes around and place them at the centre of court and political life. Even King James had faith in Robert, for he had personally written a letter of encouragement and support that hung like a sacred relic in a black bag around Robert's neck.

Essex House was becoming a focal point for all the disaffected people in the country, with men coming from Wales and even Ireland to show their support for the earl or, at the very least, wanting to find shelter and food for a few nights.

Their true and various reasons for inhabiting the courtyard of Essex House were unimportant to Henry Wriothesley, who did not care whether they were true believers or simply men who had nothing better to do, but he did his best to convert them to the Essex way of thinking. He gave permission in Robert's name for a Puritan preacher to deliver a sermon criticising the pro-Spanish policies of Cecil and citing Calvinist doctrine that claimed men were entitled to depose a monarch who had failed to serve God and the country. The men grew rowdy, openly bearing arms and speaking treasonously against the Queen and her Council.

Reports of what was happening began to make their way to the Council and they caused great alarm. To try to calm the unrest at Essex House, the Council had the Lord Treasurer dispatch a letter to Robert, warning him in the friendliest language of the dangerous waters he was heading into. Robert read the letter with contempt, tossing it across to Henry to read for himself.

'They are just trying to delay the inevitable,' Henry said contemptuously. 'They can see how much support we have here and they are frightened. We need only rouse those men out there and we can take the court.'

Robert laughed. 'We will show that hunchback, will we not, Henry?'

'We certainly will, Robert.'

XXXIII

Lettice had arrived at Essex House. She had been at her home in Drayton Bassett but the letters she received from both Robert and her husband who was with him had worried her. Their letters contained words that were blatantly treasonous, and she knew that Elizabeth's Council ensured they had spies in households they considered disloyal. What if Robert's and Christopher's letters had been intercepted? They could be arrested for simply writing such things. She had to stop them in whatever they doing. It was reckless, it was stupid, it was dangerous.

'Mother, you must stop this,' Robert emphasised his words with a gesture of finality. 'I have had enough of being ruled by a woman.'

'I am not a woman, I am your mother,' Lettice reminded him. 'Do you want to kill me, Robert? Because that is what you'll do if you carry on like this.'

'My dear,' Christopher leant towards his wife and took hold of her arm, 'do not agitate yourself.'

'And you,' Lettice shook his hand off, 'what do you think you are doing leading my boy into such danger?'

'I? I am leading no one, Lettice. Robert is perfectly able to make his own mind up about what he must do.'

'And what must he do, husband, eh? Tell me that?' Lettice demanded.

Christopher turned away, wincing at Lettice's mounting shrillness. He raised his eyes to Robert and the two exchanged an exasperated glance.

'Mother,' Robert said, lowering his voice and hoping that Lettice would do the same, 'all I am doing is demanding my rights as a peer of this realm, as an earl and scion of one of the country's most ancient lineages. I am being denied all this and it is damaging me. I have no money. I have no power, cut off from the Queen.'

'But Christopher told me that Elizabeth will allow you to return to court,' Lettice cried, 'as long as you submit to her conditions.'

'Her conditions!' Robert cried, his eyes widening and bulging from their sockets. 'Her conditions are as crooked as her carcase.'

'Robert, hush,' Lettice entreated with a sideways glance at the two liveried servants who stood in the shadowy corners of the room.

'I will not hush, Mother. Have you not told me, time and time again, that Elizabeth is a bitter hag? Well, I did not believe you. I thought you were hurt by her treatment and spoke only in anger, but I have come to see over the last few years that you were right. I have been her companion, her friend. I have been her representative, her champion. I have gone into battle and risked my life, all in service to her, and how does she repay me? With complaints and accusations, with demands for money, by treating me like a child in front of lesser men, and this, this final insult, by banishing me from the court.'

'It is dangerous to talk so,' Lettice said, her face crumpling, almost in tears. 'Christopher, tell him.'

'No, Lettice, I will not,' Christopher said, emphasising his resolution with a slicing gesture. 'I have done your bidding in most things since we were wed, but not in this. Robert is right. This is no position for a man to be in.'

Lettice saw that it was useless. Even her husband was intent on putting the family in danger. 'What do you mean to do?' she asked wearily as she wiped her moist eyes with a silk handkerchief.

Another glance between Christopher and Robert. 'Do you truly wish to know, Mother?' Robert asked. 'Perhaps it would be better to remain ignorant.'

'No, you tell me,' Lettice glared at him. 'I want to know how reckless you plan to be.'

'Not reckless, I promise you.' Robert knelt in front of his mother and took her hands in his. 'The country is with me, Mother. You should see what happens when I go out into London. I am cheered, as you said you were, do you remember? You were cheered for being my mother. Well, *I* am cheered, Mother. You came through the courtyard, did you not? Well then, you must have seen how much support I have. The courtyard is full of men who believe I can bring them freedom from the crippling policies of Cecil and they urge me to act to remove him from power. I cannot ignore them, Mother, for their sakes. I must do something.'

'What are you going to do, Robert?' Lettice asked again.

'I have a small army out there, Mother,' Robert said with a half-smile. 'I, we, are going to march on the court and remove Cecil ourselves.'

'March on the court?' Lettice rasped. 'Are you mad?'

Robert did not care for the insinuation. He jerked away from her, seating himself on the floor, his back against a table, his legs drawn up and his hands grasping his head. 'It is not madness, Mother. Why can you not see the good I am trying to do? With Cecil gone, there will be no more supposed peace treaties with the Spanish. England will be allowed to be great, as she is destined to be.'

'And you, my darling? Do you have a role for yourself once Cecil is gone?'

'I will take up my rightful position, Mother,' Robert shrugged. 'I will replace Cecil as Elizabeth's chief minister and tell her how England should be ruled.'

'Tell her?' Lettice raised an eyebrow.

Robert paused. 'Advise her.'

'My darling,' Lettice held out her hand to Robert, but he did not take it. 'Do you suppose Elizabeth is going to let you remove her trusted minister and step into his shoes? Do you not think she will see you as a threat to her throne?'

'The throne is Elizabeth's, I know that,' Robert said, 'but I will be the power behind it.'

'You mean to marry her?'

'Of course not,' Robert spat, disgusted at the idea. 'I have a wife already, Mother.'

Lettice knew that wives could easily be got rid of, but said nothing about Frances. 'And if Elizabeth will not allow you to rule her?'

Robert scratched his chin, itchy beneath his beard, and stared at the tiled floor. 'She will have no choice.'

ঌ ঌ ঌ

The theatre was empty, for no play was to be performed that afternoon. Only Richard Burbage and Augustine Philips were in the building, sorting through the company's properties to take an inventory.

'I do not like it,' Burbage said, slamming the lid on the chest that held the company's scripts. 'The Earl of

Southampton, you say?'

'Special request,' Philips nodded, holding up a leather bag. He shook it and it jingled. 'We get the takings, plus an extra forty shillings.'

'But it is an old play. We haven't performed *Richard the Second* for years. I warn you, Augustine, we will not be able to remember all the lines.'

'I told the earl that and all he said was that he was sure we would manage. I've said we will do it now, Dick. I cannot go back on my word. Not with his money in my hand.'

'I don't like it,' Burbage said again. 'It's an odd thing to ask. He is a close friend of the Earl of Essex, you know. There is something behind this.'

'You are probably right, but I did not ask and I do not want to know. As far as we are concerned, we have had a request for a certain play from a noble patron and the fee is handsome. We are players, after all.'

'Well,' Burbage sighed, giving in. 'I'll dig out the scripts and bring them to The Mermaid.'

Philips deposited the leather pouch in a strongbox kept under the eaves and pocketed the key. 'I'll see you there.'

'And when was the play performed?' Cecil asked Lord Treasurer Buckhurst. He was working at Cecil House rather than the palace due to a severe head cold and he had summoned the Council to meet in his study. He planned to return to his bed when the meeting was over.

'Yesterday afternoon, Sir Robert. There was a sizeable audience, the majority of them friends of the Earl of Essex. Lord Mounteagle, Sir Gelly Meyricke, Sir Charles Blount.'

'I see.' Cecil looked around the room at his fellow

counsellors. 'I do not believe that we can afford to ignore this incident, gentlemen. The play was deliberately chosen to illustrate to the people the deposition of a monarch. This, coupled with the reports we are getting regarding the activities at Essex House, and it is quite clear the Earl of Essex and his friends are planning a rebellion. Do you agree?'

His fellow counsellors voiced their agreement and it was decided that they would send a message to Robert, requesting his presence before them to give an account of himself and the activities at Essex House. Cecil gestured to his clerk to write the request and the letter was dispatched to Essex House before the hour was out. It seemed his bed would have to wait.

The messenger was sent away from Essex House, and so prevented from delivering the Privy Council's request. Cecil dispatched the Council's Secretary Herbert to insist that he be given admittance and brought before the earl. Secretary Herbert could not be ignored as a humble messenger could and was ushered into Robert's presence. But Robert was unimpressed by the Council's summons. Who did they think they were telling him to present himself and answer their questions? The time for that, when he would have slunk along to the court and submitted to the Council's questioning, was gone. He was the Earl of Essex. He had an army in Essex House. He had men ready to follow him into whatever he chose to lead them. Let the Council go hang themselves. Robert sat back down and told Herbert that it was out of the question for him to leave Essex House. Could Herbert not see that he was ill? And besides, he distrusted the Council's motives. Once outside the walls of Essex

House, Robert said, he would not put it past the Council to have him murdered in the streets and blame it on a villain.

Astounded by Robert's words and unable to do more, Herbert returned to the Council and gave a report of the meeting.

By this time, midnight was approaching and Cecil, blowing his nose noisily into a linen handkerchief, deemed it best to wait until the morning to act further. Robert feared for his life, Cecil scoffed. What, or who, in God's name did Robert think he was threatened by? Cecil went at last to his bed, his mind busy with wondering what Robert's next move would be.

Robert did not go to bed. He and his fellow conspirators stayed up making plans for the morrow, buoyed up with the promise Henry had wrung from the city's sheriff of one thousand men to aid his rebellion. No one questioned the veracity of this promise. The sheriff said he would provide men, so men would be provided. Did not all free-thinking men, men of vision, men who loved England, want to act against a government that was appeasing the Spanish?

Robert and his rebels were resolved to march on the Palace of Whitehall the following morning.

XXXIV

February 1601

Whitehall Palace seemed almost deserted. Courtiers, whose only occupation was to stay at court and live off its bounty, sensed that something important was afoot and kept to their rooms. The palace guards had a more alert look about them than usual and they gripped their halberds tighter.

Cecil had advised Elizabeth to stay in her private apartments and she did not argue. This action of Robert's had been fermenting for months and in all that time she had been living on her nerves. But now the moment had come, she felt strangely calm. She may not have thought it possible five years earlier, but now she had complete faith in Cecil, in his planning and capabilities, and there was only the smallest concern that he would fail to put down the uprising.

It was what she wanted and had expected, so she had been surprised and angered by Cecil's desire to talk with the rebels to reach an amicable understanding. She and Cecil argued, Elizabeth shouting that she did not need to conciliate Essex. He had a duty, as her subject, to bend his knee and bow his neck to her. The rebels should be arrested and imprisoned. But Cecil had reminded Elizabeth of Robert's popularity and that harsh treatment would only rouse sympathy for him and damage her. She had reluctantly agreed that calm persuasion would be the best course.

Cecil had dispatched a deputation to Essex House to discover Robert's exact intentions and to warn him of the danger he would find himself in if he attempted to carry out a rebellion. But Cecil's policy of persuasion failed. Robert claimed the deputation had been sent to kill him and his companions and drew the deputation inside the walls of Essex House and locked them up.

Robert had men enough to make his rebellion a true threat to Elizabeth, but as with so many of his ideas, the plot was uninformed, unplanned and lacking a strategy. The discontented men congregating in the courtyard of Essex House could not understand why their leaders did not march directly on the court, but Robert and his co-conspirators did not consider their confusion and gave no explanation that there were weapons in the city that they needed. Such men were followers and should be content to do as they were told.

Robert, Henry and Lord Mounteagle rode through the streets of London, shouting out their battle cry of 'For the Queen. A plot is laid for the life of Essex.' But the people were confused, bewildered at these knights and nobles on horseback, waving their swords in the air. They either closed their doors upon them or just stood and stared.

When Robert and his rebels entered the city, they found that a heavy chain had been drawn across the street at Ludgate to cut them off. Robert had not been prepared for opposition, believing what he had been told, that the people were behind him and would hold off the Queen's men. He began to panic. A severe pummelling began inside his head, making his vision swim. His body became drenched with sweat and made his skin itch. He could not bear it. There, in the middle of the street, he called out, 'I must change my shirt, my body burns.'

Henry and Mounteagle stared, amazed, at one another.

'Damn your shirt, Essex,' Mounteagle yelled.

But Robert was insistent, and to calm him, Henry pulled him inside a merchant's house and demanded a clean shirt from the astonished mistress. He waited with growing impatience and anxiety while Robert washed the sweat from his skin and pulled on the fresh garment. Mounteagle remained in the street, guarding the door, cursing Robert for such folly.

While Robert tarried with his wardrobe, Cecil had taken action. He sent out his brother to proclaim in the London streets that the Earl of Essex was a traitor to the Queen. The streets were emptying as merchants packed up their stalls and goods and sought safety behind their doors. Soon, all that were left were either followers of Essex or the Queen's men.

'I am called traitor,' Robert cried, his voice thick with emotion, with astonishment, bewilderment, indignation.

'They are the traitors,' Henry retorted, pressing his face to the window to see what was happening. 'Come, Robert. We have tarried here long enough. We must return to the streets. The citizens know not the truth, we must tell them. Come, Robert, come.'

Henry helped Robert buckle on his breastplate, and grabbing their swords, they rejoined Mounteagle.

'We must answer this lie,' Robert said. 'Go you, Mounteagle. Cry out that Sir Robert Cecil has sold us to the Spanish and—'

He was prevented from saying more for there came the sound of armed men, their boots ringing on the cobbles. All three men turned to see a troop of the Queen's soldiers, the Lord Mayor at their head, with his sword in his hand and pointing straight at Robert.

'My lord, you and your associates will throw down your swords and come with us.'

'We are not traitors, sir,' Robert declared.

'You are traitors, my lord, to wander the streets so armed. You have spoken treasons and I am charged to secure your surrender.'

'Robert,' Henry hissed, 'what shall we do?'

Robert's breath was coming fast. What was he to do? Surrender? No, he could not countenance it, surrender was for cowards. But what to do? And then it came to him. The deputation. Yes, that was it. He had hostages at Essex House. He must get back there. He whispered his plan to Henry and Mounteagle, and before the Lord Mayor could prevent them, they had run down Lombard Street, past St Paul's and come once again to Ludgate. *God's Death, I had forgot the chain*, Robert realised. His head was agony and he wanted to bang it against the wall in his torment.

But, mercy of mercies, he was not abandoned. In the narrow street, Robert was suddenly joined by friends, his stepfather, Sir Christopher Blount, amongst them, men who had been promised a fight and were determined to bloody their swords.

But the Queen's men did not just bear swords but pistols too, and they used them. The air became thick with smoke. Blount was shot in the cheek, and for good measure, knocked on the head by a queen's man. Another man was shot dead. Others were injured in their arms or legs.

Robert turned and ran back the way he had come, ducking down an alley to head for the river. He fell into a boat moored on the bank and Henry and Mounteagle jumped in behind. They grabbed the oars and rowed back as fast as they could to Essex House.

Yet more misery awaited them there. They found that the hostages had been released and had been free to return to court to tell their sorry tale. Within half an hour, Essex House was surrounded and Robert could not fool himself any longer. His rebellion had failed and only one place was being made ready for him – a prison cell.

But was it to end thus? Had he so mistaken his power? Was he not the man he had thought he was, the man his friends had assured him he was? Yet he could not deny the evidence of his own eyes. Even now, Henry was throwing all his papers on the fire - his letters from King James, his lists of arms, and details of the plot that he had been foolishly persuaded to make. The fire banked high, spilling out smoke into the chamber. With the Queen's men banging on the doors, Henry grabbed Robert and dragged him up the stairs to the roof.

'We are done for, Robert,' he said breathlessly, slipping and sliding on the leads. 'We must surrender.'

'Then what did you bring us up here for?' Robert cried despairingly.

'We cannot surrender until we have agreed on terms,' Henry said, peering over the side of the roof. 'They would take us and clap us in irons else. But we are no common men, Robert, and I will not be taken as such.'

'You have more heart than I,' Robert said, drawing Henry to him and holding him close. 'You are the lover of words. You must use them wisely now.'

So, Henry spoke for two hours until an agreement was reached. Dejected, exhausted, Robert and Henry descended and unlocked the doors of Essex House. Henry had negotiated that, though he and Robert were to be arrested, their wrists and ankles were to bear no shackles.

Elizabeth, waiting in her silent palace, had refused to

retire to bed until she heard from Cecil's own mouth that the rebellion had been put down. At midnight, she crept beneath her bed covers, smiling into the darkness at the easy defeat of the Earl of Essex.

XXXV

The morning came brightly, bleeding through the cut-out diamonds and stars in the wooden shutters, proving to Elizabeth that Gloriana was not burned out yet. She basked in the sun's warmth, even as the dust motes floated around her. She even had a smile for Cecil as he came to bid her good morning.

They breakfasted together, Elizabeth enjoying the taste of her food for the first time in weeks. Before, with rebellion threatening, it had tasted like ash in her mouth, but now the bread and meats tasted sweet. They tasted of life.

Elizabeth had been put on trial by Robert. He had demanded of her people: 'Who do you want? An aged, cruel queen or a young, noble-hearted man?' And they had answered 'Elizabeth'. They had refused Robert the glory he craved. He was crushed, he was nothing. He was dust beneath her feet.

Curse the Pygmy, she thought as Cecil set his plate aside and picked up his ever-present folder of papers, *must he go on about the matter? Must he regale me with talk of men, of arms, and of surrenders? Must he spoil my joy with talk of how close I came to losing my throne?*

'So, London is secure?' she asked irritably.

Cecil resented her tone. Why should she snap at him so? Had he not saved her throne for her? 'We have brought in five hundred men from Middlesex to guard the centre of London and they are now stationed at Charing Cross. Three hundred from Essex are stationed in the east of London and three hundred more at Southwark. There are plenty of others throughout London as well. Your capital is entirely secure, madam.'

'And Essex's treason has been proclaimed?'

'Yes, and notices are being posted even now. The Privy Council is selecting lawyers to prepare for the rebels' trial and letters are being drafted to all the peers of your realm to come to London immediately to serve at the trial. Lastly, orders have been given to all the clergy to preach sermons denouncing the Earl of Essex.' Cecil glanced up at Elizabeth. 'Are the arrangements to your satisfaction, Your Majesty?'

Elizabeth slid her gaze towards him. 'They are, Pygmy. You have done well.'

'Thank you, Your Majesty. I am only sorry that it came to this pass.' Cecil meant it. He thought it was an ignominious ending for Robert, although he had had no desire to see his rebellion succeed, and Cecil's heart was heavy.

'I think I am partly to blame,' Elizabeth sighed, pushing her plate away. 'I should have seen the kind of man he was. He has his mother's blood, after all.' Her mouth turned down at the thought of Lettice. 'I am so very glad Leicester is not here to see it. His heart would have broken to see me treated thus.'

'Is it not likely he would never have allowed it to happen?' Cecil suggested, knowing that praise of Leicester was certain to please.

Elizabeth smiled and closed her eyes in memory of the man she had loved as no other. It was an answer.

'Will you wish to attend the trial, madam?' Cecil asked a few moments later when she did not speak.

His words brought her back to the present. 'No. I will hear your report. What? Why make you that face?

Cecil fiddled with his knife. 'I did not think to attend, madam. I am not needed after all as a judge…' He left the sentence unfinished, feeling uncomfortable beneath Elizabeth's accusatory eyes.

'Do you not want to see him brought low, Pygmy? Is this not what you have wanted your entire life?'

'With respect, madam, no,' he said, indignantly. 'If things had been different—'. He broke off, his throat tightening. He looked down at his small delicate hands. 'When our paths first crossed, the earl and I, I was a queer, solitary thing, proud and disdainful of boys like him who could sport and laugh because they were perfect. No deformation touched them. And I had plenty of perfect creatures to compare myself to. My father's house was home to many of his wards of court. And then the earl arrived and though he too was perfect and so unlike me he was, on occasion, kind. I say on occasion. When it was just he and I. He changed when the others were there, became more like them, and I knew he resented the time he had spent with me. You will think me pitiful, madam, but I even tried to buy his friendship. I made him gifts of books, praised his wit. I even laughed with him when he mocked me. And then he was gone and I was left with the others.'

Cecil touched his cheeks, concerned that he had allowed some tears to fall, but they were thankfully dry.

'I missed him,' he shrugged and gave a little laugh. 'So you see, madam, despite all his insults, his dealings against me, I cannot rejoice in his downfall. There is something of the boy who thought Essex was wonderful in me yet.' He drew a deep breath. 'I do not want him to see me at the trial because I do not want him to think that I am gloating.'

He sniffed, expecting Elizabeth to speak. The speech he had just made had been difficult and he thought, expected, hoped, her words would be sympathetic.

'You are a fool, Pygmy,' Elizabeth said. 'Were your positions reversed, he would swing the axe himself.'

৬ ৬ ৬

Cecil had lied to Elizabeth and he had lied to himself. He found that when the time came, he could not keep himself from attending Robert's trial. He needed to see Robert, needed to hear what he said with his own ears, not read it in a report. He entered Westminster Hall before the spectators had filed into the rear of the chamber before it was populated with nobles in their ermine clad red gowns and before the clerks and secretaries had set up their desks and before the accused had been brought in and made to sit inside a square box like any petty felon.

Cecil had hidden behind a curtain and listened as the treason charges against Robert and Henry Wriothesley, who were being tried together, were read out, as they were cross-examined, as they gave their excuses and pitiful lies. He listened as Henry Wriothesley showed himself to be both a coward and a liar, to deny all knowledge of Robert's plotting and even his own part in the rebellion. Cecil listened with a cold feeling as Francis Bacon stood to give evidence against his former master, but could not help but be impressed by his cousin's demeanour and statesmanlike mind in the face of Robert's accusations of treachery. *Perhaps*, Cecil thought, *he had been wrong not to find a place for*

Francis.

Through it all, Cecil remained silent. He was ashamed of Robert. This was not the boy he had once admired, nor was he the man who had promised so much. This Robert was a man who was far from seeing things as they truly were, who veered from bursts of confident talk to mumbling admissions of guilt. Was this wretched man the people's champion?

Cecil wished for it all to be over, that an end could be made of this farce of a trial whose judgement had already been made. But his breath caught in his throat when he heard Robert making an extraordinary accusation against him, Cecil.

'I was told that Master Secretary Cecil had said to a fellow counsellor that the Infanta of Spain's claim to the English throne was as good as any other,' Robert declared defiantly.

Cecil could not believe that Robert had spoken such an untruth. But God a'mercy, he was saying it again and louder this time. Each word was as a blow to Cecil and he could stand it no longer. He drew the curtain aside and, in the astonished silence that followed, limped towards Lord Treasurer Buckhurst, who was in charge of the proceedings. Not without causing himself some pain, Cecil fell to his knees.

'Forgive me, my lord Buckhurst, but I beg you to let me answer my accuser, who hurls a foul and false report at my head.'

Buckhurst waved him to proceed. Cecil rose and moved to stand before Robert, who looked him straight in the eye, unrepentant.

'My lord,' Cecil began, hearing his own voice quaver, 'I acknowledge that the difference between you and I is great. For wit, I give you the pre-eminence. You have it in abundance. For nobility too, I concede. I am not noble, yet I am a gentleman. I am no swordsman – there also you have the advantage. But I do have innocence, conscience, truth and honesty to defend me against the scandal and sting of slanderous tongues. Here, in this court, I stand an upright man and you as a miscreant. I protest before God, I have loved you and made much of your virtues, told Her Majesty that your virtues made you a fit servant for her, if she would but call you to the court again. And had not I seen your ambitions turn towards usurpation, I would have gone down on my knees to Her Majesty, would it have done you good. But you have a wolf's head in a sheep's coat. You are in appearance humble and religious, but in disposition ambitious and cunning. God be thanked, we now know you. And my lord, were it but your own self who betrayed the Queen, the fault would have been less. But you have drawn noble persons and gentlemen of birth and quality into your net of rebellion, and be assured, their bloods will cry vengeance against you.'

'Ah, Master Secretary,' Robert said, unimpressed by Cecil's scathing speech, 'I thank God for my humiliation, that you, in the ruff of all your bravery, have come here to make such a speech against me this day.'

'Indeed, my lord, and I now humbly thank God that you did not think me a fit companion for you, for if you had, you would have persuaded me to betray my queen as you have done others. But I challenge you to name the person who told you of my supposed preference for the Infanta of Spain. Name him if you dare. If you do not name him, we can only believe your claim to be a falsehood.'

'It is no falsehood,' Robert protested. 'I can easily name the man. He stands here beside me. Henry Wriothesley, Earl of Southampton. He knows I speak no untruth.'

Cecil and Robert both turned to look at Henry, who seemed to shrink beneath their gaze. His mouth opened, his breath came quickly. 'I… I cannot say.'

'Come, Henry,' Robert urged, his brow creasing in confusion. 'Speak the truth.'

'I do,' Henry protested, pulling his arm free from Robert's gripping hand. 'I cannot say I ever heard that Master Secretary Cecil spoke of the Infanta of Spain.'

'But Henry, you told me so.'

'I did not, my lord, and you cannot make me say I did.'

Robert stared at his friend, uncomprehending. What was the matter with Henry? Why would he not confirm his words? Had he been wrong? But he was sure Henry had said those very words.

'So,' Cecil said, 'your words are proved to be a falsehood after all, my lord.'

Robert fell back into his chair. He had nothing more to say. Even Henry, his closest friend, had betrayed him.

Cecil waited in the antechamber to the Queen's apartments. He clutched the transcript of the trial to his chest, wishing he could rip the papers to shreds and thereby pretend the last few weeks had never happened. *I wish you were with me, Father. I fear the Queen will have her revenge and Essex will die.* He wanted his father by his side because his father would tell him that such a judgement was just, that Essex deserved to die, and he would believe his father. His conscience would be salved.

The doors opened and one of Elizabeth's ladies gestured for him to enter.

Elizabeth was in bed, her nightcap tight on her head and her face free of any paint. It startled Cecil to find her so and he forgot to bow, failed to speak.

'Guilty, I presume?' she said, not looking up.

'Indeed, Your Majesty,' Cecil stammered. 'Both Essex and Southampton sentenced to death.'

'There were none of my nobles who were moved by Essex's words?'

'None. The verdict was unanimous.' *As we knew it would be*, Cecil thought. The guilty verdict had been decided before ever Robert and Henry set foot in Westminster Hall.

Elizabeth, at last, looked at Cecil. 'What is it you have there, Pygmy?'

'The transcript of the trial. I thought you might care to read it.'

Elizabeth paused, staring at the document, before telling Cecil he could leave it. Cecil placed it on the table by her bedside.

'What has happened to the world, Pygmy?' Elizabeth asked quietly.

'Majesty?'

'I have done nothing but serve this country of mine every day I have sat on my throne. I have made so many sacrifices, Pygmy. I would not place England at the mercy of a foreign power, which meant that I could never marry a man of my own degree, and to marry a man of a lesser degree would have meant civil war. So, I remained a maid. Never to be a wife or a mother. I have signed the death warrants of those near to me in blood who coveted my crown and still it is not enough for me to sit safely on my throne. What have I done wrong that my subjects should treat me so?'

'You are loved, Your Majesty. The failure of the earl's rebellion proved this.'

'Does it? I think it proves nothing of the sort. He, the wretch, and his friends believed the people would join them in rebellion, and several thousands of my subjects did join them, your reports have told me that. So many discontents, Pygmy.'

Cecil sighed. 'The people are fickle, Your Majesty. Many of them have known no other sovereign but your gracious self. They believe their lives could be better than they are. They are mistaken.'

Elizabeth was silent, but nodded at the door, telling him that he could leave. Cecil bowed and left, glad to be out of her presence.

Elizabeth heard the door click shut behind Cecil and she watched her attendant snuff out the candles and settle onto her pallet at the foot of the bed.

Elizabeth tugged the bedcovers higher as her body grew cold. She felt wounded, as though Robert had stuck a blade in her side and her blood was trickling out. She had thought herself loved, adored, but she knew now that was not true. Cecil was right, her people were fickle. They always had been. She had seen their changing moods all her life, long before she became queen. How had she become blind to their nature?

But I am still Queen, and I will be Queen until I die. I have fought hard for my throne and no one is going to take it away from me.

XXXVI

The Reverend Abdy Ashton perched himself on the end of the wooden table and looked over at Robert, standing by the small narrow window that looked out onto the cobbles of the Tower courtyard. 'Are you certain that you wish to see no one, my lord? Not even your wife or your mother?'

Robert shook his head.

'Your soul is heavy,' Ashton said, opening his Bible.

'I am to die, Reverend,' Robert said sadly, his voice breaking. He rested his head against the stone window jamb and closed his eyes. 'How do you expect my soul to be?'

'Indeed, my lord. You are going out of this world, but you do not know what it is to stand before your maker. Unburden your heart. Make confession of your sins.'

'Confess?' Robert turned to him and Ashton could not help but start at the pale skin and red eyes, the look of fever. 'Oh yes, I need to confess. They blamed me, Reverend, at the trial for it all, but it wasn't me, it was Henry. Henry Wriothesley. I thought he was my friend but he betrayed me. He stood by my side and denied that he had ever advised me to rouse the city. Denied that he had ever said Cecil was a true servant of Spain. Untrue, Reverend, untrue.'

'And the rebellion, my lord?' Ashton prompted. 'What were your true intentions?'

Robert sat down next to Ashton and Ashton smelt the stale sweat on his unwashed body, proof that Robert had been neglecting himself as the Lieutenant of the Tower's reports to the Council had claimed.

'My intentions were not what they said,' Robert said, looking into Ashton's eye. 'I never wanted the throne for myself. I just wanted to free the Queen from Cecil.'

'But your popularity with the people, my lord. The hiring of the players to perform *Richard the Second*, a play which is concerned with the deposition of a king.'

'That was Henry's idea,' Robert said savagely, 'not mine.'

'But you were communicating with King James?'

'What of it?' Robert demanded. 'We all know the Queen cannot live forever. What harm was there in making myself known to the one who would succeed her? Many at court have done the same thing.'

'Can you name them?' Ashton licked his lips in anticipation.

Robert rattled off a list of names, not forgetting to include his stepfather and his sister, Penelope. So many names that Ashton knew he would not be able to remember them all and told Robert so.

Robert's eyes grew brighter. 'Bring me pen and paper and I will write their names down. They too must be punished as I. I want Elizabeth to know everything. I want her to know how ill-advised I was. I want to make a true confession, Reverend. I want my soul to be cleansed.'

'It will be, my lord,' Ashton said happily, laying out

the small table with the writing tools. 'God loves a repentant sinner.'

❧ ❧ ❧

It was late and a single candle burned in Cecil's study. Cecil was reading Robert's confession that Reverend Ashton had delivered up to him when a shadow fell over him. He looked up, startled.

'Has the wretch written to me?' Elizabeth asked.

Cecil got to his feet. 'No madam, he has not.'

Elizabeth wandered around his study, picking up books, pretending to read. 'I thought he would plead for his life.'

'I think he is resigned to death, madam. Reports from the Reverend Ashton and the Lieutenant of the Tower say he is in a very dejected state of mind. He does not sleep, he does not eat, but prays continually.'

'Then death will be a mercy, will it not?'

Cecil despised her for the callous remark. Would she not even show a hint of compassion, the smallest shred of feeling for the man who had once stayed by her side through the dark hours when her nightmares came, who had made her laugh and kept her mind off growing old?

'However, his mother has written to the Council. She begs for her son's life.'

'She wants him to go free?'

'She begs the same punishment for her son as Henry Wriothesley. Life imprisonment. She says she will be forever in your debt and praises your most gracious majesty.'

'Of course, she does,' Elizabeth nodded in satisfaction. She moved back towards the door. 'The She-Wolf turning hypocrite to save her cub.'

'What shall I tell her?'

'Tell her nothing, Pygmy. I am glad that she is upset. I want her to know what it is to suffer.'

༄ ༄ ༄

'And you wrote to her?' Dorothy almost screamed at her mother.

Like Lettice and Penelope, Dorothy had travelled to London for the trial of her brother and was staying at Essex House.

Lettice sniffed and wiped her reddened nose. 'I have already told you, daughter, yes, I wrote to Elizabeth.'

'And?'

'And I begged her, you hear me, I begged her not to hurt Robert and Christopher. I pleaded with her to let them both stay in the Tower, like that bastard Wriothesley. And nothing. I received a letter from Cecil saying the Queen refused to listen.'

Dorothy fell onto the seat beside her mother. 'How can she? After all Robert has been to her. How can she let him die like this?'

Lettice began to cry again, rocking back and forth with her head in her hands. Dorothy looked across to Penelope who was sitting by the window, looking out at the rain. 'Pen, you must do something. I know he said you were involved in the plot, but you must do something.'

'Do you think I care that he tried to implicate me?' Penelope sighed. 'He's my brother, too, Dorothy, and we know that Robert has always said things he doesn't think about. He didn't mean it, I know that. And I have written. I wrote to the Council, the same as Mother. They gave me the same answer.'

A tear escaped from Dorothy's eye and she wiped it weakly away. 'Perhaps,' she said, 'perhaps Elizabeth means to make Robert think that she will go through with his execution, and then issue a reprieve. Pen? Do you think so?'

Penelope didn't think so. She had had experience of Elizabeth too and, like her mother, knew that Elizabeth could be cruel. But she met Dorothy's eye and gave a small smile. 'Maybe, Dorothy. I don't know. She loved him once. Maybe she still does. Maybe she'll realise she can't kill him.'

Lettice heard her daughters talking and refused to allow herself to hope. She was sorry for her husband, of course, but her heart was breaking because of her son.

Oh, how she hated Elizabeth. She thought she had hated her before but it had been nothing compared to how she felt now. Her son, her glorious, beautiful son was sentenced to die by Elizabeth's written command and there was nothing she could do to stop it. She had even thought of offering herself in Robert's place, wondering if her death would appease Elizabeth's wrath, but she knew her cousin too well. Elizabeth wanted her to suffer, she knew. Well, she *was* suffering, and it felt like she would die from the pain in her heart. She felt it everywhere, in her bones, in her head, in her stomach. She couldn't eat, she couldn't think, she couldn't do all the things she should be doing as mistress of a house. What did her house matter anyway? Her son was going to die. She knew that children died; she herself had lost a child in its infancy but that had been through illness. She had been able to cope with that, only blaming God for taking him away, and the pain had eased with the passing of time. But this, this was different. Robert wasn't ill, he was in the prime of his life, and that life was being deliberately ended. This was pain unlike any she had ever felt before. It was being powerless and knowing the exact moment when Robert was due to leave the world. To know that one minute before eight o'clock on the morning of Ash

Wednesday he would be alive, but that at one minute past eight, his beautiful head would have been severed from his body and his blood would be dripping through the planks of a scaffold.

And her son would be no more.

XXXVII

Tower of London

Robert was so very tired. He had not slept, for he had been told that he was to die in the morning and he felt that, despite his confession, his soul was still stained. So, he had spent the night on his knees in prayer, only the cold light of the moon for company.

There was no crowd around the scaffold, no one to cheer a traitor or cry, 'God bless you.' Just a few nobles present to witness his death.

He climbed the steps to the platform and bowed to the clergymen who stood grouped, ready to give him solace before his head was off. 'Oh God, be merciful unto me, the most wretched creature on the earth,' he murmured and moved to the centre, his black boots becoming covered with the sawdust that had been sprinkled over the wooden planks to soak up his blood.

Robert looked up at the grey sky above the White Tower. His mouth was dry and he had to swallow several times before he could speak.

'My Lords, and you my Christian brethren, who are to be witnesses of this my just punishment, I confess to the glory of God that I am a most wretched sinner, and that my sins are more in number than the hairs of my head; that I have bestowed my youth in pride, lust, vainglory, and many other sins, according to the fashion of this world, wherein I have offended most grievously my God. The good which I could have performed, I have not done, and the evil which I should not, I have done; for which I humbly beseech our Saviour Christ to plead for me. Especially for this my last sin, this great and bloody, infectious sin, whereby so many, for love of me, had ventured their lives and souls and have been drawn to offend God, their sovereign and the world. Jesus, forgive me, the most wretched of all. The Lord grant Her Majesty a long reign and bless her. I beseech the world to have a charitable opinion of me for my intention towards her Majesty, whose death, upon my word and salvation and before God, I protest I never meant. Yet, I am justly condemned and I desire all the world to forgive me, even as I do freely and from my heart forgive all the world. I beseech you all to join with me in prayer, so that my soul may be lifted up above all earthly things.'

Robert's fingers fumbled at his neck, trying to untie the cord of his black velvet cloak. He called for his manservant, Williams, to help him, then remembered that he was not at home at Essex House, Chartley or Wanstead, and would have to manage himself. His fingers began to obey him and he removed his cloak and ruff.

He knelt on the straw, his lips hardly moving as he recited the Lord's Prayer, and he was grateful to them when he heard the spectators praying, too. Only then did he remember his doublet and took that off too, revealing a scarlet waistcoat, the only point of colour in that drab scene. He turned to the executioner, his stomach lurching at the sight of the anonymous black mask hiding the man's face. He swallowed, trying to rid his throat of its lump.

'I forgive you. You are welcome to me, for you are the minister of justice.'

The block was only a few inches high. He laid on his front, feeling the sawdust prick his palms and fill his nostrils with a sweet, woody smell. He placed his neck in the cut-out curve, feeling the pressure against his Adam's apple. He was asked if he wanted a blindfold and he replied that he did not. One of the clergymen on the scaffold with him began reciting the fifty-first psalm. Robert listened intently, closing his eyes as the words 'cleanse me from my sin' floated in the air above him.

'Executioner,' Robert said, hearing his voice tremble, 'strike home. Come, Lord Jesus, receive my soul and into thy hands, I commend my spirit.'

The axe fell and Robert felt an intense, sharp pain in his shoulder. Such agony! He screamed. The second blow came, hitting him in the shoulder again and cutting off his scream. He could make no noise. His throat was too tight, the pain too great. The axe fell for the third time, hitting its mark at last, severing the neck and ending Robert's suffering.

The executioner, distraught beneath his black mask at his bungling, picked up Robert's head almost tenderly and held it aloft, feeling the trickle of hot blood down his forearm.

'God save the Queen.'

Bibliography

Borman, Tracy *Elizabeth's Women: The Hidden Story of the Virgin Queen*

Greenblatt, Stephen *Will in the World: How Shakespeare Became Shakespeare*

Hibbert, Christopher *Elizabeth I: A Personal History of the Virgin Queen*

Keay, Anna *The Earl of Essex: The Life and Death of a Tudor Traitor*

Lacey, Robert *Robert, Earl of Essex: An Elizabethan Icarus*

Shapiro, James *1599: A Year in the Life of William Shakespeare*

Smith, Lacey Baldwin *Treason in Tudor England: Politics and Paranoia*

Somerset, Anne *Elizabeth I*

Weir, Alison *Elizabeth the Queen*

The Queen's Favourite

Born into an ambitious family, Robert Dudley is determined to climb high. Thrust into the world of the Tudor court when still a boy, he learns to cultivate useful relationships and finds none more so than his friendship with the young Princess Elizabeth. But when his father's attempt to crown Lady Jane Grey in Mary Tudor's place ends in failure, the Dudley family are branded traitors and imprisoned in the dreaded Tower of London, some never to leave.

Pardoned and released, an unhappy Robert retires to the country. But when Queen Mary dies, hope revives and he heads for London. For England has a new queen. Elizabeth Tudor is on the throne and she has not forgotten her childhood friend.

But their friendship soon deepens and Robert finds himself the object of the virgin queen's desire. The throne of England seems to be within Robert's grasp.

Only Elizabeth stands in his way.

Can Robert fulfil his father's ambition to see a Dudley on the throne of England?

Can Robert ever become King?

Book 1 in *The Tudor Court* series.

When the Siren Sings

London, 1938.

When young and handsome Daniel Beck leaves prison, he knows what he's going to do. He's going to play it straight.

At least, that's the plan. But then he meets Phoebe Merrill, a poor little rich girl, and despite his best intentions, falls in love. But Danny forgets the old saying of 'Everything that glitters is not gold'. His golden girl may have the face of an angel, but there's a devil inside.

Talking his way into a job with Phoebe's father, Danny leaves the big city for the leafy countryside of Richmond and The Larches, the Merrill family home. Believing he's fallen on his feet, Danny allows himself to become romantically involved with the women of The Larches, unable to resist their pull. So, when Phoebe asks him to murder her father, Danny finds he can't refuse.

But what does he really know about the girl he loves and her motive for murder?

Just what is Danny letting himself in for when he surrenders to her Siren song?

Join my mailing list to receive your FREE and EXCLUSIVE eBook, ***The Poet Knight and His Muse***, a short story about Sir Philip Sidney and Penelope Devereux and one of the greatest love poems of Queen Elizabeth I's reign.

It is completely free to join and I promise I will never spam you – I'll only be in touch when I have something I think will be of interest to you. You can easily unsubscribe at any time.

Enter this address into your web browser to be taken to my sign-up page:

http://www.subscribepage.com/ebook-subscribe

21491172R00152

Printed in Poland
by Amazon Fulfillment
Poland Sp. z o.o., Wrocław